WITHDRAWN

JOURNEYS' END

A Wartime Romance

Summer 1939. Leonie Harcourt, nearly eighteen, finds herself pregnant by her Parisian lover, Luc Gosselin, in a London preparing for war. She is dispatched to an unknown aunt's farm in Somerset. Luc doesn't return after the war, but throughout all the years ahead Leonie keeps what he gave her to take care of – a small locked suitcase – and it is this that will reconnect her at last with the Gosselin family...

Sally Stewart titles available from
Severn House Large Print

The Enchanter's Wand
Over the Sea to Skye
Prospero's Daughters
Roman Spring
A Time to Dance

JOURNEYS' END

Sally Stewart

Severn House Large Print
London & New York

This first large print edition published 2010
in Great Britain and the USA by
SEVERN HOUSE PUBLISHERS LTD of
9-15 High Street, Sutton, Surrey, SM1 1DF.
First world regular print edition published 2008 by
Severn House Publishers Ltd., London and New York.

British Library Cataloguing in Publication Data

Stewart, Sally, 1930-
Journeys' end.
1. World War, 1939-1945--Social aspects--Fiction.
2. English--France--Fiction. 3. Paris (France)--
History--1940-1944--Fiction. 4. Somerset (England)--
Fiction. 5. Love stories. 6. Large type books.
I. Title
823.9'14-dc22

ISBN-13: 978-0-7278-7835-9

Printed and bound in Great Britain by
MPG Books Ltd, Bodmin, Cornwall.

Journeys end in lovers meeting,

Every wise man's son doth know

William Shakespeare

One

In the summer of 1939, in an untidy Parisian studio, Luc Gosselin sat sketching a girl who couldn't help smiling at him, even though he'd asked her not to.

'Stay still, girl, for pity's sake. It's almost finished.'

The command, delivered in the French they always spoke together, was as sharp as the pose she'd been given to hold was uncomfortable, but neither sharpness nor discomfort mattered; she was with Luc. That was the important thing.

Told at last that she could relax, she stretched her cramped body in the happy certainty that he was watching her. Then she pointed at the shabby, velvet-covered couch pushed against the only empty wall the cluttered studio possessed.

'If I were a professional model I suppose this is the moment when you'd throw me down on that and make passionate love to me,' she suggested hopefully.

'Of course,' he agreed with only a faint tremor of amusement in his voice, 'but since you are in fact the schoolgirl protégée of my good friends the Bernards, we shall drink a decorous cup of coffee together instead.'

She sighed a little as if to say that another of life's opportunities had been lost, but moved across the room to inspect his sketch of her face. Caught half in profile, its entranced gaze was fastened on some moment of delight that only she could see. She stared at it for a while in silence.

'You could call it "Happiness",' she suggested quietly at last. 'That describes my life here with Tante Genevieve and Professor Bernard. I'm never going back to London. I hope my father realizes that. My stepmother won't mind; she couldn't wait to pack me off to the nuns as soon as I was old enough and she was able to give up pretending to look after me.'

Luc heard no self-pity in her voice, but no exaggeration either; she simply spoke the truth. 'Is that what made you hate her so much?' he asked. 'The banishment to the convent?'

Unexpectedly Leonie Harcourt shook her head. 'No, I loved the nuns – I suppose because most of them were French and reminded me of Maman. I hate Christine because she took the place that belonged to my mother. Added to that, although she's elegant and clever she has no heart; there's an empty space where it should be. Here, with Genevieve and Pappi Bernard, and dear Max Reiner in his atelier under the roof, I feel loved again. It's important to feel loved.'

She was right, Luc thought, and she spoke

of what she knew from experience painfully bought. He watched her sip the coffee he'd given her, aware that she was suddenly lost in some remembrance of a time when her French mother was alive to fill their home in London with warmth and gaiety. Not yet eighteen, she was still the schoolgirl he'd just called her, even though she was learning fast how to tease him with her emerging beauty. But the uncertain, lonely creature who'd arrived in Paris the previous year was already transformed, and he found himself hoping that he would still know her when her adolescence had finally been left behind. She was intent on becoming completely French, unaware that traces of some patrician style and steel still spoke of her English father. Luc occasionally provoked her by saying so, but not today. She was a girl of moods as swiftly changing as an April day, and now she was looking wistful again.

It seemed that her thoughts had travelled into the future along with his own. She waved a hand around the studio's comfortable, familiar disorder. 'Promise me you'll stay here, Luc. I need people to be where I can find them ... nothing must change. Paris has to remain unaltered, too; I love it just as it is.' She frowned over what she was going to say next. 'Pappi Bernard looks sad when I tell him that, and so does my darling Genevieve, but nothing dreadful is going to happen, is it? I know the Germans have insisted on all their displaced people being brought back into what they call the Fatherland, but that doesn't seem unreasonable.'

He smiled at the word but shook his head. 'Tell the Austrians that it's not unreasonable to have been annexed by their neighbours, *ma petite*. Tell the Czechs they mustn't mind having had their country dismembered!'

Leonie's frown deepened. 'I wasn't thinking of the Anschluss,' she admitted, 'and of course Pappi's wife, Lilli, was an Austrian, and dear Max Reiner is her nephew. But at least he's safely here in Paris, and we have nothing to worry about.'

Luc nodded, reluctant to upset her with a less optimistic glimpse into the future. 'True enough. We have the Maginot line between us and Germany, not to mention all the strength of the French army, and your English Prime Minister who has promised peace in our time. So let us agree that there is indeed nothing to worry about.' But it hadn't sounded quite convincing enough, he thought, so he spoke again in a different tone of voice.

'Time you went home, *ma chère*. I have serious work to do instead of dawdling here with you.' But he softened the remark by touching her cheek gently with fingers that left a faint smear of charcoal on her pale, clear skin.

She didn't argue, content to know that at least he hadn't said she mustn't come again. He wasn't quite in love with her yet; she knew that, but he would be one day – she knew that too with equal certainty. All she had to do was wait. She would soon grow old enough for him, and wise enough and beautiful enough. She just needed a little more time.

With the summer term at the Lycée over, she was free to revel in the joy of living in Paris. The Bernards' old house on the Île de la Cité, lovely in itself, was also a magnet for Left-Bank intellectuals and artists alike. She might be too young to contribute very much, but she was nevertheless there, and properly aware of the privilege of sharing in the perfect life that Genevieve and her father, a professor of Greek at the Sorbonne, had created. There might be – if she admitted it to herself – a slight sense of tension in the air, a faint hint of forced gaiety in the friends who wandered in and out; but it seemed that no one saw any need to despair. The war to end all wars had been fought and painfully won twenty-five years before. The shadow hanging over them would dissolve, just as the mist floated off the river's glimmering surface as the sun rose each morning.

It was sad that Luc should have suddenly decided to go down to the South to paint – a hastily-scrawled note had warned her not to call at the studio, because he would be away for the *mois de vacances* – but the days were still filled with things to do. She loved setting out for the markets each morning, armed with Marthe's shopping-list and her old wicker basket. There were the bookstalls along the quays to haunt in search of bargains and, best of all, expeditions with 'Tante' Genevieve – not an aunt at all, in fact, but her dead mother's lifelong friend and her own dear godmother. Genevieve spoke to her sometimes of the young, beautiful Cécile Lefevre who'd selected so unexpectedly from her host of suitors an aloof English diplomat and gone with him to live in London. She'd died there when Leonie was nine years old, and godmother and child had since shared the view that Edward Harcourt and London were to blame – in Paris she would surely still have been alive.

Genevieve, apart from being the kindest, wisest companion Leonie had ever known, was also an interior decorator of renown. Equally as happy to trawl flea markets as the expensive galleries of the rue du Faubourg Saint-Honoré or the August sales at the Salle Drouot, she seemed to hold all the enchanting magic of the city in her square, ugly hands.

But, for a girl who had guessed her godmother's secret, Genevieve's crowning attraction was to be unavailingly in love. The charming, painting-obsessed man who lived and worked in the atelier upstairs needed her, of course. Without her he might sometimes have forgotten to eat or bathe or shave. But Leonie felt sure that Max Reiner – Pappi's nephew by marriage – would never want a wife. That was how great artists were – selfish and strangely unaware of their power to hurt other people. Genevieve knew this and it was probably why she treated Luc merely as one of Max's students when he came to the house – Leonie wasn't to be encouraged to repeat her own mistake. Giving one's heart to a man who didn't even notice the gift was a recipe for too much grief. Leonie saw no need yet to explain that whatever her future held – grief or joy – it would lie in the hands of Luc Gosselin.

But without him in Paris the long, hot days of August began to drag and for once she wanted time to pass more quickly. The hint of thunder was always in the heavy air, threatening a storm that loomed but never quite arrived.

Then one day it did, in a terrible and unlooked-for way. She came back from shopping earlier than usual to find Genevieve deep in conversation with her father. A letter lay on the table in front of them, and it was so clearly what they were discussing that she made to leave them alone again. But Genevieve's lifted hand told her to stay.

'Come and sit down, *ma chère* – there's something we must talk about.' She glanced at her father, but he faintly shook his head and she had to go on herself.

'There was a letter from your father this morning. Leonie dear, he wants you to go home ... very soon.' It was as far as she got before she was fiercely interrupted.

'Tante, this is my home now. You said I could always stay ... you and Pappi said that,'

Leonie insisted in a voice made hoarse by sudden shock. She stared from one to the other of them, unwilling to think that she could no longer believe them. 'Am I a nuisance ... don't you want me here?'

This time it was Professor Bernard who spoke. 'You could stay forever, child, if the decision concerned only us. But you are still a minor. Your father is your legal guardian – he has the right to say what you must do. He wants you back in London.'

'But why?' she almost shouted. 'He's always away working, never there, and my stepmother certainly doesn't want me.'

Genevieve touched the letter lying on the table with fingers that trembled slightly. 'Your father says there's going to be a war, and he's a diplomat – he should know if anybody does. He thinks you would be safer in London ... and writes that you must leave very soon.'

Leonie's face relaxed into a blinding smile. 'Well, if that's all it is then of course I needn't go. Even if my father is right, Germany won't dare to interfere with us here. We talked about it, Luc and I, before he went away. France isn't some small, helpless country to be trampled on. Germany was beaten to its knees once before and will be again.'

The brave words dropped into the silence in the room. Then the professor spoke again, with such quiet, sad authority in his voice that she knew she'd sounded too loud and altogether too shrill.

'My dear, the Germans were beaten last

time it's true, but at appalling cost. In our desire for the revenge we thought was deserved, we inflicted wounds on them that have festered ever since. I share your father's belief that they want to go to war, and that you should therefore go back to London.' It was as much as he could bring himself to say. He lifted his shoulders in a little gesture of defeat, then walked quickly out of the room and took refuge with his nephew upstairs.

Leonie stared beseechingly at her godmother. 'Doesn't Pappi understand? I don't want to be safe in London – I want to be here with you. This is my mother country, not England. And in any case my father could easily be wrong.'

Genevieve tried to smile at her. 'Then you will come back, *n'est-ce pas, ma chère?* We shall be here waiting for you, I promise.' She hesitated for a moment, but decided that the subject of her goddaughter's friendship with Luc Gosselin couldn't be ignored. 'Perhaps you're afraid that Luc won't wait ... is that what upsets you most?'

Colour tinged Leonie's pale face but she answered defiantly. 'He was having to wait for me to finish growing up in any case; he understands that.' She saw the doubt in Genevieve's face and shook her head. 'You think he's a charming wanderer, living on Père Gosselin's wealth while he learns how to paint. It's not true, tante – he is *très sérieux* underneath ... certainly about painting and probably also about me.' She went to stand beside her godmother. 'If I must leave can I not stay until he gets back to Paris ... to say *au revoir* at least?'

Genevieve nodded, hearing in the words an entreaty that she couldn't help but yield to. Nothing had happened yet; it might not happen at all. The child deserved a few days' grace, surely, and Edward Harcourt's letter had been a little too peremptory for Genevieve's liking – so typical of an Englishman accustomed to giving orders to lesser mortals.

But before a week was out came the dreadful news of German troops marching into Poland. Edward had been right – Great Britain and France, both having pledged to support the country that was now being invaded, were forced to declare war on Germany.

There could be no delay now, Pappi said, Leonie must get ready to leave. Two days later, with a letter for Luc left in Genevieve's keeping, she said goodbye to them at the Gare du Nord and turned her white, anguished face towards England.

Two

Afterwards she remembered very little of the day's journey. The train was uncomfortably crowded and too hot, but that was only a small addition to her weight of misery. Like Jane Eyre, the heroine of an English novel she'd once read, she could feel the cord connecting her heart to its true home stretched to breaking point. If it snapped she might bleed to death, just as Maman had probably done when she was condemned to live in London.

To exchange Paris for what she remembered as a dour, grey city was hard enough; to lose Tante Genevieve and dear Pappi Bernard for a father she scarcely knew and a stepmother she hated was much worse. But even more heartbreaking was her anxiety about Luc. She'd insisted that he'd be waiting when she was free to return to France – pride had demanded that. But what if it wasn't true? What of all the young women still allowed to be there who were already desirable enough to steal him away?

She closed her eyes against the prick of tears and thought instead of the speech she would make to her father, because he must be made to understand at once that she had come through *force majeure* to stay as little time as possible.

But first there was the bustle of arriving at Calais where the ferry was already moored alongside the quay. She followed the rest of the passengers on board, threaded her way through the piles of luggage that littered the deck, and found an empty seat. No need to seek shelter in one of the crowded saloons; the English Channel (such arrogance – why not the French Channel, she wondered) lay quiescent under the late-summer heat. An hour later they were approaching Dover, and she stood up, impelled by the urge that seemed to fill everyone else to watch the chalk cliffs of the Kentish coastline materialize out of the afternoon haze. The young man standing beside Leonie waved a hand at them.

'Lovely to be back, isn't it?' he suggested, despite the fact that her white face looked anything but joyful.

'Is it?' she asked indifferently, and then turned away before he could recover from his surprise and think of something more to say.

Throughout the journey she'd become aware that she was now listening to clipped English voices. Even so it was a shock to hear herself addressed as 'Miss Harcourt' by the Customs officer looking at the labels on her luggage. Even her name sounded different from the soft, agreeable 'Arcour' that French pronunciation had made of it.

A window seat on the train to Victoria

enabled her to watch the countryside slipping by, but how small and cramped it looked compared with the lovely spaciousness of France. There were too many hedges, far too many buildings, and the sprawl of London's suburbs had surely grown worse since she went away. But with the journey almost over all she could think about now was her arrival at the house in Green Street. She hadn't seen Christine Harcourt at all since leaving London, and her father had only once visited them on the Île de la Cité during an official stay in Paris. But that evening with the Bernards had only confirmed her intention not to like the father she scarcely knew.

At Victoria Station she was helped with her suitcases by a courteous fellow passenger who beckoned to a waiting porter, then lifted his hat and walked away. There was just time to think gratefully of Pappi Bernard, who'd pressed English money into her hand at the Gare du Nord, before the porter was draping himself with her luggage.

'Cab, miss?' he asked briefly. 'Be a queue, I 'spect – always is when the boat-train comes in.'

She followed him along the crowded platform, deafened by the noise, and still not attuned to a different language. It took her a moment to realize that the elegant woman standing by the barrier was her stepmother.

Christine spoke first to the porter, instructing him where to find her taxi driver waiting outside in the station forecourt. Then she turned to look at her stepdaughter. Taller surely and, in appearance at least, no longer the miserable hangdog schoolgirl who'd refused to accept their life together on any terms but her own.

This young creature even wore her school blazer and pleated skirt with a different air. She ignored the fashion for complicatedly waved and curled hair; instead, a simple, straight bob made a becoming frame for features that were emerging into beauty – clever Genevieve Bernard's guidance, no doubt. The only thing that hadn't changed was her stepdaughter's wary, measuring glance that gave nothing of herself away.

'You've grown,' Christine Harcourt said, aware that the greeting must seem inadequate and probably patronizing. What was needed was an affectionate hug, and a warm 'welcome home, my dear'. But, even if she could have managed that, Leonie's own attitude would have warned her against attempting it. They were still not friends, and perhaps never would be.

'You shouldn't have bothered to come and meet me,' Leonie forced herself first to think in English and then to say. 'I was going to take a taxi – I have some English money.'

Even to her own ears it sounded ungracious, but already she seemed to feel the old deadening lack of warmth that was what she remembered about the tall, beautifully groomed woman beside her.

'We mustn't lose sight of the porter,' Lady

Harcourt said hurriedly, 'and anyway it's impossible to talk at railway stations – such noisy, unpleasant places.'

Five minutes later, settled in the taxi with Leonie's luggage stowed on board, she turned to look at her stepdaughter.

'Your father would have come himself but he's rather unwell at the moment. It's no surprise, of course. He's been killing himself with work since before he went to Munich with Mr Chamberlain last year.'

Leonie gave a little shrug. 'Perhaps they needn't have gone. The agreement didn't achieve very much, did it?'

'It bought us some much-needed time,' Christine said sharply. 'We may soon be grateful for that.'

She smoothed a wrinkle out of one beautiful suede glove with the fingers of the other hand, then spoke again, with something that sounded almost like diffidence for once.

'Leonie, I realize that you didn't want to come back to London and probably still refuse to believe that there was anything to come back for. There's very little sign that we're at war, apart from the barrage balloons floating in the sky above us. But I ask you to believe that your father didn't bring you home just in order to make you unhappy. He believes that you'll be safer here in the bad times that are coming.'

It was an overture of sorts from a woman not given to making them. Leonie recognized it as such, but too much resentment suffocated her; she could do nothing in return but say briefly, 'I'm sorry my father's not well,' and then stare out of the window.

The taxi driver navigated the traffic rapids of Hyde Park Corner – she was beginning to identify places now – and slid into the calmer waters of the Park and the East Carriage Drive. She remembered the parks certainly – the green lungs that enabled London to breathe, hadn't someone said? – and then the wide double thoroughfare of Park Lane that they were turning into. Here, while they waited for the streams of traffic to part for them like the waters of the Red Sea for the Israelites, she had time to think of what she'd left behind: the lovely old house on a quiet island in the middle of the Seine. From her bedroom window she'd been able to watch the rising sun turn the river from grey silk to silver, and the towers and spire of Notre Dame etched against a moonlit sky. The tall, narrow house in Mayfair that they were pulling up at now would be a poor substitute for what she'd lost. She could only cling to the memory of Luc's smiling face and repeat in her mind what she knew he would say to her. *'C'est la vie, petite – pas toujours exactement ce qu'on veut!'*

Indeed it wasn't what she wished for, life in this unfriendly place with a woman she disliked. But she would endure it because Luc would expect her to. Wars didn't last for ever, and they'd still be young when she was free to go back where she belonged.

Inside, the house at least became more familiar; she even remembered its smell, compounded of wax polish, cigars, coal fires, and the flowers her stepmother arranged so professionally. Something else was familiar, too – the figure of a small, thin man who walked into the hall from the kitchen quarters.

In alpaca jacket and striped trousers he wore the usual uniform of an upper servant, but this was Smithy, her father's Cockney batman in the earlier war, his devoted henchman ever since, and her own friend as well. Perhaps because he remembered their home in Kensington Square when Cécile Harcourt had been alive, he'd never done more than settle for armed neutrality with the captain's new wife. He carried out her orders, but entirely in his own way, and she knew better than to complain; Edward would never consider getting rid of him.

He came forward now, not quite certain about this modish-looking young girl who'd replaced the unhappy youngster he remembered. But Leonie held out her hands, ready to smile for the first time in days.

'Smithy, it's me – don't you recognize me? I can't have changed all that much,' she insisted hurriedly.

His answering grin wiped away her impression that he looked much older, as well as tired and sad. 'Smartened up a lot, I'd say, miss, and about time too! Still, it's nice to 'ave you back again.' Then he spoke in a different tone of voice to the woman behind her.

'The captain's 'aving his little rest, Madam – said to tell you he'll be down later on in time for dinner.'

Even now his master remained for him the 'captain', not Sir Edward, and he failed more often than he remembered to address Christine Harcourt as anything but simply 'Madam'. She always chose to ignore the error, thinking that she thereby scored a point in the private duel they fought.

She merely nodded at him now, and then spoke to Leonie. 'We still dine at eight but life has become more informal – don't bother to change. You can unpack and relax after your journey before you meet your father. Alice will bring you some tea. I don't suppose you've eaten much today.'

Leonie could have said that she'd eaten nothing at all – grief, resentment and nervous dread had combined to overcome any desire for food. She *was* hungry now, but already felt like an unwanted guest, required to be no more of a nuisance than she could help.

Smithy filled the awkward moment by going to fetch her suitcases from the front porch.

'Come with me, miss, if you please,' he said in a faint parody of the well-trained servant that Christine Harcourt expected him to be. 'Alice will follow shortly with the tea.'

Leonie glanced at her stepmother but *she* was only giving her attention to the messages left on the hall table. The guest need simply do what she was told and follow Smithy upstairs.

The bedroom he led her to was familiar. Nothing in it had changed except that heavy black material now hung between the window and the silk curtains.

'Blackout,' he explained briefly. 'If you don't put it in place *before* you switch the light on we'll have the warden down on us like a ton of bricks.'

He stared at her white face, feeling a sudden shaft of pity. Not much of a homecoming ... probably no welcome at all from his captain's lady-wife downstairs.

'Your *pa*'ll be pleased to see you,' he said pointedly ... 'been looking forward to it, I know.'

Her tremulous smile thanked him for what she thought was a fib kindly meant, but all she said, was, 'Why must he rest in the middle of the afternoon – is he really unwell?'

'Worn out, if you really want to know,' Smithy said fiercely ... 'been overdoin' it for years, always chasin' about, one foreign place after another. They don't leave 'im in peace even now – keep sendin' papers to be looked at.'

Alice arrived with the tea before he could go on, but when they'd left her alone Leonie thought about the conversation the maid had interrupted. Smithy's thin face had been full of angry sadness, and it occurred to her now for the first time that he must love the man he'd been talking about. But however Edward Harcourt might seem to a loyal servant, she couldn't see her father in those terms. For the moment he still had control of her life. Her affections were another matter, and but for him she'd still be in Paris with her true friends.

She roused herself eventually to unpack the clothes that must tide her over until her trunk arrived from France. Among them was the leather-bound notebook that Genevieve had given her as a parting present – something, she'd said, in which to record passing impressions and events. Putting words to them might be a relief when life in England got too much for her! That had been Tante's brave attempt at a joke but now, for the first time since childhood and her mother's death, Leonie buried her face in her hands, overcome by a sudden storm of weeping. As she'd been then, she was suddenly more lonely than she could bear ... it was going to be too long, this banishment from the people she loved. The cord attaching her to them could not be made to stretch so far.

At last, exhausted by sobbing, she grew calm enough to wash her face and hands, and tidy her hair. It was time to jump the hurdle of meeting her father, and it would be a little easier to do this with her stepmother present than to have to face him alone. But when she walked into the small family sitting room on the ground floor only Edward Harcourt was there. He stood up slowly as she walked across to him to brush her cheek against his own in minimal greeting. Then she stepped away, struggling to hide a sudden sense of shock. She remembered him as a man of finely chiselled features but now his face was gaunt to the point of emaciation, and his fair hair had turned to silver. She knew his age – not quite fifty – but he seemed to have become an old man.

'Smithy said you're not well,' she managed to say, to break the awkward silence in the room. 'I'm sorry, Papa.'

'I'm a little tired, that's all.' The subject of his health dismissed, a faint smile touched his mouth. 'Smithy also said *you'd* turned out better than he expected! I can see he's right.'

Edward Harcourt waited for her to sit down, and then sank back into his own armchair. She hadn't responded to what he'd just said, and her shuttered face told him how resentfully she accepted being there. Her eyes were fixed on the hands gripped in her lap – tell-tale, white-knuckled hands that hurt him.

'My dear, look at me, please,' he asked gently. 'I know how much you loved being in Paris. Genevieve tried to be tactful, but she warned me that you'd hate being made to come home. It probably even seems unnecessary – life looks normal at the moment – but believe me when I say that it's better for you to be here.'

She gave a little shrug she'd learnt in Paris – it wasn't, he thought, an English gesture. 'I'm here because you sent for me, but I *did* want to stay there, and I'd like to go back as soon as I can.' That, she reckoned, made the position quite clear.

He stared at her, aware of a stubborn determination not to accept any alternative he could offer. The rejection hurt him but he couldn't blame her for it when he knew with aching sadness that his remarriage hadn't ever been accepted by his only child. Genevieve had also mentioned a young man who seemed to matter a great deal, but how could *that* grief be touched on except by a loving, sympathetic woman like Genevieve herself?

It was Leonie who spoke next. 'You know that I was going to be enrolled at the Sorbonne – Pappi Bernard had it all arranged. What am I going to do now – go to some English school? I think I'd hate that, even if they'd have me.' She suspected him of having given no thought to the matter, and waited for him to have to say so. But it seemed that she was wrong.

'No more school,' he said unexpectedly, 'but while the Sorbonne is out of reach my stopgap idea is that you should meet an old friend of mine, Dr Hoffmeyer. Johan left Austria at the time of the Anschluss, being unable to tolerate his German neighbours. He's a noted scholar, as well as a charming man, but he must earn a living here by taking in students. Your French is probably as good as his, but he could teach you German and Italian as well, and other languages are always useful to know. Does that appeal at all?'

The question so diffidently asked made it hard to insist that nothing he could suggest would appeal. She was even finding it difficult to go on disliking him. Instead of the aloofly courteous stranger of the past she confronted a man who seemed too tired to argue with. She was about to concede that languages might at least be useful when he unintentionally clinched the matter himself.

'I should point out that your stepmother is not in favour of the idea. She lumps Austrians with Germans, I'm afraid, and much prefers the *émigré* Poles who are now flocking into London!'

Leonie's strained face suddenly relaxed into a smile. 'Lessons with Dr Hoffmeyer will suit me very well,' she said firmly as the door opened and Christine Harcourt walked into the room.

Three

Life seemed normal, at least for the moment her father had said, but Leonie recorded in her diary that it wasn't really true. There was nothing normal about a city emptied of its young children as trainloads of them left for safer places in the country. Air-raid shelters were being hurriedly built, sandbags now protected public buildings, and even the windows of their own house – like everyone else's – were criss-crossed with tape as a precaution against flying glass.

She wrote to Genevieve in Paris that she was now equipped for life in London – with ration book and a gas mask that smelled as disgusting as it looked grotesque. And she was becoming accustomed to the church bells' silence and the blackness outdoors when evening came. But they all seemed to be prepared for a war that hadn't begun; the Phoney War, it was being called.

There was, of course, Russia's brutal attack on brave little Finland, and everyone hoped that this David, especially, would trounce Goliath once again; but that unequal northern struggle had nothing to do with the conflict they were supposed to be involved in.

The war that no one seemed to want to fight would soon be over, she wrote to Luc Gosselin; she would be back in Paris before the cat could lick its ear – an expression that Smithy had recently taught her to use, she explained proudly.

For the moment, though, it was an unexpected pleasure to discover that she was beginning to like her father very much, even if she was aware that as *their* friendship ripened so her relations with Christine Harcourt soured. She didn't know that Edward was largely to blame by pointing out to his wife that Leonie was growing more and more like her dead mother. Christine was enjoying the war; she was the driving force on all manner of committees. But it chafed to know that her own absence from the house wasn't missed as long as Leonie was there to reminisce with her father about Paris, a city he seemed to love as much as she did.

'She shouldn't be in London at all,' Christine was driven to insist one morning. 'I was right to suggest that she'd be far better off with your sister down at Frantock. She could be useful there – help Elizabeth with the evacuees that have been foisted on her. Here she spends hours with your friend Hoffmeyer, listening to his tales of life in the days of the Austro-Hungarian Empire. How useful is that for heaven's sake?'

'Johan talks to her in the languages she's there to learn,' Edward pointed out gently, 'and they speak French together as well, which makes her happy.' He smiled at his wife, hoping to persuade her frown to fade. 'My dear, she's no more a country girl than you are! I think she'd hate being buried in rural Somerset.'

'At her age she should go where she's sent,' came back the sharp answer. 'She's becoming precocious, Edward – I'm afraid our visiting friends make too much of her.'

Their 'visiting friends', he knew, were the young men now flocking into London from abroad, to whom Christine enjoyed offering hospitality while they were missing their own homes. His drawn face looked suddenly anxious at what she'd said and she hurriedly amended it.

'There's no harm in their attentions, but the Poles especially are very charming, and she's still an impressionable schoolgirl.'

'I'll talk to her,' he said after a moment, too aware of his earlier mistake to mention that he would miss her very much if she agreed to go to Frantock.

When a suitable opportunity came, he approached the subject as diplomatically as he could by asking her how much she remembered of being taken as a child to visit the Somerset village where he'd been born.

Leonie hunted through childhood memories already relegated to a distant past that she seemed to be no longer concerned with. 'I remember an old stone house,' she said finally, 'and the lovely smell of lavender and roses along the path to the front door.' Then another recollection surfaced. 'I *think* I remember Tante Elizabeth. Was she a tall, fair-haired lady surrounded by dogs?'

Edward nodded. 'She's surrounded now by children – evacuees from London who find life in the country not at all what they are used to.' He hesitated, and then went on. 'It might be a good idea for you to go and lend a hand – what do you think?'

She knew exactly what to think: the idea was her stepmother's way of getting rid of someone she didn't want in the house. The girl who'd made such a fuss about coming back to London could probably be persuaded easily enough to leave it again now.

Leonie looked at her father's hands, almost transparent in their thinness, lying on the arms of his chair. She didn't need the doctor's visits or Smithy's increasing sadness to warn her that his captain was losing ground day by day. But she knew now that even if the war ended tomorrow she wouldn't be able to go back to Paris while he was still alive; she'd have to wait for Luc until her father no longer needed her.

With his question still hanging in the air, she finally answered it. 'I think I'd rather stay here; I've got used to London now. Dr Hoffmeyer reminds me of Pappi Bernard – he even knows Max Reiner from the days when they were in Vienna together – and I think our lessons cheer him up. So I won't go to the country if you don't mind.'

The decision, announced so gravely, made

him smile. More and more she reminded him of Cécile, and he found it wonderful that the happiness of getting to know her should have been given to him to light these closing months of his life.

'Then they must manage without you at Frantock,' he said in the quiet voice that used as little of his remaining strength as possible. 'But I hope you'll visit it again one day – it's a lovely, peaceful place.'

For a moment he was tempted to say that he wanted to be buried there, but at only seventeen she was justified in being frightened at the thought of death. Christine knew his wishes, and he felt sure he could rely on her to carry them out.

The first wartime Christmas came and went. Finnish David was finally overcome by the Russian Goliath, and by the time the spring arrived Edward Harcourt had slipped away from them as undemandingly as he had lived. So quiet a man might have been expected to leave only a small emptiness behind; but Leonie saw her own sadness mirrored in Smithy's stricken face. Even Christine Harcourt mislaid her usual self-control when the moment came to say goodbye to her husband.

Leonie remembered the image she'd given Luc of her stepmother – so long ago it seemed now – of a woman without a heart; *that* would need correcting when she saw him again. Still more unfair had been her own resentment against her father. She understood now that he'd married again largely for her benefit. Perhaps he could have chosen a woman she'd have been able to like more easily, but if she'd been a less unforgiving child Christine Harcourt might have been a different stepmother. It was a painful question to ask herself even now, but it needed an answer.

Her father's funeral was, as he'd wished, to take place privately in the village church at Frantock, but by the morning of the day before it was clear that Leonie would have to be left in London. A bout of influenza that threatened to turn into something more serious made the Harcourts' doctor insist that she was far too unwell to travel. Knowing that it would leave a spare seat in the car, Leonie hoarsely pointed out to her stepmother that her father had been Dr Hoffmeyer's dearest friend. 'He's very sad,' she added. 'Could he not go in my place to the funeral?'

Christine Harcourt merely waved the suggestion aside. 'I don't think so,' she said briefly. 'Your father asked for a private funeral.'

The cortège set off early the following morning but almost as it was on the point of leaving Smithy knocked at Leonie's door. He'd brought the small leather-bound book which she knew had been always on her father's desk.

'Thought you might like to follow the service in this,' he said gruffly. 'I don't know as I make sense of all the words, but the captain did.'

Left alone again, she found the pages for the Burial of the Dead. Catholic-reared, she wasn't familiar with the majestic language of the *Book of Common Prayer*, but now she could understand why Smithy had brought it for her to read.

> I heard a voice from Heaven saying unto me, Write, for henceforth blessed are the dead which died in the Lord ... for they rest from their labours.

Her other unexpected comfort came at the end of the long, lonely day when Christine reappeared, apparently to make sure that Cook and Alice had looked after her properly. But almost on the point of leaving the room again, she said, 'We took your friend, Dr Hoffmeyer, with us, by the way. I think it did him good to be there.'

It was probably that unlooked-for concession that made Leonie seek out Smithy when she was well enough to go downstairs. She found him in his pantry, polishing the already gleaming silver as though his life depended on it.

'Stop working, please,' she said gently. 'My stepmother is out and I want to talk to you.' She hesitated for a moment, not sure how to go on. 'You know how our family life has been since Maman died,' she said finally. 'Was it my fault, do you think?'

He laid down his polishing cloth while he thought about the question.

'You *was* a little varmint,' the honest answer came at last, 'but the captain didn't blame you. He knew you was missing your mum. And when things didn't work out and you were sent away to school 'e made sure you went where the nuns spoke the French lingo.'

Leonie blinked away sudden tears, fingering the jug that Smithy had just so vigorously polished. 'We almost left it too late, my father and I ... but not quite,' she managed to say. 'I have that to be grateful for, but I wish I knew what to do next.' Dark eyes that looked too big in the thinness of her face mutely asked for help he didn't know how to give. 'I don't think I can stay here, because my stepmother and I still can't quite like each other, but I have no idea where else to go. My father suggested Somerset but I don't know my aunt and maybe *we* shouldn't get on either.'

'It's still up to 'er Ladyship, I reckon,' Smithy felt obliged to point out, 'seein' as you're not grown up yet.'

Leonie's face broke into a sad smile. 'I'll be eighteen in a week's time – grown up enough to choose to go back to Paris if it weren't for this stupid war.'

He agreed that, put this way, it *was* a nuisance, but since he could only repeat his advice that she must talk to her stepmother, there the subject rested.

But her birthday was still two days away when the 'stupid' war suddenly became serious instead. On the ninth of April they awoke to the news that not only were German troops invading Denmark, but German warships were sailing across the Baltic Sea to Norway. The phoney war was over at last.

More dreadful events followed swiftly after that: by the beginning of May Holland and Luxembourg had also been overrun, and a British Expeditionary Force had been hurriedly sent to support the Belgian army.

On her next visit to Johan Hoffmeyer she watched his finger stab the map of Europe spread out in front of them.

'Here, child,' he said in the French they usually spoke together, 'is the only frontier left that matters,' and he traced the route of the Maginot Line between France and Germany. 'This is what your mother country must rely on to keep her safe.'

Leonie stared at his troubled face, seeing in it the doubt that Luc's had hinted at months ago before she'd left Paris.

'Why shouldn't France rely on it?' she queried sharply. 'Everyone says what a military wonder it is.'

Dr Hoffmeyer's expression didn't change. 'My dear, it may be wonderful indeed but I'm afraid it's not complete. For safety's sake it should have reached the northern coast but it stops far short of that – something to do with the terrain, I understand, that wasn't suitable for the underground workings. But add to that what we now know of the way Germany is fighting this war – with aeroplanes and fast-moving tanks – and then judge how safe the French frontier is.'

Leonie thought of Luc and the Bernards in Paris and felt fear grip her heart. She wanted to shout that her Austrian friend was an exiled old man in despair over what had happened to his own country. But that was only part of the truth; he was an historian, a scholar trained to weigh evidence and, from it, reach balanced conclusions.

'Will Germany invade France next?' she asked quietly. 'Is that what you're saying?'

'Inevitably, yes,' he answered, but his hands steadied her shaking fingers. 'Even so, *liebchen*, we don't give up hope. Two great countries, Great Britain and France, are pledged to support each other, and Nazi Germany is not invincible. All its victories so far have been comparatively easy.'

She seized on that comfort, thinking that what he said was true. It allowed her to smile at him as she got up to leave. *'Á bas les Allemands!'* she offered as a kind of prayer, 'and *Vive la France*, and this country too.'

But either heaven wasn't listening or Johan had underestimated the enemy's invincibility. By the end of May the Belgian king had instructed his troops to lay down their arms, and the British Army was fighting a desperate rearguard battle towards Dunkirk, the only Channel port now left open to it. The German tank onslaught *did* sweep round the poorly protected north of France, and by the middle of June their troops had entered Paris.

Leonie listened to the dreadful news in the kitchen at Green Street. Cook and Alice wept, Smithy's worn face was full of angry despair.

'Bleedin' Germans,' he said fiercely, forgetting himself in the stress of the moment. 'Thank Gawd the captain's not 'ere to see what's happenin'.' He managed to bite back what else he might have said, but Leonie guessed and put it into furious words for him.

'I think you'd like to say bleedin' French as well, but just don't say it in front of me.' Her dark eyes glared at him, and he had to remember whose daughter she was.

'Lovely people, your mum's,' he conceded quickly. 'Nothing wrong with *them*, but I reckon their generals need shakin' up a bit, that's all.'

She accepted this in the spirit in which it was offered, but had to admit that he'd been right, when Field Marshal Pétain, now in charge, all too quickly signed an armistice taking France out of the war.

'Don't hate the French even now,' she pleaded to her downstairs friend. 'My father would ask you to remember what they suffered last time. Marshal Pétain saw the carnage at first-hand; perhaps he's right to believe that they simply couldn't bear it again.'

Smithy nodded, privately thanking the Almighty that instead of an ancient, useless soldier, or the exhausted, heartsick Neville Chamberlain, at least his own people had now got a fighter to lead them in the person of Winston Churchill. But Leonie's white face made him cast around for what relief he could give her.

'No need, at least, to worry about your friends in Paris,' he said gently. 'There'll be no trouble now with the Armistice signed.'

She sweetly thanked him for the comfort with a kiss on his cheek, and then went upstairs to bring her diary up-to-date. Even just handling Genevieve's gift seemed to bring her and Paris closer, at a time when she needed all the reassurance she could get that the life she had known there *would* survive the nightmare that was happening.

Four

The beautiful, bow-windowed drawing-room on the first floor was rarely empty now. It had become a recognized meeting place for many of the foreigners in London. Some were too old to fight, but others waited to be made use of in whatever battles lay ahead. Those who spoke little or no English were consigned to Leonie to look after. No linguist herself, Christine Harcourt thought this could be her stepdaughter's contribution to the war effort. She was a less than patient hostess herself to guests who couldn't make themselves understood, and she was ready to leave the more unrewarding incomers to a girl who, after all, had nothing else to worry about.

Leonie gave them English lessons willingly enough; she had a fellow-feeling for the ones who desperately missed being where they belonged, and helping them blotted out some of her own anxieties about the future. Invasion fever filled everybody's mind, and it no longer seemed a question of if, but only of when, Hitler would send his storm troopers across the Channel.

Despite this, General Charles de Gaulle, self-proclaimed leader of the 'Free French', was urging as many of his own countrymen as could make their way to London to join him there.

Some of those who now did so fetched up in Green Street and joined what Christine Harcourt liked to refer to as her circle of allied friends. It made for welcome noise and bustle in a house that would otherwise have seemed over-large and too empty, but Leonie confessed to Johan Hoffmeyer that it did nothing to lessen the loneliness at her heart's core. She'd given up trying to write to Luc or Genevieve; no replies came back now, and she was afraid that some known connection with England might even harm them. The certainty was growing that she would never see them again, and that, she explained gravely, left her facing a future of lifelong loss.

On the brink of tears at the sad conviction in her voice, her friend struggled to sound firm. '*Ma petite*, you are much too young to give up hope. Even if we agreed – and I do *not* – that your Parisian friends are lost to you, there will be other people for you to love. Life does not end when you are eighteen. It is what your father would say, but now I must say it for him.'

She smiled because he was kind enough to feel agitated for her, and didn't explain that hoping against all reasonable hope was what was so painful; letting go of it at least enabled her to accept that life couldn't replace what she had lost.

'At least I'm old enough now to join one of

the women's services,' she said, switching to a subject he would find less distressing. 'It wouldn't feel like leaving home. In fact, away from Green Street I shall feel closer to what *was* my home with Papa and Maman in the funny little house we lived in years ago. It's time I talked to my stepmother again about joining up; she can't overrule me this time.'

She felt happier at the thought and walked home across the Park framing in her mind what she would say – unless too much provoked, no reference to her dislike of the house she was going towards, and no hint that she thought her stepmother tiresomely overplayed her new role of international hostess. She would simply insist that she needed to feel more useful and had reached the age when she could decide things for herself. The phrases were ready when she walked indoors, but had to wait because Christine Harcourt was out, attending yet another committee meeting.

The following morning Leonie took her usual early walk through the Park before the London air got tainted with traffic fumes. The barrage balloons floated like silver fish in a strange blue element of sky instead of sea, and she stood still for a moment, shivering despite the warmth of the morning, imagining the horror of the air attacks the balloons were supposed to help prevent.

She didn't love London – it was too big, too masculine a city – but she was slowly discovering in herself an immense pride in it. Its history had been long but *now* surely was its great moment, and she must hate as much as Smithy did the people who threatened it.

Back in Green Street, she found their front door open – the signal to any would-be visitors that they were welcome to come in. The most attentive of them, Colonel Stefan Zamoyska, was already there, in his capacity of unofficial host and stand-in for the lady of the house. In Leonie's unforgiving opinion, the Polish gentleman smiled too much and stood too close to her when he had something to say, but she tried to remember that she wasn't the only lonely person living there; her stepmother must be missing Edward Harcourt even more than she was herself.

The colonel bustled towards her now to say in the flowery German he found easier than English that the *gnadige fraülein* – herself – was needed in the drawing room upstairs. She climbed the lovely, curving staircase, weighting the chances of finding her stepmother there. If it was some lost, tongue-tied Dane or Dutchman needing help, the chances were very small. But Christine Harcourt *was* there, talking to two young men who were neither Danish nor Dutch. The room went dark for a moment, and Leonie made a desperate grab at the door she'd just pushed open. She wasn't hallucinating, or going out of her mind, and she must even strive her hardest not to faint, because it wasn't a stranger but her mother's cousin, Jules Lefevre, talking to Christine Harcourt, and the tall figure beside him was, could only be, her longed for Luc.

She ducked her head until the faintness passed, and took a deep breath. More times than she could remember she'd imagined meeting him again, but never like this, in a room full of people, with Christine Harcourt looking on. Someone spoke to her. Asked, she thought, if she felt unwell. She managed to smile and shake her head, and then threaded her way across to where the new arrivals were being made welcome. It was Jules who turned and saw her first, while Luc still struggled to talk to his hostess in the English he'd almost forgotten.

'Leonie, ma chère petite cousine,' he abandoned words in order to kiss her on both cheeks and give her a suffocating hug. She emerged from it tearful but smiling, and then held out her hands to Luc, the only gesture she could manage. For the moment there was nothing she could find to say. The reeling world had righted itself again, but she needed time, and the warm strong clasp of his hands, to be sure of what was happening.

'Mademoiselle Harcourt speechless for once?' he asked in a voice that wasn't quite even. 'I don't believe it. That's *not* how I remember you!'

He'd given her the small respite she needed, and now she could frame words and address them to her stepmother. 'Have they introduced themselves properly? My cousin, Jules Lefevre, and my ... good friend, Luc Gosselin.' Then she turned to the men. 'Tell me, please, about Tante Genevieve and Professor Bernard. You must have seen them ... are they all right?' A gleam of humour lit her pale face. 'If it's easier you're allowed to speak French here – a lot of people do!'

It was Jules who accepted the offer, with a little apologetic bow to his hostess. 'They are both well, my dear, and send you so much love. It was Genevieve, of course, who said that we might come and ask for you here.' He looked round the room, and then raised Christine Harcourt's hand to his lips. 'This kind lady makes many of us refugees welcome, I see.'

Pleased by the charming gesture, she whisked him away to meet the most senior of his compatriots who happened to be there, and it left Leonie and Luc free to stand and stare at one another. He looked older, she thought, and very tired, but he was still Luc, her one and only love.

'We heard the General's broadcast,' she said huskily, 'is that why you and Jules have come?'

'It was hard to know what to do,' Luc admitted, 'stay and try to take care of people there, or answer de Gaulle's call. But we can't leave it all to the British ... I suppose that's why we're here.'

She nodded, resisting the temptation to stroke away the sadness in his face and what she sensed was his despair. He was an artist whose purpose in life was to observe and recreate beauty, but events were forcing him to face the prospect of trying to kill his fellow creatures.

'Tell me about the Bernards,' she said quickly. 'It's so long since I heard from them. Are they really all right?'

It would have been a hard question to answer, even if his mind wasn't occupied in registering the change in her. In less than a year since she'd left Paris – admittedly a very extraordinary year – the charming, wayward schoolgirl had grown up. Dark hair and eyes were unchanged, but now the lovely bones of her face were clearly visible, and extreme slenderness made her seem taller than she was. She had grown beautiful very quickly. But it hadn't needed more than his brief conversation with Christine Harcourt to confirm what he already knew – stepmother and daughter could have had nothing in common with each other except the man who was no longer there.

'I'm sorry about your father, *petite*,' he said gently. 'That news was the last we had, and Genevieve asked me to say that she was happy to have been proved wrong about him.'

Leonie nodded, then returned to the question he hadn't answered. 'Is it very bad for them in Paris now?'

'They manage,' he said slowly. 'Life is supposed to go on normally, but what a travesty of the truth that is when we're no longer masters of our own city. You can't imagine what it's like to watch German soldiers goose-stepping along the Champs Élysées and face the fact that there's nothing you can do about it.'

'Not quite true,' Leonie said firmly. 'You can do what you have done – come here to help us fight *les Allemands*. Mr Churchill is very firm on that point: we *shall* fight them.'

He didn't contradict the proud little boast – let her believe in miracles as long as she could. 'You've become more English,' he merely pointed out and saw her smile at last.

'Only for the duration, Luc!' He looked puzzled, and saw her smile at last. 'It's a stock phrase here now – whatever we have to put up with is "only for the duration"; afterwards everything will go back to normal.' She stared at him, suddenly grave again. 'We have to believe that if we're going to win.'

A glance across the room confirmed that her cousin was still deep in conversation, and she could hold out her hand to Luc. 'Jules is being taken care of. Will you come with me? There's someone I want you to meet.'

She led him out of the room down to the kitchen quarters where Smithy sat repairing a clock that refused to chime. He inspected the man who followed her into the room but waited for her to speak.

'Smithy, you have to meet my dear friend from Paris, Luc Gosselin. Luc, may I present Mr Albert Smith, my father's brave soldier in the last war and his dear friend thereafter.'

The 'dear friend' looked put out. 'She always talked a lot of nonsense and still does,' he grumbled. 'Truth is I was the captain's servant, in the war and after till 'e died.'

'You're both right, I think,' Luc said with a faint smile, 'and now you're his daughter's friend as well.'

Smithy nodded, aware of the expression on Leonie's face. She looked enchanted, like a child gazing at some precious treasure; but she wasn't a child, she'd become a young woman now, and he knew what the look meant.

'Luc's an artist,' she said next, 'but for the moment he's come to join General de Gaulle. Maman's cousin has come as well – he's upstairs talking to my stepmother.'

'So now you reckon we might be able to win the war, I suppose,' Smithy commented. He stared at Luc and saw understanding and humour in the other man's face. He was French, of course, but probably not much wrong with him apart from that. A smile finally lit his own lined face. 'Pleasure to meet you, I'm sure, but now I've got work to do, and you're supposed to be with the quality upstairs.'

Obedient to the hint, Leonie turned to look at Luc. 'We've been dismissed, I think, and Jules will be wondering where we've got to.'

As they climbed the stairs she thought of something else. 'You must stay with us while you're here. I'm sure my stepmother would want you to, and there *are* spare bedrooms.'

He halted and turned round to face her. 'My dear, we aren't free to do what we please. It's disorganized at the moment while the authorities work out what to do with us, but we *are* under military orders. We're billeted at a school where the pupils have been evacuated. The beds are rather small, but we're comfortable enough. We'll come and see you again as soon as we can.'

She had just been reminded, very gently she realized, that war was war; he wasn't there to make her happy or restore her wavering faith in the divine order of things.

'I was going to volunteer for something myself,' she answered gravely after a moment, 'but I shan't for as long as you're in London – that would be asking too much of me.'

There was teasing in his smile, but something much more serious as well. 'And I shall try not to worry about all these handsome, gallant Poles Lady Harcourt invites to this house! You and I have our future to look forward to, do we not?'

It was too soon and it was more – much more – than he had meant to say; but his introduction to Smithy downstairs, her only friend, had made him sharply aware of how alone she was. He also understood much more clearly than she did how precarious their future was. But, as if the Holy Grail had been put into her hands, he saw the answering radiance in her face and couldn't regret what he had said.

They went on up the stairs together hand in hand, and found Jules waiting for them anxiously. It was already time for him and Luc to leave, he said, and they left at once.

Five

In everyone's memory afterwards it remained a summer they would never forget – the oppressive atmosphere of uncertainty and dread oddly counterpointed by a succession of lovely, sunlit days when life should have been easy but was not.

They were all, Smithy reckoned, living on their nerves, but Leonie was doing more than that. In his considered opinion her Frenchman should have stayed where he belonged; one less to fight for the General maybe, but that would have been better than watching a girl ride a seesaw of joy and fear that even made *him* dizzy.

At least the young man mostly stayed away from the house. Perhaps he understood what damage he could cause – Smithy was prepared to give him credit for that. But one Sunday morning he arrived just as Leonie was setting out for mass at the little Catholic church she favoured in Farm Street. Smithy, watching him smile and take her hand, wondered if she'd listen to a word the priest said.

They came out afterwards into sunlight that seemed all the more golden after the candlelit dimness of the church. Its adjoining garden was unkempt, but a little, hidden oasis of tranquility that they were both reluctant to leave. With Luc's jacket spread out for them on the untidy grass, Leonie watched him stretch out full-length and close his eyes. After a little while she leaned across and lightly kissed his mouth.

'Why did you do that?' he asked, still not looking at her.

'I wanted to see you smile,' she answered. 'Do you hate being here so much – is that why you look so sad?'

'I was thinking how much I hate communal life,' he said more or less truthfully. 'I'm going to make a very bad soldier, I'm afraid.'

'A temporary soldier,' she insisted firmly. 'When the war is over *you*'re going to become a great painter, and I shall be your devoted handmaiden, looking after you as Tante Genevieve looks after Max Reiner. Only, unlike Max, you'll have to look away from your easel occasionally, long enough to notice that I'm there, because I'm not as selfless as my darling godmother.'

Luc opened his eyes then and smiled at her. 'It's a promise, *chérie* – you *will* be noticed.' But his face soon looked haunted again and she thought she knew why.

'I'm sorry I didn't ask about your family,' she murmured. 'You must be worried about them if they're still in Paris.'

'My father is not,' the answer came quickly. 'He couldn't bear the sight of his beloved restaurants filled with German officers. My brother and sister don't seem to mind; they even manage to welcome our invaders.'

The bitterness in his voice kept her silent for a moment, and she knew she must choose her words carefully. 'Perhaps they haven't much choice,' she ventured at last. 'And there must be *something* of Parisian life left to pick up when the war is over.'

'Generously enough said for both of us,' he commented. 'Well done, *petite*.'

She winced a little at the jibe, but shook her head. 'Not well done at all. That's why I have to be more careful now about judging other people. I was quite wrong about my step-mother, and completely wrong about my father.' Then her lovely smile reappeared. 'Fortunately I'm not wrong about you ... about us!'

The sudden, joyful certainty in her face brought him upright to look at her, and to take hold of her hands in a grip that hurt.

'My dear, don't ... please *don't* think too much about that lovely future day when I'm a famous artist and you're my pride and joy. I'm afraid it's a long way off at the moment.'

'Oh, I realize that now, among other things,' she said firmly. 'I didn't know my father loved poetry until I found in his books that he'd marked lines that had a special meaning for him, like this one – "Look thy last on all things lovely every hour... " Well, that's what I do now, all the time. I know I may lose what I find most lovely, but at least I'm intensely alive. That's how I want to be, not breathing but hopeless and dead inside.'

It was a declaration of faith and love, he realized – foolhardy perhaps but brave. He kissed the palms of her hands and folded her fingers carefully over them for safekeeping. Then he pulled her to her feet, aware of their seclusion and how easy it would be to start something there that he had no right to finish.

'I must walk you home to your Mayfair mansion, my little love, before I return to my more humble school hall. We have lectures scheduled for this afternoon.'

She fell into step beside him but kept tight hold of his hand. 'Do you mean what you said about being a bad soldier? Couldn't you be something else instead?'

The anxious question made him smile naturally at last. 'What shall I suggest – painting murals on the walls of the general's quarters? I'm afraid it doesn't sound quite dashing enough for the warrior I'm supposed to be! Jules, by the way, sees himself as a brilliant fighter pilot. Any day now he'll be sent up to Scotland to learn how to fly a plane.'

'But *you* won't do that, will you?' Leonie's voice sounded urgent now. 'Promise me you won't do that.'

'No, *chérie*; that would be *too* dashing for me. I shall have to find a happy medium. That's what my English friends here say. They seem to have a great faith in it, and so shall I.'

She smiled because she knew that he

wanted her to, and then they walked the rest of the way in silence, both of them aware of the minutes ticking away before they were separated again.

The door of the house opened as they reached it, and Christine Harcourt and her Polish squire, Colonel Zamoyska, came out.

'We've been to mass – in Farm Street church,' Leonie explained, to fill a silence that felt awkward.

'Of course ... the good monks,' her stepmother said vaguely, never sure of how or with whom Catholics chose to worship God. Then she included Luc in her smile. 'I'm sure Cook can find you some lunch, Mr Gosselin,' although she was even less sure about that, food rationing being what it now was.

But Luc answered for them both. 'Thank you Lady Harcourt, but I must rejoin my companions.' He kissed Leonie on both cheeks, murmured '*À bientôt, petite,*' and strode off down the street.

'*Very* abrupt,' her Ladyship commented, 'one can't tell with the French – they're either that or much too effusive.'

'But never the happy medium, of course,' Leonie agreed sweetly, and went inside and closed the door.

There were dreadful things happening on the Continent and, added to them, the daily news of mounting losses among the precious Atlantic convoys. Even so, it seemed to Leonie that the war was a distant nightmare on the far side of the narrow sea that kept England, for the moment at least, uninvaded. Then something occurred to make it more real and propel her into a serious quarrel with Smithy.

He'd been very careful not to rub salt into her wounds about the French Armistice. But news of the order given to destroy the French fleet sheltering at Oran was a different matter. He didn't even try to hide his jubilation and looked unmoved when she began to fly at him.

'We're supposed to be on the same side,' she stormed. 'How *can* we expect Frenchmen to come here and fight when we attack them like this? I hate my father's country – perfidious Albion indeed!'

Smithy sounded calm and unimpressed. 'That's 'cos you know even less than I do about what's what.' He held up his hand to stem the tirade that was coming. 'Now you just listen to me. We've got the Eyeties against us as well now that the brave Duce reckons it's safe to join in, so there's a war to fight in North Africa as well as everywhere else. I don't know how much good they are, but Italian ships added to the French fleet might have dished us in parts of the Mediterranean. I'm prepared to upset a few Frenchmen to stop that happenin' and so, thank Gawd, is Mr Churchill. He gave them the choice – join us or be sunk. The French admiral chose wrong, that's all.'

It was a long speech for Smithy, usually a

man of few words, but even in the middle of her own distress Leonie heard the conviction that had prompted it. He *did* know more than she did, she had to admit, and had given four years of his life to fighting the very people who were threatening them now.

'Well,' she sniffed, blinking away angry tears, 'I'll take back the perfidious Albion bit, but I still shan't know what to say to Luc when he comes next.'

Part of the trouble, Smithy realized full well, was that her Frenchman *didn't* come. It stood to reason, of course; he wasn't in England just to keep paying social calls. But it was hard to have to point this out to a girl who couldn't help but keep one eye on the street in case he should come walking along.

'When you see 'im, keep off the bleedin' war altogether,' was the best advice Smithy could offer, 'talk about somethin' more cheerful, I should.'

She nodded and gave him a little kiss, to show that they were still friends, but resentment continued to rankle, and she went to visit Dr Hoffmeyer expecting to get sympathy from him. To her pained surprise he was quite as firm with her as Smithy had been.

'My dear, your old friend was quite right. This is no time for sentimentality, I'm afraid. Your Prime Minister understands that better than anyone, and I hope that even the French people you love will do so as well.'

Unable to answer for what Luc would understand, she went back to Green Street to discover that she'd missed Jules Lefevre, come to say goodbye before he left for Scotland. Her stepmother's tone of voice suggested that it served her right for not staying at home where she might have been useful, and Leonie retreated to her own room to weep in private for the lost chance of hearing news of Luc.

At the end of another week, fearful of missing him, she refused to go with her stepmother on a duty visit to a relative who was thought to be dying. They parted company on cooler terms than usual, glad to be rid of each other for a few days.

Christine Harcourt was still away when a quiet knock sounded on the front door one evening. Smithy, listening to the nine o'clock news broadcast in the kitchen, didn't hear it, but Leonie – crossing the hall – did. She was tempted not to open the door so late in the day, but the gentle knock was repeated and she was suddenly sure she knew who waited there.

It *was* Luc, holding a small suitcase in one hand. She beckoned him inside and quietly closed the door.

'My stepmother is away,' she murmured, 'and Smithy's downstairs. We won't disturb him – he can't bear to miss a word of the news.'

She led Luc into the small, ground-floor sitting room and turned to smile at him, pale face now radiant with joy.

'It's ages since you came, but I shan't complain now that you're here,' she promised. 'Can you stay this time? *Please* say yes. Surely it's too late to go back to your wretched school.'

'It's too late to have come at all,' he said ruefully, 'but we've been hard at work until now.' He hesitated for a moment, then went on in a voice he tried to make as casual as possible. 'I'm here to say goodbye, *petite*, not to stay.'

'Not ... the fighter-pilot thing,' she murmured. 'Oh, Luc, I thought you promised not to.'

He shook his head. 'No, not that. I can't really tell you very much about it, but I'm going back to France.'

'To France? But you've only just escaped from there. You can't go back – it's much too dangerous.' Her voice broke at the thought of it, and her eyes were suddenly full of fear.

He led her to a sofa, and pulled her into his lap, holding her close.

'Listen please, *chérie*. It won't be dangerous at all because I'm going to the south. There are no Germans there – it's unoccupied France, still governed by Frenchmen.'

'So what's the point of going?' Leonie muttered, not unreasonably, he thought. He kissed the tip of her nose because she sounded merely cross now, and then smiled lovingly at her.

'This is what I'm not supposed to talk about, *chérie*, so please forget what I say. People there are already forming into groups

– *résistants*, they're called – to feed information back to the authorities here, and make life difficult for the Germans should they break the armistice terms and begin to interfere. But these groups need help in organizing themselves and they need supplies which will be dropped to them from the air. I know the countryside, and I can talk to them, and to the people here. I'd be a hopeless soldier, but this is work I *can* do.'

Leonie asked her next question with the calmness of despair. 'When do you leave?'

'Within a day or two – it depends on the weather now. We shall be put ashore at night from a British submarine. Exciting, *n'est-ce-pas*, for an unadventurous artist like me?'

She couldn't smile, but promised herself that at least she wouldn't weep. 'I'd go with you if they'd let me – isn't there something I could do?'

He gently kissed her trembling mouth, and felt her lips cling to his, making it hard to draw away.

'*Chérie*, I'm a French citizen with a right to be there; you're not.' Then he looked down at the small suitcase at his feet. 'There *is* something you can do for me – take care of this. My father gave it to me before I left Paris. He was very vague about what was inside – family papers, he said, that would come in useful when the war is over. There wasn't time to ask about *them* or about the key he forgot to give me! We'll break into it together when I come to take you back to France.'

Leonie nodded. 'Of course I'll take care of it,' she agreed, but spoke as if her mind was much more concerned with something else. She was half-frightened by what she was going to say next, but still quite sure that it had to be said, as calmly as possible.

'Will *you* do something for me?' she finally asked. 'Will you stay here tonight? I don't mean in a room by yourself, I mean with me.'

He couldn't pretend not to understand, or try to brush away a suggestion that wasn't meant to be serious. Life was too precarious now for pretence of any kind. More than ever now they were, as her father's poet had said, looking their last on all things lovely every hour of every day. But he managed to smile at her as he shook his head.

'*Chérie*, I can't do that. It would be very wrong of me.' He sought desperately for something that would not only convince her but also lessen the hurt of being rejected. 'Think what your friend Smithy would say ... He'd hate the French – with good reason – even more than I suspect he does already!'

'He didn't hate my mother,' Leonie said firmly, 'and in any case I don't care what he thinks.' Her composure was threatened now but she forced herself to say what she didn't really believe. Crushed disappointment was her only weapon left – the one he might be too kind to withstand.

'Not too young any more, but still not attractive enough – why didn't I realize that before you had to point it out to me! Poor

Luc, you must have been hoping for so long that I'd stop loving you when I grew up. But now that I *am* grown up, I'm still offering you something you don't want.'

His hands gripped her thin shoulders and shook her almost roughly. 'Don't say it ... don't think it, not for a moment. You're far lovelier than I could possibly deserve. But you're still only eighteen, *ma petite*, and I am just about to leave you here alone because I have no choice.'

She could even smile at him now, reassured on the one point that mattered. 'It's *because* of that, Luc, that I beg you to stay. I know as well as you do that the work you're going to do is dangerous. I even realize that unless God is very merciful I may not see you again. But I shan't ever accept anyone else, so if you won't stay with me tonight I may never know what it is to give myself completely to the joy of being loved.'

He held out a moment longer; could just – he thought – have resisted the wave of longing that flooded through his own body. But *her* need couldn't go unanswered. He stood up with her in his arms and carried her upstairs. They could have met Smithy trying to bar her bedroom door and it would have made no difference to him now; she *must* know that she was loved before he went away.

She awoke to the dimness of early morning in the room and memory of the night just past seeped in like an incoming tide of delight.

She hadn't known, couldn't have imagined, the joy of what had happened. She smiled at the recollection of what Luc, teasing her but shaken, had said about convent-reared lovers, and pitied from the bottom of her heart the nuns who would die not knowing what it was to be tenderly, passionately loved.

She stretched out her hand to touch him again but, beside her, the bed was cold and empty. There was only a scrap of paper torn from a notebook lying on his pillow.

'My love, this is the coward's way of saying *au revoir* – I couldn't bear to wake you, kiss you goodbye, and then have to go out weeping into the street. Remember that I love you, and wait for me, please. Luc.'

She read and reread the few lines, then lay watching the dawn light creep slowly into the room. It was hard to believe, but the sun was still rising, her heart was still beating, even though Luc had gone. Another line of poetry her father had marked slipped into her mind – 'Thoughts that lie too deep for tears'. As always, poets went to the heart of things. She would travel with Luc on his journey back to France, keeping him company in her mind, but there'd be no relief in weeping.

Today, she finally remembered, her stepmother was due home. It seemed strange to think that neither *she* nor anyone else in the house would realize that yesterday's Leonie Harcourt had become a different person. They never would know, she told herself, but not because she was ashamed of having spent a night with Luc. Having even one other person aware of it would use up some of her secret hoard of joy, and she might need it to last too long to be able to spare a single bit of it.

She went downstairs at the normal time and found Smithy scratching his head in the hall.

'I could 'ave sworn I bolted the door last night, same as usual. Must be gettin' old and careless.'

She managed to answer without blushing. 'Don't worry, Smithy, I won't split on you when her Ladyship gets back.' Then she smiled at him and repeated one of his own sayings. '"What the eye don't see the 'eart don't grieve", *n'est-ce-pas*?'

He nodded but didn't smile, and stared at her a little too long for comfort. Nothing more was said, but she knew he'd guessed the truth about the door that ought to have been bolted and wasn't.

Six

There was no point now in staying in Green Street. Leonie came to this conclusion having faced the certainty that Luc must remain in France until the war was over. She was left to an existence that she couldn't bear. Smithy's outward manner to her hadn't changed but she knew that his good opinion had been lost. Added to her stepmother's usual polite indifference, it made her feel that she was living in a cold and empty vacuum. The warmth and kindness she'd known in the Bernards' house had become a distant memory, and the thought of Luc brought more anguish than relief. His pretence of going off on some 'Boy's Own' adventure had been a brave try at concealing the truth – what he was being sent to do was dangerous. She could only endure it by finding something demanding to do herself.

This time she didn't repeat her earlier mistake of talking about it first; she simply volunteered for service in the WRNS and then waited to be called. It was only when the enlistment papers were in her hand that she made her announcement at breakfast one morning.

'Fait accompli,' she said to her stepmother with a faint smile. 'I'm going to become a Wren! I have to report to Devonport this afternoon.'

If she'd expected any angry protest or show of regret she would have been disappointed – if anything, Christine Harcourt's expression looked relieved. But, much to Leonie's surprise, she *did* say one unexpected and disarming thing.

'You'll be glad to escape – you've never felt this was your home.' It was too accurate to be denied, but before she had to say so her stepmother spoke again. 'I didn't intend it to be like that ... I hoped there would be more children here, but...' Her hand brushed away the rest of what she couldn't say, and Leonie suddenly understood what had made her the disappointed woman she was: she'd been married to a man who couldn't forget the wife who had died.

'I didn't make it easy for you,' Leonie quietly admitted. 'Smithy pointed it out to me and he was right. I'm sorry it's too late to change things now.'

Christine Harcourt smiled, but didn't comment on what had just been said. 'Friends at a distance from now on?' she suggested instead. 'You'll come back here when you're allowed time off from shoring up the Navy! Home or just house, this is your base until you can return to Paris.'

Leonie nodded, thinking that whatever else her stepmother might lack, she didn't lack honesty. Warmth she couldn't pretend to wasn't offered, but a kind of friendship was. It was something, at least, to take away.

They exchanged a kiss on both cheeks at parting. Cook was tearful, and Alice enviously aware that chronic short-sightedness would keep her chained to domestic duties. Smithy loaded Leonie's suitcase into a waiting cab and gave her a fierce hug, but his only parting shot was, 'Should've been the Army – the captain would've liked that.'

'Nicer uniform in the Wrens,' she managed to say, 'especially the hat!' Then she jumped inside and stared unseeingly out of the window until they reached Paddington Station because her eyes were full of tears.

Life at Devonport was not unlike being back at the Convent – different mentors, different uniform, but the sense of being in school again was comforting and irritating at the same time. It was a far, uncomfortable cry from life in Green Street, but for that she was grateful. Less easy to deal with was the feeling that her fellow recruits, mostly older in years, still seemed like schoolgirls emotionally. As a result the friendships that were quickly formed didn't include her. She thought *them* childish, they thought *her* stand-offish, and half-foreign as well. Her officers reckoned her intelligent, and promotable when she'd grown out of the habit of querying orders she thought unreasonable.

Then one morning she failed to appear for

parade, and the girl who slept next to her reported that Leonie had been sick when she got up. The doctor's examination revealed beyond doubt that Wren Harcourt was pregnant. He made no comment on the word 'spinster' among her enrolment details, but her reaction to his news puzzled him: shock would have been natural in the circumstances. Instead, she seemed apologetic for having wasted the Navy's precious time, but indifferent to almost everything else.

'You'll be dismissed, of course,' he confirmed, 'but what will you do then? You must talk to the child's father, I suppose, or at least to your family.'

A wry smile touched her mouth for a moment, but she agreed calmly enough that her family would have to be told, and he was left to assume that the father was already untraceable. It happened in wartime ... It was one of the sad, inevitable consequences of the lives young people were now leading.

In front of her fellow Wrens she was calm when she left Devonport, but on the train journey back to London dizzying waves of anxiety and fear mixed with joy made her feel wretchedly sick again. Her stepmother, as her next-of-kin, had already been informed of the reason for her dismissal. Although she couldn't be sure of the reception she would get in Green Street, the likelihood was that warmth and reassurance would be missing, unless Smithy decided that she was more sinned against than sinning; but she would have to correct him about that.

As usual, the house seemed to be full of people she didn't know. Christine Harcourt's 'allies club' was a recognized meeting place now, where the lost and lonely made free of her hospitality. They did not, Leonie realized, include herself when she came face to face with her stepmother.

'I know why you're back,' was the extent of her own welcome. 'The Commanding Officer wrote to me.'

Christine Harcourt stared at the girl in front of her, looking for some trace of shamed regret, but all she could see was white-faced exhaustion mixed with pride. 'I imagine there's still time to terminate the pregnancy,' she went on coolly. 'Is that what you want to do?'

'No, I do not.' Afraid that she'd shouted the words, Leonie repeated them more quietly. 'No, I do not. The child is all I may ever have of Luc.'

In turn she watched her stepmother's face and thought she saw a kind of bitter envy there. No pretence of comfort on offer; at least Christine Harcourt had the virtue of consistency. But her anger couldn't be allowed to fall on someone else.

'Don't blame Smithy. He didn't even know Luc came to the house while you were in Oxford – much less that I begged him to stay a night before he went away.'

It wasn't dislike, but anguish surely, that she saw now, as the memory of an earlier conversation came back to her. The longed-for children her stepmother had been denied must make her own condition unbearable.

'You don't want me here,' she said, almost gently now. 'I'll find somewhere else to live.'

'You'll go to Frantock – it's already been arranged with your aunt.' She recognized the refusal that Leonie was about to put into words and spoke again herself in a less hostile tone of voice. 'You'll need something to do, and Elizabeth needs help – she sounds exhausted. In any case, I have a duty to your father to keep you safe. Air raids have already started here and they're only the beginning of what we can expect. For the sake of your child, at least, go to Frantock, please.'

Leonie could see no way out of the corner she'd been boxed into. Somerset might look like the end of the world, the end of life itself, but the truth was that she had no real alternative.

'Very well – Frantock it is,' she finally agreed. 'Now I'd like to go and lie down – it was an uncomfortable journey.'

She had got as far as the door when her stepmother's voice halted her. 'Will you tell Luc Gosselin about the child? I suppose that what I really mean is, will he acknowledge it as his?'

Lower lip bitten too sharply, Leonie had the taste of blood in her mouth, but she managed not to weep in front of the woman watching her.

'I shall tell him when I can. For the moment

he's back in France working for us as an undercover agent.'

Christine lowered her sword, suddenly reluctant to say that if he survived at all, the chances of his remembering one night spent with a lovesick teenager were small indeed. Instead, she sounded sharp again. 'Go and lie down for heaven's sake. Alice can bring you a cup of tea.'

She wondered why her stepdaughter's face suddenly relaxed in to an odd smile, unaware that Leonie was replaying the memory of her return from Paris the previous year, and her stepmother's offer of an ever-useful tray of tea. The sun might fall from the sky, the world might come to an end – but through every catastrophe dear, short-sighted Alice would be delivering the inevitable cup of tea. Leonie's smile now was born of the sudden conviction that, against whatever odds, these people she lived among and half-belonged to *would* win the war after all ... because it didn't occur to them to give in.

That night she heard the banshee wail of the sirens for the first time and – following Smithy's urgent knock on her door – spent the next six hours on a camp bed in the cellar, listening to the drone of enemy bombers overhead and the answering boom-boom of the anti-aircraft battery hidden in the park. Frantock began to seem less like the end of life now and more like her best hope of preserving it.

When morning came she set off once again

for Paddington, now en route to Somerset, but this time Smithy took it upon himself to escort her to the station. Very little was said along the way, even when they passed sickening signs of bomb damage, but at Paddington it was obvious that the train was going to be delayed and so some conversation would be required. He'd said nothing so far about the reason for her sudden return from Devonport but she knew that nothing else *could* be said until the subject had been dealt with.

'I'm sorry,' she finally muttered. 'I expect you think I've let you and my father down.'

He stared at her thin face, seeing the sadness she found hard to put into words. 'Nothin's normal now, so what I think is neither 'ere nor there. But I'll tell you this: the captain would've liked a grandchild, so mind you take care of it.'

She nodded, and then reached up to kiss his cheek, acknowledging that friendship was intact after all. 'I hope this is going to work – Frantock, I mean. I know nothing about the country, and my aunt knows very little about me except that I'm in disgrace.'

'She's part of your family,' Smithy pointed out, 'bound to be all right. As for the country, I think your pa wanted to live there 'imself one day ... said it was peaceful! Mind, we only went once, but I couldn't sleep for the din the animals made all night – give me London any time.'

Leonie's fleeting grin appeared as she remembered the noisy night they'd just spent in the cellar, but then she grew serious again. 'What will *you* do, apart from always keep in touch with me, I hope?' There was no need to mention that he would soon be too old to go up and down numerous flights of stairs a dozen times a day.

Smithy waved the problem away. 'Die in 'arness is what I'll do. I promised the Captain I'd stay with 'er Ladyship, so that's all there is to that.'

A flurry of whistles suddenly broke out, and the rest of what he might have said was lost because the train was finally about to leave. Leonie leaned out of the window for one last shouted request. 'If there should be any word from France, Smithy, you'll *promise* to let me know?'

'I'll bring it in person,' he answered hoarsely, and then stood waving his hat until the train was out of sight.

She expected an anxiety-ridden journey but, thanks to the past night's sleeplessness, she dozed for most of the way. The train was pulling into Taunton station as she woke up, and there was barely time to heave her luggage onto the platform before the guard was blowing his whistle for departure. Someone would collect her but that was all she knew. The minutes lengthened and everyone else had drifted away before a large man galloped towards her.

'So sorry ... it *is* Leonie, isn't it? When we rang they said the train was running very late

– it must have made up time.' Looking at her uncertain expression his own weather-beaten face offered a friendly smile. 'I'm your uncle by marriage, by the way – Michael Wentworth.'

Her hand was lost in a huge paw that felt calloused and rough. A working farmer, she realized; not someone who left the hard grind of looking after his land to other people. It was a small fact to hold on to amid her almost total ignorance of the people she was being foisted on. There was only her memory of an old stone house and a tall, fair-haired woman with a retinue of dogs. But there were children now, her father had said – as much of an unknown quantity to her as the dogs would be.

'I've come to help, not be a nuisance,' she said gravely to this pleasant stranger, 'but I'll have to learn about living in the country.' She sounded self-possessed, but her face was very pale, and – accustomed as he was to handling animals – he recognized the fear that made her hands tremble.

'You'll learn soon enough,' he said gently, 'but first you look as if you need fresh air and wholesome food. It beats me how anyone manages to survive in London at all, especially now.' He was decking himself with pieces of luggage while he talked. 'One more for you,' he said, handing her a holdall in addition to the small leather suitcase she kept a tight hold on, 'then we can go. The car's outside. Not supposed to use it, of course, but we're some distance from Taunton, and I thought you might not fancy a long ride in a pony and trap!'

With nothing more to say for the moment, Leonie followed him outside to where an ancient Humber waited in the afternoon sunlight. Her first impression of her aunt's husband was that he was a large, kind, gentle man, and the image needed no alteration for as long as she subsequently knew him. She supposed he must have been told why she was there, but his manner simply suggested that she'd come to pay them a long-overdue visit.

Half an hour later they approached the house she remembered, but she hadn't remembered its glowing colour.

'It's golden,' she said suddenly, surprised out of a long silence. 'I'd forgotten that.'

'Because it's built of hamstone, quarried out of a hill a bit to the south of where we are on the edge of the Levels – golden indeed with the sun on it,' Michael Wentworth agreed. 'Otherwise it's Blue Lias locally, which is grey, but we reckon it doesn't compare with this.' She smiled at the pride in his voice, and he saw that she would be beautiful when she looked happy.

'The front door's open,' he said. 'You go in and find your aunt while I drive the car round to the yard.'

Now her heart was beating uncomfortably fast again, but there was the lavender-edged path she remembered, and she must walk along it to meet Elizabeth Wentworth.

Familiarity went awry, of course, because the woman awaiting her in the hall was prematurely silver-haired now, and had shrunk to being no taller than Leonie herself. She looked for some resemblance to her father – the thin, straight nose perhaps, and deep-set eyes. Yes, there *was* a likeness.

'Welcome to Frantock,' her aunt said coolly. 'It's a long time since you were here.' She didn't sound hostile, but her husband's friendliness was missing. Her good opinion would have to be earned, Leonie realized, and her affection might be even harder to achieve.

'My stepmother asked me to say that she would have liked to come herself, to see you again, but she is very occupied with helping people who use the house as a kind of meeting place – they're foreigners who've had to take refuge in London.'

'Very praiseworthy I'm sure,' Elizabeth said in a noncommittal voice. Then, because she was a direct, plain-speaking woman, she came to the point. 'I know, of course, why you've had to leave the Wrens. I won't pretend that I approve of conceiving children out of wedlock, but I accept that in wartime normal rules of behaviour are subject to great strain.' Then the pallor of the girl in front of her made her add something else. 'I also realize that life since your dear mother died has been difficult, and you're still very young. At least you've had the courage to keep the child – I hate abortions.'

'It didn't need courage,' Leonie heard herself say steadily to this formidable aunt. 'I *want* the child, and I pray night and morning that Luc will survive so that he can know about it. If you can't believe that I don't want to stay here, even if I *am* supposed to help you with the evacuees.'

There was silence for a moment in the cool, flower-scented hall while Elizabeth considered the girl she had accepted reluctantly as another burden she didn't really want. Edward's daughter, of course, so she couldn't have been refused, but she looked too out-of-place, too defiantly different, for Christine Harcourt's solution to the problem to work.

'Of course you must stay,' Elizabeth said more gently all the same. 'Yours won't be the first or the last illegitimate baby to be born in Frantock and that is all we need ever say on the subject. Now I'll take you upstairs. You look as though a rest would do you good before supper.'

Leonie fought down a half-hysterical bubble of laughter, waiting for the inevitable offer of tea; but it didn't come and she followed her aunt up a beautiful, shallow-treaded staircase to the floor above. She was led into a simply furnished but charming room, its windows open to the lovely view outside – cattle-dotted meadows neatly hedged, tall clumps of trees whose names she didn't know, and more distantly the gentle green Somerset hills.

'The children will be back for their tea

soon,' Elizabeth said, 'but you won't hear the noise they make up here. Lie down for a while, I should.' Then she went out and quietly shut the door.

The bed looked inviting, but the cushioned seat, surely intended as a vantage point, drew her back to the window again. Tired and heartsick as she was, the peace of the place registered after the bedlam of London. She'd have to remember to tell Smithy he'd been wrong about that. But how, or even if, she could become a country person seemed doubtful, and she suspected that nothing less would be needed to fit into Elizabeth Wentworth's ménage. How long her stay was to be she had no idea. Was she there 'for the duration', or only until her child was born? The future with Luc was what her heart and mind must cling to, but oh, dear God, how far away it looked and how very uncertain.

Seven

The summer wore on, and the Battle of Britain was fought and won in the skies above the hop fields and orchards of Kent and a Channel that Leonie no longer resented being called 'English'. It was the battle that history would remember, but Leonie saw herself as also living through an important struggle of her own.

Outwardly nothing changed; despite whatever clothes the weather obliged her to wear, she still had the Parisian flair learned from Genevieve Bernard that marked her out from the local women. But slowly and painfully she was adjusting to the country's different heartbeat. No longer irritated by the measured pace at which people walked and talked, she began to notice what went on around her, and to learn from Michael Wentworth the names of plants and trees, and the behaviour of the animals they shared the land with. She fell in love with the old stone farmhouse that felt so richly lived-in, and came more gradually to terms of mutual respect and liking with her redoubtable aunt.

The evacuees, initially, had something to do with this. Even they, though noisy and untidy, had slowly responded to the atmosphere of the house. They no longer referred to the vicar's wife, with whom they'd crossed swords early on, as 'that old cow', and – without having to be told – now closed farm gates and went round the edges of newly sown fields. But they were homesick for London's back-streets and bored when it wasn't their turn for village classrooms that couldn't accommodate them and the local children at the same time.

They barely knew where France was, and refused to believe Leonie when she said that its inhabitants spoke a language of their own. She persisted – explaining that to them the farm would be *la ferme*, the house *la maison*, and so on – and gradually the game caught the children's fancy and they demanded a French lesson every morning.

Her patience with them came as a surprise that Elizabeth commented on over supper one evening. 'I've graduated from being the Missus to Madame, thanks to you, but the real boon is that they forget to be naughty when they're interested in something.'

Leonie smiled but answered seriously. 'It helps to take their minds off what is happening in London. Even though they don't talk about them they know about the bombings and that people like their parents are getting killed.'

'Of course they do, poor little tykes,' Michael Wentworth agreed. He swallowed the last of the cider in his glass and then stood up, work for the day not finished even now because a sick cow needed attention.

Leonie watched the smile he exchanged with his wife as he went out and felt a stab of aching envy. He and Elizabeth had each other; Luc, as only the shadowy companion of her mind, wasn't nearly enough.

'Did you always plan to be a farmer's wife?' she suddenly asked Elizabeth. 'And know for certain that you wanted to stay here?'

Her aunt looked up from the apple she was peeling. 'Good heavens, no! I was going to be a concert pianist, like a second Myra Hess.'

It was all she seemed inclined to say but Leonie persisted. 'So why weren't you?'

Elizabeth held up her right hand, missing the top joint of its little finger. 'It was bitten off when I was fifteen. My boxer puppy was being attacked by a much larger dog and I tried to separate them. I rescued the puppy, but never touched the piano again.' She saw the expression on Leonie's face and shook her head. 'Don't look so tragic – I should only have been averagely good, unlike Myra Hess! And as things turned out it was all for the best. My brother James was killed on the Somme in 1916, and although Edward came back from that war it was clear that he was destined for a brilliant professional career – so I was the one to stay here. Michael came to help my father manage the farm. It seemed sensible for us to marry, and gradually – and very unexpectedly – I fell in love with him.'

'And lived happily ever after,' Leonie suggested with a touch of envy.

'Not entirely happily – but after three miscarriages I gave up hoping for children.'

The calm statement made no claim for sympathy, but Leonie heard the echo of a pain that her aunt chose to keep hidden from the world. Silenced by it, she said nothing at all, but Elizabeth spoke again herself.

'What about you? All I know is that you went to Paris to stay with your godmother, and obviously met a young man there.'

It was hard to begin but, as dusk filled the room with an intimacy that seemed to make confession possible, Leonie found herself describing Tante Genevieve and Pappi Bernard and, of course, the great artist-to-be who was Luc Gosselin.

'I have to believe they're safe and that Luc will come back,' she finished unevenly. But she shivered despite the day's warmth that lingered in the room. 'We hear of terrible things happening to Jewish people, and Pappi's wife, Lilli, came from a Jewish family in Austria.'

'But he is a French citizen, my dear,' Elizabeth said firmly. 'There's no likelihood at all that he or Genevieve Bernard will be harmed.'

Leonie's nod agreed and there the conversation ended. When Michael Wentworth came back to find them still sitting there in the dark, she got up to say goodnight and left the room.

'Problem of some kind?' he asked, aware

that his wife had found it harder to warm to their guest than he had.

'Not a problem – just my niece and I getting to know each other at last. It's about time we did,' Elizabeth admitted, calmly stacking supper plates on the table.

Another Christmas came, bringing memories of the previous year and her father's advancing illness. But this year Leonie knew that at least she was awaiting a birth, not death. The long-expected invasion hadn't come and the Italians were being defeated in the Libyan desert. There was even a faint hint of optimism in the air, despite the savage bombing of provincial cities now as well as London.

Her swollen body was becoming burdensome, but they were still several weeks short of the date she'd been given when labour pains began and she was hastily driven to hospital. Her tiny daughter was born alive, but too prematurely to survive, despite the loving care she was given. A week later a tiny coffin was interred in the family plot in the churchyard, and Lucienne Harcourt was laid to rest alongside her grandfather.

As usual, nature took no note of human tragedy; the resurgence of spring seemed especially lovely, but every tree breaking into vivid green leaf, every new lamb nuzzling its mother, was an affront to a girl whose life seemed to have come to an end.

'She's given up,' Elizabeth said to her

husband one evening after Leonie had gone, early as usual, to her room. 'Her body is recovering because she's young, but mind and spirit refuse to mend. I try to console and I even try to bully, but she simply nods and goes on listening to the voice in her head that says there's no point in living because Luc is probably dead as well. We need a miracle and please, dear God, send us one soon.'

It arrived a month later in the shape of a tall young man in 'hospital blues' instead of RAF uniform, who limped into the garden where Leonie sat pretending to read. Dazzled by the bright sunlight, it took her a moment to recognize him; then she was on her feet, running towards him.

'Jules ... I can't believe it, but it *is* you.' Her voice broke on the words as he swung her off her feet. Then, setting her down again, he gently smeared away the tears that had begun to trickle down her cheeks.

'Your aunt told me to look for you out here.' Shocked by the gauntness of her face, he added quietly, 'I'm so sorry about the baby, my dear.' Without realizing that he did so, he'd spoken in French, and she answered in the same language.

'I can't talk about it, even to you,' she muttered. 'Tell me your news instead – you've been wounded, that much I can see.'

'Shot down at last, but I'd been very lucky until then,' he confessed, 'and I was even luckier to get out before the plane caught fire.'

She led him to a cushioned bench and registered the change in him. The young, laughing Jules now looked older than his years, and stress and pain had engraved lines on his face that shouldn't have been there. He was a man who'd seen too many of his comrades die and gone on risking his own life all the same.

She leaned over to kiss his cheek and managed to smile at him. 'I'm very proud of you.' It was an effort to keep her voice steady as she went on. 'I've had no news of Luc, but I knew I couldn't expect any.'

'I came because I can do a little better than that,' Jules said, and saw her thin body stiffen with the shock of sudden hope. 'I went to Green Street first, of course, but your step-mother told me where you were.' He gripped her trembling hands and held them in his warm ones. 'Luc is all right, my dear. I found friends in London who told me how to contact the people at this end of the operation he's running. When I explained who I was they were prepared at least to tell me how well he's doing. So, if you must feel proud of someone, feel proud of Luc!'

She closed her eyes and he feared she was about to faint, but when she ducked her head colour seeped back into her face. At last she could look at him again.

'When the baby died I was sure Luc was dead as well,' she said simply, 'but perhaps God is going to be merciful after all. Let's go indoors, because I must tell my aunt – she's been far more patient with me than I deserve.'

Elizabeth listened to the news, thanked God privately for the timely miracle, and then insisted that Jules must stay for as long as his sick leave lasted. He was reckoned a hero by the evacuees, of course, who suddenly became their normal noisy selves again after weeks of muted sadness in the house. They followed him about like shadows and even agreed to learn to sing the 'Marseillaise', which he played for them on the piano in the drawing room.

'The right spirit is there,' he insisted to his hostess with a grin, 'so who cares if the accent is terrible!'

When the time came to say goodbye they insisted on piling into the car to see him off at the station, so there could be no sad leave-taking there. But they stood waving until the train was out of sight and then the smallest of them, Evie, burst into tears and refused to be comforted.

Growing strong again, Leonie knew that she had yet to face the question that hung at the back of her mind: what was she to do now? More easily acknowledged was the change in herself that made going back to her stepmother's house seem like returning to a comfortable prison. The alteration had been so gradual that she scarcely noticed it happening. She couldn't have recognized the moment when she first began to look with pleasure at cloud patterns or a starlit sky, couldn't have said when she stopped being afraid of the two big shire horses that Michael Wentworth kept as much for sentiment as for their usefulness about the farm. But, little by little, she had begun to feel at home in Frantock and even heard herself claiming proudly to a stranger one day that the blue lias of the nearby villages couldn't compare with its golden hamstone. She made a joke of it to Elizabeth, and then abruptly spoke the question in her mind.

'Tante, I've probably been here longer than you bargained for – isn't it time I went back to London?'

'It's only time if you want to go,' Elizabeth answered calmly after what seemed like a long pause. 'Nothing was ever said about when you were to leave ... I suppose it seemed to depend on what was happening in London.'

'But now all Germany's armies are being hurled against Russia instead of us,' Leonie pointed out, 'and the air raids seem to have ceased. Even the children are going back to London.'

'I know – we shall be thankful to see them leave and we shall miss them very much!' She halted for a moment, then went on. 'We should be very sad to see you go, but it was always understood that you'd only be here while a refuge was needed.'

'I don't need that any more,' Leonie answered, 'but I don't want to try to get back into the Wrens, and I don't belong in my stepmother's house. Uncle Michael is short-handed; couldn't I help him? I'm not afraid of cows any more – I've even grown to like them.'

The earnest statement made Elizabeth smile. 'Bravely said by a girl used to living in cities! We're promised two land girls, so you won't have to work your fingers to the bone, but this is your home – stay forever, or at least until Luc comes back.'

'Thank you ... thank you very much,' was all that Leonie could find to say, but it was enough for Elizabeth Wentworth, in whose considered opinion less was always more and better where displaying emotion was concerned.

There was enough to contend with, as it was, in listening to each day's news broadcasts – being cast down by the hideous carnage on both sides in Russia, by Germany's grip extended all over France, Italy and Eastern Europe now, and by the desperate struggle in the wastes of North Africa where a brilliant German general – the 'Desert Fox' – and his battle-hardened men had replaced the defeated Italians. Then, almost at the end of the year, came the final, devastating news that Japan had joined the so-called 'Ring of Steel' and savaged the American fleet at Pearl Harbour.

'There's no end to the horror; the whole world is being engulfed in war,' Elizabeth said in tears as the wireless was switched off. But she saw Michael shake his head.

'My dear, it's the *beginning* of the end,' he promised her, 'because it means that America must *fight* the war with us at last, instead of just helping on the side. I know things look black, and they may look blacker still before we're through, but we shall win now – have no doubt of it.'

He was proved right in the end, but there were three more years of bitter fighting to endure before Germany, bombed and starved and fought into submission in Russia, France and Italy, laid down its arms. General de Gaulle entered Paris at the head of his Free Frenchmen and the nightmare of the Occupation was over.

In Frantock the church bells rang out for the first time in nearly six years, and a shabby, tired and rather less than well-fed congregation filed into the ancient pews to thank God that the killing was over; technically at least, Europe was at peace again.

Waiting as patiently as she could for news of Luc, Leonie agreed when her uncle explained that conditions on the Continent were bound to remain chaotic for some time to come. She went on calmly with her share of the farm work – much of it relieving him of the burden of form-filling that he considered such a waste of a farmer's time. She helped Elizabeth and tended her father's and Lucienne's graves in the churchyard as usual. But heart and mind clung to the prospect of Luc, directed to her by Smithy in Green Street, walking along the path to the front door. She thought that, like Cio-Cio San in '*Madame Butterfly*', waiting for Pinkerton, she might have to hide for a moment or two so as not to die of joy at their first meeting.

Eight

A year later Japan surrendered to the Americans and, technically at least, the world was at peace. But Luc still hadn't come and the letters that Leonie wrote to the Bernards also fell into the limbo of lost things. She made enquiries in London, but the veils of wartime secrecy were still hard to penetrate, and no one that she talked to admitted responsibility for the work Luc had been involved in. They insisted the organization would have been disbanded by now in any case.

It was time, she explained to her aunt, to go to Paris herself and look for them. She'd been told to wait, but she could bear it no longer.

'I've been expecting you to say that,' Elizabeth admitted, 'but how can it be done? It's such a pittance that we're being allowed to take out of the country – how will you manage for money?'

'I shall say I don't need any because I'm going to stay with friends.' Leonie looked desolate for a moment. 'I'm far from sure of that, of course, but the francs I brought back from France in 1939 will keep me going for the few days I need to be there.'

She chose to travel as she had done before,

by train and ferry. It had the merit of being cheaper than going by air, but also the gradual approach seemed necessary. She needed to get used to the idea of being back in France.

Paris wasn't the city she remembered. The springtime scent of rain-washed lilac was still there, the same mixed smell of coffee, Gauloises, and cheap red wine floated out of every bar-tabac she passed – no change there. Unlike London, there were no gaping holes where bombs had fallen. Paris had been declared an 'open city', safe from being destroyed. The alteration, Leonie finally decided, was in its spirit – shabby and subdued, it seemed traumatized by too-vivid memories of what had happened in a way that London, bombed and flattened, hadn't been.

She went first to what had been Luc's studio, and a sort of studio it still was. But now a group of scruffy-looking musicians interrupted their rehearsal for long enough to explain that they'd moved in six months ago; there'd been nothing to suggest who the previous occupant was except some paint splashes on the floor that they hadn't bothered to remove.

She went next to the Île de la Cité, and her anxious heart lifted at the sight of the Bernards' old house. It looked cared-for and lived-in as it always had, but the young woman who answered her knock was not Tante Genevieve. Suspicious at first of the stranger at her door – surely another changed attitude caused by the war – she listened to Leonie's explanation of why she was there, but shook her head at the end of it; No, she hadn't known the Bernards. Her husband had bought the house when it was left empty and almost derelict after the war. German officers had lived there; that was all she knew about its past.

'I'm sorry I didn't know your friends,' she added more gently, seeing the pain in her caller's face. 'I could make you some coffee – ersatz, I'm afraid! – if you'd like to come in. You look tired.'

Leonie thanked her for the kindness but refused the offer, explaining that her time in Paris was very limited. Afraid of using up her precious stock of francs, she trudged to the university, where surely she would find someone who knew Professor Bernard. Made stubborn by anger and despair, she refused to believe what she was told: that the Professor had simply gone, leaving no forwarding address. But she was defeated by the polite, stonewall indifference of the man behind the desk, who merely repeated his deep regret that he was unable to help her.

She turned away at last, and walked through the throng of students in the hall. Almost at the door a voice behind her spoke.

'Excusez-moi – un moment, s'il-vous-plait.'

She spun round to find a middle-aged woman just behind her, who quickly explained that she'd heard Leonie's conversation with her boss. Mam'selle's French was very good, but was she not English? She smiled when Leonie admitted to being half-English at least.

'I thought so – you stayed with the professor before the war. My name is Berthe Marchal, by the way.'

'Can *you* tell me anything about him and his daughter, Genevieve?'

The hoarse question made the older woman nod. 'Yes, but not here. Come share my usual lunchtime seat with me – it's not far away.'

Leonie fell into step beside her and they walked quickly through the Place Dauphine. Finally settled on a bench by the river, Mlle Marchal gave a little sigh of relief as if the lovely view in front of them, silver water reflecting the towers of Notre Dame, gave her some much-needed comfort. Then she turned to look at her companion, and Leonie read the expression on her face.

'I knew Professor Bernard very well,' she said quietly. 'He was a fine scholar and the kindest of men. It's a shame we shall never be able to live down that people like him and his daughter should have died in the way they did – in a concentration camp.'

'Because of...' Leonie's voice almost failed her and she had to try again. 'Because Pappi had a Jewish wife and Genevieve a Jewish mother?'

Berthe Marchal nodded. 'That is how things were here, you must understand. *They* might just have been left alone, but the professor's nephew, Max Reiner, was hidden in their house, and some *cochon* who wanted to keep in with our occupiers betrayed them. That is also how things were.'

The bitterness in that brief sentence made Leonie reach out to grasp her companion's hand for a moment. 'I think I knew something like that had happened,' she said at last in a low voice. 'I kept pretending it might be all right, but they would never have given dear Max Reiner up – I knew that.'

She stared at the lovely view without seeing it, mind filled instead with the obscene horror of the wagons that had carried her friends and thousands like them to be slaughtered. Again a phrase her father had underlined in one of his books came back to her – 'chaos is come again'. Never since the beginning of the world could there have been such chaos as they had just lived through.

At last she said, 'Does it help you to remember all the people here who lived bravely and risked themselves for others?'

'Yes, it does,' Berthe Marchal answered slowly, 'and I even try to make myself believe that there were many Germans like that too – which only goes to show the futility and madness of war.'

Not much given to making gestures, Leonie nevertheless leaned over and kissed the other woman's cheek. 'I must go now, but thank you for talking to me.' Then, half-turning to leave, she said one more thing. 'The professor's name should be honoured at the university, not forgotten.'

'It will be – give us time,' Berthe Marchal said.

Leonie nodded and walked away, tracing in her mind the route she must take to the Rue de Ravignon, home of the first and best-loved of the restaurants Luc's father had established. She remembered what Luc had said about his family: Roland had refused to stay and watch the change of clientele, but his elder son and daughter had made the newcomers welcome, so presumably their restaurants had prospered. But arriving in the street, what appeared to be a small cinema stood where the restaurant had been.

She moved on in search of the bistro that had been the haunt of students and Left-Bank intellectuals alike. It was now some kind of municipal office staffed by people who knew nothing of the Gosselin family. But the third of Roland's restaurants, *was* still functioning. She went in and sat down wearily at a formica table – how he would have hated that! – and ordered a bowl of onion soup. The ancient waiter admitted that the patron was on the premises, and she waited with a mixture of hope and fear for Emile Gosselin to arrive. But it was a stranger who came towards her.

'*Je suis le patron – vous voulez parler avec moi?*' he asked brusquely.

'*S'il vous plaît, monsieur.*' She gestured to him to sit down, and he did so with the same wariness that she'd noticed in other people. Then she began to explain that she'd come looking for Emile Gosselin or his sister, but already the man was shaking his head.

'You've had a wasted journey, I'm afraid – they left here more than a year ago. Went down to the south, I believe, but I can't swear to that.'

Hope extinguished yet again, Leonie thought it scarcely worth asking her next question. 'You have no address for them, *monsieur* ... no idea where they might be?' Again he shook his head.

She pushed aside the half-empty soup bowl, and put coins on the table which he pushed back towards her.

'You've not eaten enough to pay for,' he said with a kind of rough kindness. 'All I *can* tell you is that the Gosselins were not popular here; they'd been too friendly with the Germans during the Occupation. People didn't forgive them, and they knew it was time to leave.'

Leonie nodded. 'Yes, I did hear about that. It's not Emile I want to find, but his brother, Luc. He came to London to join the Free French, and was sent back here as an agent. That's how I come to have lost him!' She did her best to sound ruefully amused, but the man in front of her saw the desolation in her face.

'Try the Sûreté, Mam'selle – they might be able to help,' he suggested.

She nodded, and held out her hand. 'I will, and thank you for your kindness. They'll be my last hope, I think.'

'Bonne chance,' he said as he walked with her to the door.

Too tired, now, to walk, she took the Métro to the missing persons bureau and half an hour later repeated her enquiries to yet another stranger. But this one took pity on her and excused himself while he made a telephone call. He returned with a name and address written on a piece of official paper.

'This will get you in to see someone who might be able to help you. His job is to trace people like your friend, involved in the resistance.'

Clutching the piece of paper as if it was her passport to heaven, she went out into the street again and, this time, hailed a taxi. With her hands clammy and her heart beating too fast, she was shown into a dingy, untidy office. The official looked as tired as she felt, but he listened to her request for help, and then flicked through a card index on his disordered desk. A little shrug warned her that it didn't include Luc's name, but at least he sounded apologetic for a moment.

'It's a huge task, you understand,' he said hopefully, 'so much information still to be found and indexed. But tell me where Luc Gosselin operated and I may still be able to help you.'

'Where? But I have no idea,' Leonie said desperately. 'Luc wasn't allowed to say ... I'm not sure he even knew where he was being taken when he left London – except that it was to be in the south.'

The official lifted his hands in the time-honoured gesture of a rational Frenchman faced with an irrational woman.

'The "south" – *where* in the south, Mam'selle? It covers half the country, *n'est-ce-pas*? Be reasonable, please.'

He sounded angry, but she was just as angry herself. 'I don't find it "reasonable" that men like Luc were sent to do dangerous work and you have no record of who they were or where they went,' she said fiercely.

He stared at her for a moment – she looked and even sounded like a Frenchwoman, but her dark-blue passport imprinted with the royal coat of arms lay on the desk, and he thought he heard in her voice the echo of generations of her countrymen telling their colonial subjects how to behave. But irritation was slain by the grief in her face, and he spoke more gently now.

'We are doing our best, you know, but it takes time, much time, to gather facts, check that they're authentic, and then piece them together to make the necessary picture. Very few records were kept at the time – written records were too dangerous – and many of the people involved are still not eager to talk to us.'

'Why not? Why shouldn't they be proud to talk?' Leonie asked.

Again his hands sketched their despairing gesture. 'Because life here is more complicated than you realize. There are private scores being settled, for one thing. For another, many of the bravest Resistants were Communists. The Government fears them now and deliberately ignores them.'

No longer buoyed up by anger, Leonie felt sad and empty and realized that her presence there was simply one more cross this tired-faced man had to bear.

'I'm sorry, *monsieur*. I've wasted your time,' she said simply. 'If Luc were still alive I believe that he would have come to find me, so I must accept that he is dead.'

There was, of course, one other possibility that occurred to the man opposite her: six years was a long time, in which Luc Gosselin might have met and married someone else. But instead of saying so he merely asked for an address where he could reach her if necessary.

Out in the street again five minutes later, she hailed another taxi and asked to be taken to Notre Dame. There were no more questions to be asked; she would just sit in the dimness of the great cathedral and pray for the people she had lost. In the morning she would go home. Home now was Frantock, not Paris, and, like Elizabeth, she would learn to be content with the life she had there.

Nine

The journey was almost over. Michael Wentworth would meet her off the train at Taunton, and until then she need only stare out of the window and try *not* to think about the discoveries of the past two days.

In the hope that sleep would help she closed her eyes but opened them again just as the train was pulling out of Paddington Station. A man had pushed open the door from the corridor and now sat down in the corner seat opposite her. She didn't object to a fellow passenger, but this one's face was grey, and he struggled to breathe as he pulled a small phial of pills from his pocket and swallowed one. Then he leaned his head back with a sigh of relief.

'Should you be here ... aren't you rather unwell?' she heard herself ask nervously.

'Not more than usual,' he answered after a moment's thought. But he gave a faint smile at the concern in her face. 'Don't worry – I'm not about to collapse at your feet. I made the mistake of hurrying for the train, that's all.'

It wasn't, she thought, all that was normally needed to reduce a man to this condition, but he'd closed his eyes now and she could look at him more closely. Not young, but prematurely aged, perhaps, by illness; his skin was drawn too tightly over the bones beneath, and a prominent nose clearly broken in the past didn't improve what she judged to be a harsh, unforthcoming sort of face.

'The name is Adam Vaux,' he said suddenly, still with closed eyes but as if he'd known that she was watching him. 'French-sounding, I'm afraid, but in fact entirely English.'

'It's not necessarily a recommendation,' Leonie replied coolly. 'I happen to be half-French.' Relieved by the glint of amusement in his face now, she thought it safe to ask a question. 'Why do you have a French name?'

'Huguenot ancestors who were pitched out generations ago by murdering Catholics and had to settle here.' Then a wry grin transformed his face. 'But you're a Catholic yourself, of course – why didn't I think of that!'

He stared at the suitcase on the rack above her head. 'You've been away, I see – where to?'

'Paris,' she said briefly, and decided to anticipate the question he was clearly framing next. 'I went looking for something that was no longer there.' Then she picked up the book on her lap, a clear indication, she hoped, that the conversation was over. But her fellow passenger simply ignored the hint.

'It's a mistake to go back looking for things,' he suggested next. 'I used to love Greece before the war, but because I know ancient Greek our half-witted powers-that-be sent me to join a band of Cretan mountaineers. We spent the entire war trying to understand one another. Where did you spend the war, by the way?'

Now resigned to the fact that Mr Vaux followed his own rules in conversation with strangers, Leonie put down her book again. 'I worked on my uncle's farm in Somerset. It's still my home.'

'Somerset,' he mused. 'It sounds very lush. I've got used to somewhere a bit more bare and stony myself – like Norman Douglas, who came back to England after months in Calabria and said he felt like a caterpillar faced with an endless field of lettuces! I think Somerset might be rather lettuce-like.'

'Both are green – the resemblance ends there,' she said shortly, but her flushed face seemed to give him only pleasure.

'Now I've made you cross, but that's better than having you look sad.'

She waited for the question that was likely to come next, but he leaned back instead and closed his eyes again – from boredom or exhaustion? She didn't know, but now felt vaguely disappointed. Crossing swords with him *had* at least been better than the images that filled her mind.

The train was approaching Taunton and she'd pulled her small suitcase from the rack before he suddenly spoke again.

'I'm sorry you didn't find what you were looking for in Paris.' The words, spoken this time without the tinge of ironic amusement in his voice, sounded sincere, as if he did regret her wasted journey.

She gave a little shrug, but had to find something to say. 'Well, at least I'm going home now. Presumably you're not if you don't know Somerset.'

His faint smile reappeared. 'A home is something I don't have at the moment, but that might be about to change. An elderly relative bequeathed me his cottage, which may *not* turn out to be an uninhabitable ruin. "*Nous verrons*", as you half-French people like to say!'

She hesitated for a moment, remembering his arrival at Paddington. 'Will you be able to manage?' she asked uncertainly. 'My uncle is meeting me, and he may be able to drop you somewhere.'

He hoisted himself to his feet to give her a formal little bow. 'I shall certainly manage, but thank you for asking.' His eyes studied her face for a moment. 'Apropos your problem, have you noticed how it often happens that if you stop looking for something it suddenly turns up?'

'Not in this case,' she said steadily. 'What I found was that the friends I looked for had died in the war.'

'So my half-baked piece of advice was merely hurtful – I'm sorry about that, too.'

He sounded so genuinely contrite that she held out her hand and made an offer of her own. 'I hope the cottage *isn't* a ruin; everybody needs a home.'

Then, as they trundled into the station, she turned to look for her uncle, and saw him anxiously scanning the windows as they went past. She stepped down to meet him on the platform and, watching them, Adam Vaux saw her smile for the first time. Yes, she *was* beautiful when she smiled. He was pleased about that – he'd rather thought she might be.

The story of her visit was told over supper, but Leonie broke the shocked silence that had fallen on her aunt and uncle to insist that she'd had to find out the truth. It could, however painfully, be come to terms with, whereas uncertainty was as corrosive as acid, eating away at any peace of mind.

'The last man I saw was kind in his own way,' she finished up reflectively. 'He even managed not to say what I could see was in his mind – that Luc might simply have forgotten me and settled down in France with someone else. But I know that isn't true. I'm sure now that he died, just as Tante Genevieve and Pappi and Max did.'

Elizabeth leaned across the table and patted her hand, and the gesture seemed to confirm sadly that she believed it too. 'We can't go on talking about it – it's too heartbreaking,' she said unsteadily. 'So listen instead, my dear, to what happened here while you were away. Your stepmother arrived quite unexpectedly, assuming, of course, that she'd find *you* here. We hadn't seen her since your father's funeral seven years ago, but she still managed to look elegant despite years of clothes rationing.' Sounding regretful, Elizabeth's mind seemed to dwell on that for a moment.

'Only she didn't come here to make you feel an inelegant farmer's wife,' Leonie pointed out. 'There must have been some other reason.'

'Oh, there was. She wanted us, but you especially, to know that she's about to marry again. Her husband-to-be is a diplomat at the American Embassy who is being recalled to Washington – hence the hasty visit. We probably shan't ever see her again.'

'I don't know what that means,' Leonie said. 'If she remarries does she cease to be my stepmother? Not that it really matters, of course; we never managed to relate to each other at all.' Then a flicker of amusement lit her face. 'She'll make a good diplomat's wife – her husband will be an ambassador in no time!' Then a different thought struck her. 'Did she say anything about the house ... about Smithy and Cook and Alice?'

It was Michael Wentworth who answered. 'The house has been sold, but a condition of the sale was that the staff should stay on. Smithy, she said, had already got the new owners firmly under his thumb!'

'Of course he would have,' Leonie agreed with real pleasure. 'Even my stepmother never quite got the measure of him, and the poor woman tried hard enough.'

'You used not to sound so charitable about

her,' Elizabeth pointed out. 'I take it you don't mind the remarriage.'

'Not a bit ... in fact I'm glad; it seems to neatly tie up a part of my life that's over.' Then she smiled ruefully at her aunt. 'All very fine for me to say that, of course. What if you and Uncle Michael get tired of having me here, but can't bear the thought of telling me so?'

In a rare demonstration of affection Elizabeth Wentworth got up to wrap her niece in a warm hug. 'I speak for both of us, don't I, Michael? This is your home, as I told you once before, and you are the daughter we didn't have. Is that clear enough?'

Leonie nodded, and then went to kiss her uncle as well. Back in her place at the table, she spoke of something else. 'I met an odd man on the train this afternoon who said he had no home. His name is Adam Vaux – does that mean anything to you? He'd been left a cottage by an elderly relative, but he didn't say where it was.'

'The name of Vaux rings a faint bell,' Michael said after a moment's thought. 'I know ... they were flax growers on a big scale donkey's years ago – produced enough of the stuff to be turned into sails for half the British fleet in Nelson's time. Was the man you met a farmer?'

Leonie saw Adam Vaux's harsh, reticent face in her mind's eye and shook her head. 'Anything but, I'd say – he looked more like an irascible and rather sickly don. He talked of having spent the war years in Crete, but I wasn't sure whether I was meant to believe that or not.'

'The family died out, I thought,' Michael said. 'Just as the need for sails did when steam arrived. A great shame, of course ... there's nothing to compare with the sight of a splendid ship under full canvas. A landlubber's vision, I have to say – they must have been hell to work and live on!' Then he smiled at his niece. 'I forbid you to go into the office this evening. The forms can wait until morning.'

She admitted to feeling very tired and went upstairs to the pleasure of being in her own room again after three uncomfortable nights in a cheap hotel. Old polished furniture and linen sheets welcomed her with the scents of beeswax and lavender, and, like old friends, her father's books lined the shelves that filled one wall. But there was something else that needed thinking about now that her heart was certain that Luc was dead.

She opened a cupboard door and lifted down the small suitcase he'd left with her seven years earlier. The worn leather top still bore the initials 'RG', but it indisputably belonged to Roland Gosselin's son Luc. That being so she knew she wouldn't return it to Emile even if she could ever find him. The 'family papers' inside would probably have been of interest only to Luc, but they weren't hers to destroy or throw away. He'd asked her to take care of them and that she must do.

With that settled in her mind, she got ready for bed, turned out the lamp, and lay watching the young moon that rose in the night sky outside her window. It was time to accept once and for all that she must live the rest of her life without Luc. But at least she had a home and people who loved her. Her strong impression was that the man she'd met on the train had neither. She could imagine nothing worse and suddenly felt close to weeping for Adam Vaux's loneliness. But she blinked away the tears, realizing how strange it was that instead of weeping for her French love, her tears were for a stranger, who, like Luc, she would never see again.

Living outside the village it was by no means a daily occurrence to go in to Frantock itself – officially classified now as a small market town, but still referred to by its stubborn residents as the village it had once been. But Michael Wentworth's birthday was drawing near, and it meant that a visit was necessary. Leonie pumped up the tyres of her bicycle and set off with a list of household needs hastily compiled by her aunt's God-fearing maid who, regarding a settlement that had street lighting and a café or two as being well on the way to damnation, rarely consented to visit Frantock herself.

It was, in fact, a beautiful place, with a noble parish church as its natural centerpiece. With the nearest Catholic church many miles away, Leonie had fallen into the habit of attending Sunday morning service with her aunt, convinced that Almighty God wouldn't mind whether she worshipped Him under the Anglican or the Holy Roman umbrella. She had come to love the majestic prose of the *Book of Common Prayer*, and the choral music that the local organist and choir offered every Sunday.

With Hannah's shopping completed at last, she walked along the pleasantly tree-lined main street to the town's second-hand book shop where she hoped to find the sort of old literary oddity that would appeal to her uncle.

Mr Folkinshaw's place of trade was about as uncommercial-looking as it was possible for a shop to be. A bow window on each side of a white front door hinted at the prim parlours of an elderly spinster. But, once inside, a determined bookworm not put off by the aroma of dust and mildew could find all sorts of treasure.

The shop looked smarter than she remembered; Mr Folkinshaw seemed to have gone to the unheard-of lengths of freshly painting his front door. She stepped inside to the usual musical jangle of the bell, ready to compliment him, but he wasn't there. Instead, seated in the old man's wicker chair and calmly completing *The Times* crossword, was her fellow passenger on the train journey home from London.

She gaped at him but finally found her voice. 'Well, good morning ... Are you ... are you ... minding the shop for Mr Folkinshaw?'

'Yes,' he agreed with an odd smile, 'I suppose in a way I am.'

'Then you aren't doing it very well,' Leonie pointed out. 'Since you aren't exactly run off your feet, why not tidy things up a little for him? He's old now, and rather frail.'

'I'm afraid he's dead, as of a month ago,' Adam Vaux said gently. 'He was the elderly relative I told you about – my great-uncle, to be exact.'

She frowned over the memory of their train conversation. 'You'd been left a cottage, you said.'

'There was a shop as well, but I didn't realize that the two were inextricably entwined like Siamese twins. I couldn't very well accept one without the other.'

He sounded apologetic, but she was aware by now that how he sounded or even what he said was no reliable guide to what was actually the case. Elusive was one way of describing him, but deceptive might be another. She stared at him for a moment while he stared blandly back. He was still gaunt and rapier-thin, but he looked better than he had on the train, and she could now see that he was still a comparatively young man.

'Are you serious about staying here?' she asked at last. 'Don't you have some ... some other ... gainful occupation?'

He smiled at her obvious hesitation over which word to use. 'Some more manly toil you wanted to say, I think. Well, I'm not sure about that, but I did teach Greek and Latin to young barbarians who wanted to be out playing rugger instead. That was toil indeed and rather more than I can manage at the moment. I came here expecting to put old Eustace's property on the market, but I fell in love with it instead, and Frantock itself seemed rather a jolly place to live in – even before I knew you lived here too!'

'I don't,' she said, unnerved by a compliment she didn't intend to take seriously. 'Manor Farm is three miles away. I only came here today to find a birthday present for my uncle. I ought to start looking for it, and *you* could do something about putting your merchandise in order.'

The new shopkeeper shook his head sadly. 'I'm afraid it's a failing in your otherwise delightful sex – you can't resist tidying things. The whole essence of a second-hand book shop is that it *should* be like this one. I'd say it's just about perfect as it is.'

She held up her hand in the gesture of a fencer acknowledging a hit. 'Then I shall save my breath to blow the dust off something I might want to buy.'

She wandered away, and he watched her stop to examine a volume here and there. Whatever sadness she'd brought back with her from France was under control now, he thought. Her slender body moved with the grace of a dancer. Even in her everyday country clothes of cotton skirt and sweater there was still a certain style about her, and the soft coral colour she wore was the perfect foil to her dark hair.

He got up and went towards her, holding out a small book in one hand.

'What about this? The life story of Dr John Dee – Elizabethan genius, wizard or necromancer, or maybe even a bit of all three! Would that appeal to your uncle?'

Leonie glanced at the first page, and smiled suddenly. 'Indeed it would – thank you; you've just made a sale.'

He wrapped it up with a care she thought was probably typical of him, and received the money that she handed over.

'You have the advantage of me,' he commented. 'I don't know your name.'

'It's Leonie Harcourt,' she said gravely. 'The Harcourts had to leave the Manor in my grandfather's time, and now we live at Manor Farm – that is, my father's sister, Elizabeth, her husband Michael Wentworth, and me.' She took the package he handed her and suddenly added, 'They're the sort of people I think you'd like. Come to dinner one evening and meet them, but you'll need a bicycle or a car to get there.'

'Alas, I have neither at the moment,' he said, but he didn't sound regretful and she was left with the impression that loneliness was a condition he'd deliberately chosen. She gave the little shrug he remembered and walked out of the shop. He watched her for a moment, and then went back to his seat. It had been stupid to reject her offer of friendship, but he'd grown used to the idea that whatever life was left to him had better be lived alone. He found himself wondering about the friends she mourned; surely, to cause the desolation he'd seen in her face, a man she'd loved had been among them.

Then, one Sunday when the worshippers had left and he was free to roam about the churchyard, he came across the grave of Edward Harcourt – Leonie's father, presumably – and beside it the grave of two-day-old Lucienne. He thought he could guess at least some of the story that lay behind it, and winced at the memory of his clumsiness that afternoon on the train.

Ten

The birthday present proved a great success, so much so that Leonie had to explain where it had come from. Then she had to further confess that it hadn't been old Mr Folkinshaw's clever suggestion because he was now dead; the new owner of the shop was his great-nephew Adam Vaux.

'Vaux? The man you met on the train?' asked Elizabeth, whose memory for unimportant trifles was, in her niece's opinion, sometimes better than it need be.

'The very same,' she had to agree, 'but I suspect the arrangement's temporary while he takes a short rest from schoolmastering. He seems to have been unwell.'

'We must meet him – welcome him to Frantock,' Elizabeth said at once. 'Shall I ring him or will you?'

Leonie hesitated for a moment. 'I don't think he'll come,' she commented finally. 'When I suggested he might like to meet you, he said he had no transport, but it sounded like an excuse from a man who prefers to be left alone. Even customers are probably a nuisance he'd rather be without.'

She thought she was talking too much, but her aunt was kind enough not to point out that she seemed quite knowledgeable about the solitary-minded Mr Vaux, and there the matter rested.

But driving through Frantock one evening, Michael Wentworth noticed lights still shining in the book shop's windows, and obeyed a sudden impulse to stop his battered old jeep and walk inside.

'Good evening,' he said with his usual friendly smile. 'I saw the lights were on, and wanted to thank you for suggesting the John Dee book to my niece – was it a lucky choice or do you have some sort of bookseller's sixth sense about what people might like?'

Adam Vaux's forbidding expression relaxed into a grin. 'It's a game I play with myself – guessing what people will look for when they come in; but I usually stop short of giving advice. Your niece, I take it, is Leonie Harcourt.'

'Yes, and I'm Michael Wentworth – I should have introduced myself, but my dear wife rightly accuses me of always putting the cart before the horse!' He glanced at his watch and then at the man who'd stood up to shake hands with him. 'Do you always stay open this late?'

'No, I simply forgot to lock the door,' Adam Vaux admitted. 'Your niece pointed out when she was here that a little tidying up and dusting might not come amiss. I denied it at the time, but I can see that she may be right. I was considering the problem of where to start when you came in.'

His visitor cast an eye round the overfilled shelves and the stacks of books on the floor for which there was no shelf space at all. 'I think you need help ... We could ask my wife who knows everyone for miles around. Why not come and meet her now? I'm on my way home. Take potluck and share our supper.' Then he remembered what Leonie had said. 'I'll run you home afterwards.'

Refusing Leonie Harcourt had been one thing, turning down *this* kindly offered invitation was something Adam found he couldn't do – it would have been like kicking a large, gentle retriever who just wanted to make friends.

'Well, if you're sure it's not too much trouble, I'd like to come – I've been wanting to see inside one of the local farmhouses. They're what I believe the experts pompously call vernacular architecture at its very best.' Having given, he thought, a reasonable excuse for accepting one invitation having refused a previous one, he switched out the lights and followed Michael Wentworth out into the cool dusk of an early summer evening.

Settled in the jeep, he turned to look at the man beside him. 'I'm sure you know that I shared a compartment with your niece on the train down from London. I think I distressed her then unintentionally, and I don't want to do so again – is the child's grave in the churchyard anything to do with her?'

'Her daughter,' Michael said briefly. 'The

father, a Frenchman, didn't come back from the war.'

Adam thought of the dates on the little headstone. 'Leonie couldn't have been much more than a child herself.'

'She was eighteen. Her father had died by then, and she's been with us ever since. It's not the life she imagined for herself, poor girl, but to us she's the child we never had.'

'Thank you – I understand now.' Then Adam changed the subject by pointing to a small American flag decorating the jeep's dashboard. 'How come?'

Michael's friendly grin reappeared. 'We housed evacuees at the beginning of the war and some American officers towards the end of it. They left the jeep behind as a rather clapped-out thank you, but it's been going strong ever since.'

A few minutes later they turned in under the archway that led to the yard and he smiled at his guest. 'Welcome to Manor Farm.'

If the sudden appearance of someone else to feed put a strain on the hostess no one would have guessed it from Elizabeth Wentworth's manner. Her niece looked less delighted, but Adam expected that. He'd been tiresome in the train and clumsy at the bookshop, and he was there at her uncle's invitation, not hers.

But supper was a pleasant meal despite the slight coolness on Leonie's side of the table. Her aunt, always forthright, asked what she wanted to know.

'Call me nosy if you like,' she admitted with a smile, 'but we're curious about you! We know you are old Mr Folkinshaw's great-nephew, but that isn't nearly enough to satisfy our thirst for information.'

Adam didn't seem to mind her directness. 'He was my grandmother's brother – a bachelor solicitor who finally gave up law to do what he'd always wanted. My father was an Oxford don who preferred translating the works of Homer to teaching them to unenthusiastic students, and my mother wrote biographies about the Romantic poets. I was an afterthought in their scholarly lives and something of a constant surprise, I think, whenever they noticed that I was there!'

Elizabeth smiled, but persisted. 'We need the story brought up-to-date, please.'

'The war came and I, a Classics teacher in my turn, was sent to the Aegean. My father, elderly by then, died while I was away. My mother outlived him, but not for very long; I think she just missed him too much. I went back to teaching – not a very strenuous job perhaps, but more than I could manage by then. Eustace died, and I suddenly found myself with a new occupation that suits me very well.' He smiled at Elizabeth. 'Here endeth the not very exciting history of Adam Vaux.'

'Not at all,' she answered. 'Here beginneth a new chapter, surely. But Michael says you need some help.'

'I need different kinds of help,' their guest

admitted. 'Some of the books are old and probably only good for pulping, others are old but look as if they might be valuable. I need a crash course in antiquarianism, if there is such a thing, to tell me which are which. I also need someone to help me remove the dust of ages that Eustace obviously didn't even notice.'

Elizabeth considered the problems for a moment. 'I can help with the dust, at least. Hannah, who works for us here, has a son who is what local people call simple. Poor Will, aged thirty now, is not exactly employable, but give him a straightforward task and he will do it until the cows come home. He'll enjoy sweeping and dusting for you. I'll organize it with Hannah tomorrow.'

Then it was Michael's turn. 'Is transport another problem? You'll want to be able to get around outside Frantock.'

'I must replace an ancient car that died of rigor mortis in my father's garage. But, immediately I have another solution. Miss Matilda Dobson, whose garden runs alongside the churchyard, has a paddock and in it lives a mare called Blossom. While coming to borrow my stock of detective stories, the gorier the better, she's decided that I might like to get about locally on Blossom. It would do us both good, she says.'

Leonie suddenly broke her long silence. 'What if the mare decides to gallop or leap over hedges – horse riding isn't necessarily a very placid means of locomotion.'

A smile of pure amusement lit Adam's face. 'In this case it is! Blossom has acquired the dimensions of a carthorse, and if I asked her to jump anything more than a puddle I'm afraid she'd turn round and laugh at me.'

'Well, she'll amble with you here across the fields anyway,' Michael said happily, 'so we can look forward to frequent visits, I hope.'

He looked at their guest's face and took note of its tiredness as well as the smile that still lingered there. A countryman himself, conditioned to hard work in all weathers, he would normally have been disconcerted by someone like Adam Vaux, so different from himself – a scholar, an indoor man even if he did know how to sit on a horse. But Elizabeth liked him – that was obvious – and Michael Wentworth needed no better recommendation than that.

'Time I ran you back to the shop,' he said with a smile, 'and that leaves my dear womenfolk free to attend to *their* duties – what an excellent arrangement!'

Adam bowed over Elizabeth's hand with unexpected formality and, watching the graceful gesture, Leonie could suddenly imagine him as an Elizabethan courtier in ruff, doublet and hose, thinking up some new intrigue that would make or break a queen. But what he said was much more mundane.

'Does Hannah's Will need collecting if he comes to the shop?'

Elizabeth shook her head. 'No, he cycles in and out of Frantock all the time when he hasn't anything else to do.'

Adam directed a little bow at Leonie and got a cool nod in return, but she left her aunt and uncle to walk with him out to the yard, and busied herself instead with stacking dishes in the kitchen.

'Nice man,' Elizabeth said when she walked in a moment later. 'Sad he looks frail, but I doubt if the Aegean was a very healthy spot during the war.'

'He spent it chatting to Cretan mountaineers, he *said*,' Leonie pointed out. 'That doesn't sound very arduous.'

'You don't like him,' her aunt commented, then her voice changed. 'My dear, you can't dislike every man who isn't Luc. It's ... it's unreasonable.'

'So it is,' Leonie agreed with a wry smile. 'Don't worry ... I'll get used to Adam Vaux in time, unless of course Blossom finds the walk over here too much for her!'

Then she blew her aunt a goodnight kiss and went to bed.

But their next encounter wasn't at the farm. A week later, having delivered Blossom's Saturday afternoon treat of a handful of sugar lumps, Adam climbed the low wall into the churchyard, and then quickly hid behind a convenient headstone because Leonie was there, arranging pinks and sprigs of rosemary on her daughter's grave. He only emerged from his hiding place as she walked past a few minutes later.

'It's a fine afternoon,' he said. 'I could offer you tea in my courtyard garden.'

'Thank you,' she replied, as gravely as he had spoken, 'but it's Hannah's day off and my turn to cook supper. I must be getting home.'

'Why not a little rest first?' He spread a handkerchief on the mossy surface of a grave. 'As toastmasters love to say, "Pray be sat", for a few minutes at least.'

She gave her characteristic shrug and sat without further argument, but seemed content to close her eyes and feel the gentle warmth of the sun on her face. Its skin was already lightly tanned, he noticed, and the tan became her very well.

'Michael told me about your daughter,' he said suddenly, 'and now I have to suppose that the person you looked for in Paris was her father.'

After a long silence she finally answered. 'I went knowing in my heart that Luc was dead. I only wanted it confirmed, I think. He'd become one of many unknown warriors buried somewhere in France. The dear friends I went hoping to find in Paris weren't there either, but they died in a concentration camp.'

Adam finally broke another silence. 'You should have bashed me over the head that day in the train – why didn't you?'

She turned and smiled at him at last. 'Probably because you looked too ill. *Are* you ill, by the way?'

He made a slightly impatient gesture as if the subject bored him. 'Let's just say that I'm not expected to make old bones. Living in mountain caves in winter is something you have to be born to; my upbringing was much too comfortable. I'm left with a small heart problem – which is why Eustace's shop suits me down to the ground.' He shook his head at the concern in her face. 'Don't feel sorry for me – I wouldn't have missed those wartime years for anything in the world – but now I'm content here. I'd no idea how fascinating it would turn out to be, keeping old Eustace's precious shop going for him. It beats schoolmastering any day.'

She heard the note of finality in his voice and knew not to ask more questions about his health.

'How is Will getting on?' she asked instead. 'Aunt Elizabeth said she'd spoken to Hannah about it.'

'I have to beg him to stop working and share my morning coffee with me. I suspect, by the way, that he's *autistic*, which is a far cry from being simple. It would explain his intense concentration on whatever it is he's doing, and his lack of response to other people – he lives in a world of his own.'

'Is he aware of being lonely?' Leonie asked after a moment's thought.

The question would only have been asked, Adam thought, by someone who knew what loneliness was, and the girl beside him had probably had more than her fair share of that.

'I can't answer for Will, I'm afraid,' he said gently. 'But on the whole, I think not. *Autistic* people aren't aware of being different, thank God.' Adam's long, thin hand now waved the subject of Will aside. 'I made a new acquaintance this week – the present owner of the Manor. You must know him, of course.'

Leonie nodded. 'James Wetherby is a nice, shy man, so perhaps he didn't explain how he and his wife – also very nice but not in the least shy – come to be living here. Their son was in the US Air Force during the war and stationed not far from Frantock. He survived the bombing raids over Germany, and fell in love with the Somerset Levels. Now he's all set to become an expert on the survival of the world's disappearing wetlands, and his parents have chosen to make their home here – one of the happier stories to emerge from the war.'

'I should have said that I made two new acquaintances,' Adam commented. 'A granddaughter came with him – very pretty, impressionable, and, like her grandmother, not at all shy.'

Leonie examined this comment for its meaning. 'I expect she found you pale and interesting,' she suggested helpfully.

'A sort of ravaged Byronic hero?' Then he glanced at his companion's face. 'Possibly, but on the whole I think Mlle Harcourt is amusing herself at my expense. Nevertheless, being invited to dine at the Manor tomorrow, I shall wheeze and pant a bit, and let it be known that I'm old enough to be Amy's father.'

Leonie smiled at him with real amusement in her face. 'There will be safety in numbers because we're invited too. We exchange invitations about four times a year. My uncle and Mr Wetherby get on very well together and their wives have also become good friends, despite the fact that they continue to totally mystify one another! Amy we have yet to meet. The vicar and his wife will probably be there as well, so you can consider yourself being thrown into the deep end of Frantock society!'

'I can't wait,' Adam said truthfully. 'Life in North Oxford wasn't nearly so much fun. Are you still worrying about the supper you have to cook?' he asked suddenly as she stood up.

'Incidentally yes, but the seat is getting damp and your handkerchief is now probably moss-stained.' She handed him the green-tinged piece of cambric and then took it back. 'I'd better launder it, I think. I'll return it tomorrow.'

They walked together to the gate and she wheeled her bicycle out into the road. '*Á demain*,' she called out as she set off. Then she stopped suddenly. 'Do you need a lift to the Manor?'

'No, thank you – I have transport,' he said solemnly.

He watched her until she was out of sight, and then went back over the stone wall to the paddock to explain to Blossom that she must look her best tomorrow because they were going into high society together.

Eleven

When the moment came to set off for dinner at the Manor Adam went in the vicarage car, not on Blossom's accommodating back. He'd hesitated over accepting the Reverend Rushton's offer of a lift – he wasn't as yet a member of the vicar's congregation – but when he arrived at the vicarage he could see no reproof in the priest's gentle face. The vicar's wife, Jane, looked more capable of calling a non-attender to account, but for the moment she seemed only concerned with the proper turnout of her menfolk. Andrew, she explained, was liable to appear with a soup-stained tie, and their son, Jonathan, preferred not to wear a tie at all. Adam waited for her to inspect him as well, but after one sharp glance she allowed Jonathan to start the car.

They reached the Manor just as the farm guests arrived on foot, and Leonie shook her head as Adam emerged from the back of the vicarage car.

'I'm afraid you funked it,' she murmured. 'I expected to see Blossom nibbling Mr Wetherby's front lawn.'

'It was the journey home in the dark that I funked,' he admitted, 'not having discussed with Blossom what her night-vision capabilities are. On top of that I felt obliged to wear my best clothes.'

She glanced at his blazer and college tie. 'Very smart – I hope Amy won't be too overcome.' Then, with the hint of a smile, she turned away to greet Jane Rushton.

Inspecting in his turn the frontage of a pleasing Georgian country house, Adam now found Elizabeth Wentworth beside him.

'Are you considering the rise and fall of the Harcourt family?' she enquired. 'Farmhouse to Manor and now back to farmhouse again?'

Adam shook his head. 'This is elegant, I grant you, but I prefer where you live now.'

'So do I,' she agreed with a smile, 'but I'm glad this is in such good hands. James has even gone to the trouble and expense of buying back land that my careless ancestors sold to pay gambling debts. He intends it to stay as it was meant to be – precious wetland – not covered in concrete.' She guessed the question Adam felt wary of asking next. 'Huge government contracts during the war made the Wetherby factories a fortune, but James has a guilty conscience about that – quite unnecessarily in my opinion.'

'So he's investing his wealth in our countryside – what a nice man he must be,' Adam commented. Then his mouth twitched as he watched Jonathan's bedazzled gaze fasten upon Leonie. 'I'm afraid Mrs Wetherby's party isn't going to go quite according to plan – young Mr Rushton is here, I fancy, to entertain her granddaughter, not be enthralled by your niece. But being a fair-minded man, I'm bound to admit that it's only to be expected. He's at an impressionable age, poor chap.'

Elizabeth considered asking how her niece struck someone as blasé and ancient as himself, but their arrival had been noticed and the Wetherbys were mustering on the porch steps to welcome their guests.

They looked typically American, Adam thought: Martha matronly but elegant; James immaculately scrubbed and laundered; and Amy the picture of abundant health and prettiness. But Amy's wistful glance at Leonie's simple sleeveless dress and then at her own over-frilled blouse and skirt made Adam smile more warmly at her than he'd meant to, and she was able to feel confident again; perhaps the frills hadn't been a mistake after all.

With food rationing still in force, dinner by the standards of life in post-war, austerity England was lavish, thanks to food parcels regularly received from America, Martha admitted rather ashamedly.

'I keep telling my daughters that we're far from starving over here,' she explained, 'but it's nice to be able to share things around. We had such an easy war back home compared with you dear people over here.'

The dear people looked suitably embarrassed for a moment until Andrew Rushton smilingly explained that Frantock's hardest task had been to understand the London children sent down at the beginning of the war.

'Still, it was a remarkable social experiment,' Elizabeth insisted, 'with quite a lot learned on both sides! The boy who was the most difficult when he first arrived was the sorriest when the time came to leave, and he made us promise to let him come back when he's old enough.'

'But he'll forget that surely?' James Wetherby suggested. 'Won't city life have taken hold of him again?'

It was Michael who answered. 'I hope not, but the next two or three years will tell. He had a natural affinity with animals, we discovered. He was a scrawny little lad but he wasn't afraid of even the biggest beasts. I hope he does come back.'

Andrew Rushton smiled affectionately at Leonie, another refugee from city life he said, who now thwacked the cows' rumps with the best of them.

'Only if they don't move when I ask them to nicely,' she pointed out, 'and they mostly do.'

'Of course ... who wouldn't?' the infatuated Jonathan said too loudly.

With true kindness Adam filled the silence that followed this fervent statement. 'I'm all for pretty shepherdesses ... there's something poetic and arcadian about that. But not, I'm afraid, about slapping a cow's bottom!' He smiled at Leonie, hoping she would forgive him the laughter round the table, but she gave her usual little shrug and the conversation moved on from the more mundane details of dairy farming.

When dinner was over and they moved into Martha's white-panelled drawing room, Amy was required to pour the coffee for her grandmother. Adam took the opportunity to fill her empty place next to Leonie.

'I hope you realized that I was merely coming to the rescue of our nice young friend a little while ago,' he murmured.

Leonie offered him a cool stare in return. 'Kindness will be your undoing,' she commented. 'Amy blushes very prettily if you so much as glance in her direction, but I have to mention that your smiles are not nearly avuncular enough.' Then her considering stare swept round the room. 'Can you imagine a more disparate group of people?'

'No, but that's what is so fascinating about country society,' Adam insisted. 'Limiting myself only to the adult males – I wouldn't dare to categorize the ladies – we have a brilliant entrepreneur-turned-benefactor, a scholarly priest, a hard-working farmer, and a humble shopkeeper – all getting on like a house on fire. I'm not sure whether it says more for our inherent niceness or for Mrs Wetherby's skill as a hostess!'

For once he was offered Leonie's true opinion. 'She's brilliant at making people welcome, but I'll grant you the general niceness as well. When I was living in Paris I was in thrall to Left-Bank café society –

nothing, I thought, could be more exhilarating and grown-up and real. I don't think I could call life here exhilarating exactly, but it *is* real, and it's also unpretentious and good. I owe more than I can say to my aunt and uncle for taking me in.'

She spoke so gravely that he was left for a moment with nothing to say. Then she smiled at him. 'You could have included Jonathan in your list of males. He's not academic like the other Rushton children, but he's an apprentice stone carver, and clambering over the statues on the west front of Wells Cathedral is adult enough work for anyone!' Then she kindly offered Amy her seat next to Adam and went to discuss the making of elderflower champagne with Jane Rushton.

By the end of the evening Adam had learnt a good deal more about the people he had come to live among. James Wetherby, by means of a small telescope installed in one of the attics, was a keen watcher of the night skies; Martha was slowly re-embroidering seat covers for every chair in the house; Jane Rushton had given up a promising career as a ballet dancer to marry her gentle priest; and Amy, who disliked the man her divorced mother had newly married, was intent on coming back to live with her grandparents as soon as her college days were done. Adam suspected that this promised return was as unlikely as that of Michael Wentworth's little evacuee, but just in case Amy *was* going to reappear in a year or two's time he'd offered a small confession of his own: of a girl loved but lost to someone else during the war, and of a life of bachelorhood ever since.

Amy accepted this with mixed feelings. It was flattering, of course, to be told, and she was sad for him, most certainly she was. But couldn't he have tried a little harder to forget a girl stupid enough to choose someone else?

This thought was still on her mind some days later when she was sent to the farm to collect for her grandmother whatever vegetables Leonie had a glut of. Steered in the right direction by Elizabeth Wentworth she found an overalled figure at the far end of a beautiful walled garden. Its beds were separated by neatly clipped grass paths and trees already beginning to bear fruit grew in graceful interlocking curves against the stone wall.

Amy pointed at them with amazement. 'How clever to make them do that!'

Leonie smiled but shook her head. 'Not especially clever – gardeners have been training them like that for several hundred years! We use the French word – espalier – to describe it, so perhaps a Frenchman thought of it first!' She waved a suntanned arm round the garden. 'Welcome to my *potager* – I think it's just as beautiful as the flowers my aunt attends to.'

She led Amy to a wooden seat, where a laden trug awaited collection – a posy of mixed herbs in the centre, surrounded by small, golden-skinned potatoes, green beans, and the thick soft pods of broad beans, all neatly arranged.

'It's a work of art,' Amy exclaimed with pleasure. 'Does that come of being half-French, as Granny says you are – just *knowing* how everything should look?'

'It comes from making mistakes and learning from them,' Leonie insisted with a smile. 'When I first came to live with my aunt and uncle I was even frightened of their gentle retriever dogs! I didn't know which way up to plant a seed potato, and flowers were things one bought in florist shops. It's true I'm half-French but my pleasure in growing things probably stems from a long line of English farmers and landowners. My mother was a Parisienne – she wouldn't have known about seed potatoes either!'

Amy was silent for a moment pondering what to say next. 'I have to go home soon, to return to college in New York. I'm studying Earth Sciences so I can help my Uncle Daniel as soon as I've graduated. He's going to make it his life's work – rescuing land that shouldn't ever be built on.'

'I know,' Leonie agreed. 'We met him when he was here during the war; that was when he fell in love with this part of England. He's right – the Levels have to be protected; they're very precious.'

Amy had one more thing she wanted to say. 'Don't you think it's sad that Adam should be so lonely, living by himself? He needs some-one to take care of him.'

Leonie glanced at the wistful face beside

her, and remembered how painful it was to be eighteen and deep in love. 'Some people do prefer to be solitary,' she suggested gently. 'What looks like loneliness to us doesn't *feel* like it to them.'

'He loved a girl – in Greece, I think – and lost her; that feels like loneliness to me,' Amy insisted. 'Why won't he believe that someone else might take her place? Surely he could try.'

'You're asking the wrong person,' Leonie said after a long pause. 'I lost someone too, and no one else would do for me either – so I think Adam Vaux is right about that.'

Unexpectedly, Amy leaned across and kissed her companion's cheek. 'I'm sorry ... I didn't know. Well, I guess I'd better be on my way – I'm holding you up. But when I come back here will you help me learn some other things I don't know?'

Leonie's rare smile lit her face. 'It's a promise, and *you* can teach me about Earth Sciences, whatever they may be!'

She handed over the trug and walked with Amy as far as the lane that led back to the Manor. Then she returned to her *potager*, but for once she didn't start work immediately. Like a tiny shoot buried deep in the ground that suddenly needed to force its way into the bright air, an idea hidden in her mind insisted on being released by something Amy had said. It was a fantastic, altogether unworkable idea, but it clung to life in her mind no matter how much ridicule she poured on it. She even shook her head as if physical effort would dislodge it, but it was still there when she went back to the more useful task of digging up the potatoes Hannah needed for supper.

Twelve

As the summer waned it was time for Amy to return tearfully to New York. It might also mean, Leonie hoped, that Blossom ambled less often to the farm with Adam on her back. He was impervious to even the broadest hint that he might be neglecting Eustace's shop, and his sweet smile challenged her to pretend that the Wentworths didn't welcome his visits. A friendship had grown up between them that all three of them enjoyed. Elizabeth's only regret was that her niece seemed not to share in it – she found some task to do whenever Adam appeared. Still wrestling with her fantastic idea, Leonie merely said that one woman smiling a welcome was quite enough.

Then, one golden morning when she and Elizabeth were out searching the hedgerows for blackberries, she turned and saw her aunt idle for once, a still-empty basket in her hands and tears sliding down her cheeks. She went back at once, set the basket down, and took Elizabeth's hands in her own warm, sticky fingers.

'Something's the matter – tell me please,' she said urgently. 'Darling, aren't you well, or is it Uncle Michael – he was very quiet at breakfast.'

Elizabeth released herself and smeared away her tears. 'Stupid of me, love – nothing's wrong with us. It's the future that is such a worry. I feel so dreadfully inadequate not to have given Michael the children we need to carry on the farm – children to love the animals and cherish the land as he does. He thought at least old Tom's son would stay with us and learn to carry things on, but Ben wants to leave – says he can earn more working in a factory in Bristol. All the time this quiet desertion of the countryside is going on. Why are people such fools as not to see the value of what they have here?' Then she tried to smile. 'There, I've got that off my chest – now I'll go back to work.' But Leonie's anxious face made her say something else. 'If it hadn't been for the war we wouldn't have had the priceless gift of *you* – we don't ever forget that, my dear.' Then she picked up her basket and returned to picking fruit.

Leonie did the same, but although her fingers automatically selected the ripe, purple berries her mind was accepting something else; a decision had somehow just been made. At last she knew what she had to do.

That afternoon, changed out of gardening clothes, she cycled into Frantock and parked outside the book shop. Adam was there, sifting through a pile of books when she arrived.

'Another birthday?' he asked hopefully as she walked in. 'Business has been quiet today.'

'No – I've brought you some fruit.' She plonked down two punnets on his already chaotic desk. 'The apricots will need stewing in a little sugar syrup; the greengages are delicious eaten raw.' Then she made a little grimace of irritation with herself. This is ridiculous – I sound as if I've come to sell you something.'

'And have you?' Adam asked curiously, alert to the fact that her hands trembled, and her dark eyes were over-bright. She was trying hard for self-control, but he felt certain that a gift of fruit wasn't what had brought her there.

His quiet question hung in the air and at last she answered it. 'Well, in a way I suppose I have.'

After another glance at her face he got up and locked the door. 'It's nearly closing time – my customers must learn to come earlier in the day. We shall retire to the sitting room and sip a glass of sherry. Follow me, please.'

She was led along a narrow passage into a pleasant room she hadn't seen before. Simply but comfortably furnished, it looked what it was: the sanctum of a bachelor of taste and means.

Leonie walked over to the bow window and stared out into the street while Adam poured sherry into delicately engraved glasses. He handed her one and then waved her to an armchair. 'I can't sit down unless you do, and I hate having to drink standing up.'

She sat down, but on the extreme edge of

the chair, and he wondered how long it would take her to come to the point of her visit. At last he decided to help her.

'I'm delighted to see you,' he said gently, 'but I think you had a reason for coming – you don't normally seek my company, I'm afraid.'

She set down her glass with a bang that made him wince. 'It's difficult,' she admitted, 'but I'm getting round to it.' A fortifying sip of sherry enabled her to go on. 'I tried to tell you once how much I owe my aunt and uncle. When Lucienne died I would have died too but for them; they kept me alive by sheer loving kindness. Now I need to do something for them.' Her anguished glance met Adam's across the room. 'They had no children of their own, you see, though it wasn't for want of trying. My uncle isn't old yet, but when he is there'll only be me to keep the farm going, and I'll need a bit of help. People are leaving the land, not understanding how precious it is.'

She ground to a halt, aware that the hardest part was still to come. Adam thought it time to say something himself.

'My dear, I understand the problem but if you're thinking of offering me a job, I have to say that what I know about farming could be written on a postage stamp.'

Leonie saw the fence looming in front of her, gathered her courage and leapt over it. 'I was thinking of you as the father of a child my uncle could begin to train before it was too late.' She emptied her glass at a gulp and waited to hear what he would say.

'Let me get this straight,' Adam asked faintly. 'We – that is to say, you and I – would produce a child who could become a farmer twenty years from now. Am I right so far?'

It was easier now, she thought, to go on. 'I didn't ever consider it as a real possibility even though my aunt and uncle like you very much, until Amy repeated something you said to her. You'd loved someone and no one else would do – which is exactly how I feel about Luc. But this would be different ... a kind of business arrangement if you like.' She couldn't read the expression on his face, but went doggedly on. 'You have even fewer kith or kin than me, it seems – I thought you might like to have a child.' Her voice had grown hoarse with strain, but there were still things to make clear. 'Lucienne was conceived the only night I ever spent with Luc. I don't suppose that would happen again. You make a joke of your health, so I don't know how much of a risk it would be if we had to ... to keep trying.'

His mouth twitched at this way of putting it, but he was well aware of what the conversation was costing her in self-control. She was absurd, but valiant, and lovely in her longing to help her aunt and uncle.

'It would be a risk all round, don't you think?' he suggested gravely, not quite answering her question. She simply nodded, so he went on. 'I could only agree to our "business arrangement" if you married me first.'

He saw the shock and refusal in her face and shook his head. 'I'm not prepared to lie with someone, as the Bible charmingly puts it, unless she is my wife.'

She heard the finality in his voice but struggled against it. 'It's more than I bargained for. And in any case it wouldn't work – your job and home are here, mine are at the farm.'

'True – but no doubt we could arrange to meet occasionally,' he said with a perfectly straight face.

'I don't know how I'd explain it to my aunt and uncle without them guessing the truth,' she explained wretchedly. 'I suppose I'd have to think of some nonsense about how sophisticated we are ... leading separate lives because we prefer them that way and meeting occasionally, as you say, by arrangement.'

Nonsense it would certainly sound, he feared, but he couldn't make it easier for her. 'Say whatever you like to Elizabeth and Michael,' he said gently, 'and leave it to me to arrange things with Andrew Rushton as soon as possible. I assume that's what you want?'

She wanted above all things to shout that it was nothing of the kind. What she wanted was to escape from the room and go home and weep – for herself, for lost Luc, and for the happiness that Adam Vaux had missed. But it wasn't what she'd come for – to baulk at the last fence.

'Yes, the sooner it's done the better,' she finally agreed, and then stood up to leave.

He rose from his chair to come towards her, but she was too late to read his intention in his face, and found herself suddenly caught and held while his mouth came down on hers. She resisted for a moment, but his lips asked for a response she finally had to give, and she was trembling when he released her.

'Why ... why did you do that?' she finally managed to ask.

He might have said to wipe the desolation from her face, but instead he tried to speak lightly. 'To see whether our "arrangement" had a hope of working – it couldn't, you know, if you were unable to bear me touching you!' He made an even greater effort to sound casual. 'I think we've scrambled over *that* hurdle at least.'

Aware that sudden, aching need had betrayed her a moment ago, she was relieved, not offended, to have their first embrace described so unpoetically. Was this the moment to insist that their mockery of a marriage could end as soon as its purpose had been achieved? Perhaps not, she decided; one step at a time was all she could take, and the whole conversation had been an ordeal that left her feeling tired and strangely sad.

'I can't tell what you're thinking,' she suddenly said. 'If it seems too much like a joke to you or some sort of sordid deception, you've got to say so – *now*.'

'It's certainly not a joke,' he answered at

once. 'Let's call it a salvage effort, shall we?'

'For the farm you mean?' Leonie asked.

'Well, yes ... but maybe for you and me as well. I think we both need rescuing from the past.'

She nodded and walked towards the door, then halted there. 'A very private wedding, tell Andrew, please – not that *that* will make it any less of a deception, I'm afraid.' She stared at Adam for moment. 'You won't change your mind – about a marriage ceremony?'

'No, I won't,' he said gently. 'I don't think Elizabeth and Michael would want me to, either, leaving aside my own feelings in the matter.'

Leonie nodded again – it was all she seemed capable of now – and headed towards the front door. He waited while she climbed onto her bicycle, and watched as she pedalled away along the street. Then he went back inside, and sat down to consider a conversation that had been comic, touching and tragic all at the same time. Leonie had said herself that kindness would be the undoing of him, and there now seemed a very good chance that she'd be proved right.

Breakfast in the farmhouse kitchen, usually a cheerful meal, was more silent than usual. Leonie supposed that her aunt and uncle were still worried over the immediate problem of finding a replacement cowman for old Tom Hobbs who was overdue to retire. Her own reason for saying next to nothing was the bombshell waiting to be thrown once she could think of an acceptable way of doing it; but the more she thought about it, the worse the problem got. It was Elizabeth who finally broke the silence round the table.

'I forgot to tell you last night that I'd met Martha in town. She was bursting for us to know that Daniel is due to arrive for an unexpected visit. He's landed a job with some United Nations agency that is taking a keen interest in the preservation of places like the Levels here. That's good news, isn't it?' she asked, seeing that her husband was looking thoughtful.

'Yes, of course it is,' he admitted. 'Dan Wetherby's a nice man and a clever scientist, but I'm afraid he can't expect me not to graze livestock on our low-lying meadows in the interests of the wetland flora and fauna he reckons ought to be left in peace there! We farm as we always have done here – let winter flooding regenerate the grass in summer and move animals back to higher ground in the autumn. Farmers only had to produce food during the war; from now on, according to Dan, they've got to be ecologists as well!'

'My dear, don't worry,' Elizabeth said firmly. 'Daniel knows this is a working farm, not a rich man's hobby. I'm sure it wouldn't occur to him to embarrass us with advice we don't really need.'

She was privately less sure, though, about another possible source of embarrassment. Martha Wetherby made no secret of her heart's desire, which was to see their son married to their nearest and dearest neighbours' niece. Daniel and Leonie, reckoned Martha, were made for each other, and how neat and right and perfect it would be for the remaining Harcourt descendant to return to what had been her family's home for centuries.

Elizabeth couldn't answer for Dan Wetherby – perhaps the idea looked equally neat to him – but she was sure that Leonie, sharing calmly in his occasional visits, forgot about him the moment he went away. Having tried on more than one occasion to suggest this tactfully to Martha, Elizabeth now smiled ruefully at her niece.

'We shall have to invite them all to dinner – Martha would be hurt if we didn't.'

Leonie hesitated for a moment and then heard herself say words that she hadn't known were in her mouth. 'Perhaps she'll be less happy to come when she knows that Adam Vaux and I decided yesterday to get married.'

Fraught as the silence was, Leonie felt a hysterical desire to laugh at the expression on her aunt's face – not quite consternation, but certainly shock mixed with disbelief. Unusually, it was Michael Wentworth who found his voice first.

'You did say *marriage* ... to Adam?' he muttered. 'I did hear that aright?' He looked at his wife for help that wasn't forthcoming, and floundered on. 'He's a very nice man ... We like him, don't we, my dear?' he enquired nervously of Elizabeth. '...It's just that you've always insisted on staying single.'

Elizabeth now came to his rescue. 'It's also that you've shown no liking for Adam at all. We ought to be delighted, but ... are you sure? It's so very sudden, you see.'

Leonie's face was pale beneath its tan, but she managed to smile at her aunt. 'I know it *seems* sudden, but it's been on my ... our ... minds for some time.' She took a deep breath and soldiered on. 'It's not a whirlwind romance ... in fact, to be truthful it isn't a romance at all. We've both put that behind us. This is a sort of ... of friendly arrangement that we think ... hope ... might suit us both!'

'It scarcely sounds like a marriage at all to me,' Elizabeth said flatly. 'Is Adam going to live here or are you going to live in Frantock?'

Leonie wondered how much harder it could get. She hid trembling hands in the pockets of her skirt, and tried her hardest to sound confident and unconcerned. 'Adam must keep on the cottage, because of the shop. My work is here. We'll see more of each other, of course, than we do now ... but it will be a sort of trial to begin with, to see if we can make it work.'

Her eyes pleaded with her aunt to let the discussion rest there, however bizarre it sounded, and Elizabeth heeded the desperate request. 'Give us a little time to get used to the idea,' she said gently, 'and then we *shall* be delighted.'

Leonie managed a little smile and then walked out of the room, leaving a silence behind her that Michael was the first to break.

'I don't know what I ought to do ... go and see Adam? I can hardly forbid the banns – she's nearly twenty-eight.'

'I don't think we should do anything at all,' Elizabeth finally answered. 'Leonie gave us the explanation herself – two lonely people who've both lost the happiness they hoped for are going to try to make an unusual sort of marriage work. I shall pray that they can, otherwise she will be completely alone when we're no longer here.'

Michael considered this for a moment. 'It seems a very cold-blooded way to enter into matrimony, all the same.'

'Yes it does,' his wife agreed. 'Leonie sometimes reverts to being French, remember, and the French are much less sentimental about marriage than we are. But the truth is that she is a passionate, warm-hearted woman, and my impression of Adam is that he's anything but cold-blooded himself.'

'So you think the unusual marriage won't work?'

'I don't know,' Elizabeth answered thoughtfully, 'but if it does it won't be in the way they're anticipating.' Then a wry smile lifted the anxiety from her face. 'Poor Martha's going to be very disappointed. Bang goes her well-intentioned plan for Daniel.'

She looked up as the door suddenly opened and Leonie reappeared.

'I forgot to say that it's going to be a *very*

quiet wedding – no guests, no fuss! Adam is arranging a private ceremony with Andrew Rushton.'

'You mean we're not invited?' Michael asked.

She walked back into the kitchen and dropped a kiss on the top of his head. 'Darling Nunk – you have to give me away; of course you and Aunt Elizabeth have to be there.'

Thirteen

In the event it wasn't quite the private wedding that Leonie had intended. The Rushtons and the Wetherbys clearly couldn't be excluded, and Adam asked to be allowed to invite an old friend from Oxford, and his new friend, Matilda Dobson. Finally the bride herself decided that it was the moment for Smithy to come to terms with the country at last. Their occasional telephone conversations hadn't prepared him for the news, he said rather grumpily, but seeing as who it was getting married, he supposed he'd better help to pack her off her aunt and uncle's hands at last.

'Glad to get rid of you, I dare say,' he said as an afterthought. 'Who wouldn't be?'

Leonie refused to explain that it was hardly what was going to happen, and insisted instead that he come to Somerset the day before the wedding and stay at the farmhouse overnight. He agreed to this but refused to be met – he'd make his own way, he said.

Then, two days before the wedding date, one more possible guest appeared out of the blue – her mother's cousin, Jules Lefevre, not seen since his visit to the farm in the middle of the war. She knew that he'd continued to fly afterwards, because an occasional postcard would arrive from some Middle Eastern capital or other that he'd alighted at, but she was moved to tears to hear his voice when he telephoned from London and invited her to abandon Frantock for what he called 'an evening on the town'.

'I can't,' she said unevenly, 'I'm getting married instead! Can't you come down here? Oh, Jules – *please* come ... I would so love you to.'

'I can't stay, *ma petite* – I've to fly my princeling back to his desert kingdom. But I can't not come to your wedding – expect me by the first train of the day.'

Smithy duly arrived, having caught a train to Taunton, a bus to Frantock, and been offered a lift to the farm while he was trying to remember which direction to walk in.

She hugged him when he arrived, and told him he looked unchanged, but it wasn't true, she thought sadly. He'd been older than her father, and must be nearly seventy by now.

'It's time you retired,' she said, looking at his lined face. 'Come and live down here – you'd get used to the country, I promise.'

Smithy shook his grizzled head. 'I think I'd rather die what I was born, a Cockney, ta all the same. My lady and gent aren't bad to work for – foreigners o'course, but they can't help that.'

She took him indoors to renew acquaintance with her aunt and uncle, and then, guessing that it was what he would want, drove him in to Frantock to visit her father's grave. He stood there in silence for a while, and then looked slowly round the peaceful, tree-shaded churchyard.

'I wouldn't mind bein' buried alongside the captain when the time comes,' he said suddenly. 'Would that be a trouble to arrange?'

She smiled at him, perilously close to tears again – getting married seemed to be a more emotional business than she'd bargained for. 'No trouble at all – it's a promise,' she said unsteadily, and then took him back to supper at the farm, where her bridegroom had been invited to meet him.

It was late the following morning when a taxi deposited Jules at the farmhouse gate, so late that Leonie had begun to fear that he wouldn't come at all.

'A cow on the line, or some such ridiculous thing!' he said cheerfully as he embraced her, and then greeted the Wentworths and Smithy. 'But I'm here, and overjoyed to have arrived in time.' Deeply tanned, he was otherwise seemingly unchanged by the years since his previous visit, but Leonie sensed some sadness hidden beneath his pleasure at seeing them. She went away to change while Michael Wentworth revived him with a glass of wine, and then it was time to leave for the church.

As they walked in the organ was being softly played, an unexpected pleasure that Leonie realized she owed to Adam for thinking to arrange. Apprehensive as she felt, there was the serene loveliness of the church itself, the October sunlight falling through the stained glass windows in drifts of colour, and the organ music to quieten her stretched nerves. She was far from sure about the rightness of the sacrament she was there for, but she promised Almighty God that the vows she was about to take, dictated though they were by mind, not heart, would at least be sincere and honourable in intention.

She had insisted on waiting in a pew with her aunt and uncle, Jules, and Smithy, and only stood up as Andrew Rushton emerged, robed, from the vestry to come to the chancel steps. As she stepped forward into the aisle to join him, Adam saw her clearly for the first time – in a glowing dress of apricot-coloured silk, with a tiny pillbox hat of the same material perched on her dark hair. So lovely did she look that he almost missed what happened next. Expecting Michael Wentworth to follow her out of the pew, she seemed taken aback when Smithy stationed himself beside her instead, but her uncle's smiling nod said that this was what had been arranged – her father's faithful friend had been given the privilege that Edward Harcourt should have had. Leonie smiled blindingly at her uncle, touched Smithy's hand in gratitude, and then turned towards the man she was about to marry.

Her responses were less confident than Adam's, but she got through them without stumbling and even began to feel that, conducted as it was in a place sanctified by centuries of prayer and worship, her marriage *could* be forgiven, not only by the unforgotten memory of Luc but also by God himself. Smithy performed his part with pride and dignity, the register was signed, and she had suddenly become someone else – Leonie Vaux, the wife of a man she scarcely knew. But as if he understood her uncertainty, Adam's steady glance promised that there was nothing to fear – somehow they would make this oddly arranged marriage work.

Lunch was waiting for them back at the farmhouse, and Michael honoured the occasion by unearthing some pre-war champagne from the cellar. James Wetherby made a brief but charming speech, to which Adam replied with equal grace, and then it was time for the party to break up. The visitors from London had to be driven back to Taunton station, but Jules asked for a few minutes alone with Leonie before they had to leave.

She led him out into Elizabeth's cherished rose garden, still fragrant and colourful in late October, and smiled sadly at him.

'Dear Jules, when shall I see you again – sooner than another six years from now, please. Apart from my uncle and aunt, you're the only family I have.'

If it sounded an odd remark from a girl who'd just acquired a husband, he didn't comment on it, being concerned with what it was in his mind to say.

'Ma petite, do you remember that I made you a solemn promise years ago to tell you if I found out anything about what happened during the war?' he asked gravely.

She stared at him, warned by something in his face that the promise was about to be redeemed. 'Of course I remember,' she agreed, trying to wait for what might come next, but unable not to ask. 'Is it about Luc?'

Jules shook his head. 'No, I heard no more about Luc. But quite by chance, which is how such things happen, I met someone a little while ago whom we knew in Paris before the war. He had been a student of André Bernard's at the Sorbonne, and had visited the house on the Île de la Cité that you must remember very well.'

'Of course I remember,' she said again. 'Go on please.'

Jules hesitated for a moment, as if even now trying to decide whether to continue or not. 'When I telephoned from London and heard about your wedding I almost made up my mind to say nothing at all. But a promise is a promise, and finally I came to realize that what I'd learned might help you to draw a line under a past that still haunts you, and begin the new life with your husband that is needed now.'

She said nothing at all, dark eyes fixed on his face while Jules struggled painfully on.

'Emile and Jeanne Gosselin carried on their father's restaurants – you knew that, of course – and broke Roland's heart by welcoming

German officers. They insisted that Germans and French must learn to like one another! Genevieve accused Emile of collaborating simply out of greed, and they quarrelled very publicly. But the worst row came when he asked where *you* were in London – he said Luc had left with you something of value that belonged to the Gosselin family. Genevieve refused to give him your address, and five days later Gestapo men went to search the house and found Max Reiner hidden upstairs. The rest of the story you know.'

'Emile ... Emile Gosselin had betrayed them?' Leonie whispered.

'Yes,' Jules said simply. 'The man I talked to heard him boast drunkenly about it afterwards.' Jules stared at her stricken face. 'Was I wrong to tell you? My dear, I think now that I was.'

She shook her head, certain about this at least. 'Not wrong, Jules. I always believed that someone had betrayed them, and at least I know the truth at last, but I pray that Luc never learned that about his brother.'

There was silence for a moment, then Leonie gently put the past aside.

'You didn't answer my question. When shall we see you again? Aren't you ever going to get tired of a rootless life and settle down?'

Jules accepted the change of topic with a little smile of relief. 'I'm a vagabond by nature, *ma chère*, and the truth is that I'm happiest when I'm in the air. I shall go on flying aeroplanes until I'm too old to do it well any more, then I'll go back to Paris and die there.'

'Find a nice wife first,' she pleaded, 'you'll be lonely otherwise.'

Jules' smile was suddenly rueful. 'The girl I was waiting for married someone else.' It was lightly, gently said, but she leaned forward and kissed his cheek, suddenly sure who the girl had been.

'I must say my goodbyes,' he insisted in a different voice. 'Michael will be waiting for me to leave, and so will the splendid Smithy.'

She walked back with him into the house, and a quarter of an hour later stood with Adam and Elizabeth waving the car on its way to the station. Then, overcome by the accumulated emotions of the day, she found herself clinging desperately to the garden gate, terrified that if she let go of it she would simply fall in a heap on the ground.

What happened next she wasn't afterwards sure. Either she did faint for a brief moment or two, or Adam saw that she was beyond doing anything more rational. She was gently but firmly shepherded into the car he now possessed, and aware of being deposited a few minutes later at his cottage door.

'Why are we here?' she managed to ask.

'Because it's my home – your home too, when you feel the need of it,' he answered quietly. 'Just at the moment I think you do.'

She followed him inside like a bemused moth incapable of not following a light, and found herself led to a bedroom on the upper floor.

'This is your room,' Adam explained, in the same gentle voice that laid no stress on anything he said. 'Mine is next door. I think you need a little peace and quiet. Lie down, please. Go to sleep if you can.'

The door was shut behind him, and, suddenly thankful to the bottom of her heart just to be left alone, she looked round the room, comforted by the simplicity of what she saw – whitewashed walls; polished wooden floor; sprigged chintz curtains at the window; white cotton counterpane on the bed. She kicked off her shoes and lay down. Sleep was out of the question, of course, but just to stay in this quiet room was all she asked at the moment.

She woke to find that she'd been covered by a light, soft blanket. Summer dusk now filled the room; she had slept for several hours. Vaguely surprised to find her dressing gown laid across the foot of the bed and her slippers on the floor, she got up and put them on. The apricot dress, relic of pre-war Paris days, couldn't be worn again. It was part of the past, and the past was behind her.

She washed her face and hands in the bathroom, brushed her hair, and then went downstairs. Adam was in the sitting room, with a book on his lap that she suspected he hadn't been reading. He looked up as she walked in, but his grave expression didn't change.

'Thank you for covering me up,' she said. 'I've only just woken.'

He nodded and laid aside his book. 'Now you need some food – you ate almost none of Hannah's delicious lunch. We have to go to the kitchen, I'm afraid, via the hall. What was originally the dining room became the book shop.'

His voice was pleasant and she could feel that his intention was to be kind, but now it was kindness offered from the distance he had set between them, deliberately, it seemed. She didn't comment on the alteration, or even say that she still wasn't hungry, and simply followed him into the pleasant kitchen at the back of the house. The smell of warm bread was in the air, the table was neatly laid and a saucepan sat simmering on the hob.

He put a bowl of soup in front of her, and the first spoonful made her change her mind about not being hungry.

'It's good,' she said, sounding surprised.

'I know,' he agreed calmly. 'I only make good soup.'

She bit into the crusty bread, looked another question at him, and saw him nod.

'The secret is to sing to it, I find, when I'm kneading the dough.'

The explanation was made so seriously that she couldn't judge whether she was meant to believe him or not. In fact, she was altogether at a loss with someone who'd become this courteous stranger she was now faced with.

'I didn't say goodbye to your very pleasant friend,' she suddenly remembered to say. It seemed the easiest of the confessions she had to make.

'He's still here for a day or two,' came back the calm reply. 'Old churches inspire him to sketch them, which he does very well, and he's also keen to play the organ before he leaves Frantock. When we drove away your dear, kind aunt was inviting him to stay at the farm instead of looking for a room at a pub.'

Leonie concentrated on her soup, then pushed the empty bowl away. 'Could we stop making conversation now? There's rather a lot to say.'

'You begin,' he suggested. 'Ladies are always allowed to go first.'

Feeling like a climber confronted with a rock so smooth that no foot or handhold could be found on it at all, she took a deep breath and spoke the simple truth.

'It's probably hard to believe but I refused to think beyond today's ceremony – that was as far as my mind would go.'

'I realized that,' he answered quietly. 'But you *did* suddenly think about it after lunch. That's when I asked Elizabeth to put a few things into a bag for you and brought you here. But you aren't obliged to stay – I'll take you back whenever you say.'

She stared at him for a moment but his impassive face gave no hint of what he was feeling. It was for her to go on, it said, if it said anything at all.

'I've no right to be here – no moral right, I mean,' she tried to explain. 'For my own selfish reasons I've turned your neatly arranged life upside down, and you've been too kind to point out that my so-called arrangement is unworkable as well as wrong.'

Adam gave what she took to be a little confirming nod. 'Unworkable, I have to agree,' he said, 'but I only knew that for certain when you said goodbye to Jules Lefevre this afternoon and I saw the desolation in your face.' He managed a ghost of a smile. 'There's no harm done; we can unmarry ourselves, you know!' But her tragic expression made him go on more sharply. 'My dear girl, however much you feel you owe to the Wentworths they'd be the last people in the world to want you to ruin your life for them. You must go back to France ... be happy with Jules Lefevre.'

It took a moment for the extent of his misunderstanding to sink in, then she firmly shook her head. 'Jules is my only blood relative apart from Elizabeth, and my only link with my mother's family. But he would tell you himself that he's a vagabond, happiest when he's alone, flying above the clouds. He wouldn't thank you to suggest he ought to settle down.'

'More unhappiness for you, then,' Adam said, with sadness in his voice now. 'That's why you almost fainted when he left – I'm sorry, my dear.'

But Leonie's upraised hands dismissed his sympathy. 'I was sorry to see him go, of course, but that wasn't what had upset me so much. Jules had just told me why Genevieve and Pappi and Max Reiner died during the war. They were betrayed to the Gestapo by Luc's brother, Emile Gosselin.'

'Dear God ... how terrible!' Adam's shocked voice barely reached her. 'Are you sure?'

'Jules happened to meet a man who'd been one of Pappi's students – he was often at the house. He heard Emile boasting to his friends that he'd been responsible for getting rid of his brother's Jewish friends.'

'Was that all the excuse he needed – their Jewishness?'

'No, Genevieve had already quarrelled with him for collaborating with the Germans, but then he demanded to know where I was. He said Luc had given me something valuable that belonged to the Gosselin family. Genevieve refused to give him my address, and five days later the Germans came for them.'

'What did Gosselin imagine you had?' Adam asked after a moment or two.

'Nothing of value, that's the bitterly ironic part of it – Luc had simply left with me a little battered suitcase his father handed him when he came to London. It just had family papers in it, he thought, but he didn't even have the key. We were going to open it when he came back after the war. It's still in a cupboard in my bedroom, but I'd never turn it over to Emile – he'd have to kill me to get it.'

She spoke the literal truth, Adam realized. More than cool English blood ran in her veins, and she hated Emile Gosselin as much as she had loved his brother. He found himself wishing that Jules hadn't told her the truth, but she seemed to guess what he was thinking.

'Don't blame Jules for telling me – I'd made him promise that he would if ever he discovered what had happened,' Leonie insisted gently. 'And he hoped it would draw a line under the past – allow me to make a fresh start.'

'Which brings us back to the present,' Adam pointed out. 'I'm afraid we have to decide what we do next. Do we admit now that this morning's ceremony shouldn't have taken place, or pretend for a while and then announce that our arrangement isn't working?'

Still unable to pierce the guard he'd set on himself, she stared at him uncertainly. 'It takes two to make an arrangement. If it seemed workable when you agreed to it, why isn't it workable now?'

He gave a little sigh, as if disappointed that she couldn't work the answer out for herself. 'Because the premise it's based on is wrong,' he said patiently. 'The idea that you can draw a line under the past is exactly what is wrong. The past, added to the present, is who you *are*. You can come to terms with it or not, but in one way or another it must travel with you. Changing your name to Vaux doesn't make you any less the Leonie Harcourt who loved Luc Gosselin. If Leonie Vaux can't accept that then our arrangement is doomed before it begins.'

He saw the agonized uncertainty in her face, and spoke again before she could decide what to say. 'I made some vows this morning that still hold for me, and if you'd rather let the pretence continue for a while, the room upstairs is yours for as long as you need it. But that brings me back to the question I asked a few minutes ago – what do *you* want to do next?'

Her expression relaxed into a strained smile. 'Just at this moment I'd like to go back upstairs and sleep till morning, if you're really prepared to put up with me until then. I'd also like to say that it's not fair to leave what happens after that entirely to me, but you would very rightly point out that I'm responsible for the muddle we're in.'

Adam shook his head. 'Correction needed, I'm afraid. I may be very uncertain as to how this story will end, but I'm not in a muddle at all. However, my survival manual for venturing into the unknown recommends taking only one step at a time. So let us sleep in our respective beds, and decide on our next step tomorrow. Breakfast can be whenever you like – I don't open the shop on Sundays.'

She nodded, grateful for the small relief of talking about something as normal as breakfast. But she went upstairs fully aware of how little she understood Adam Vaux. How foolish she'd been, how inadequate had been the thought she'd given to the situation they were now in, and how carelessly she'd involved the clever, complicated and damaged man downstairs in her wildcat scheme. He'd just reminded her of the vows they'd taken, and with that thought suddenly in her mind she knelt down to pray – for the souls of the people she had loved, and for the forgiveness she seemed in such need of herself.

Fourteen

When she went downstairs the following morning the kitchen table was laid for breakfast but there was no sign of Adam. A note said briefly that he'd gone to visit his girlfriend, who was not to feel neglected now that he'd acquired a wife. Interpreting this correctly to mean that he and Blossom were ambling about the meadow together, she added her own note to his, to explain that she'd gone to the eight o'clock service in church; he wasn't to wait for breakfast for her to return.

But when she walked in three-quarters of an hour later he was grinding coffee beans, and their fragrance filled the kitchen.

'Girlfriend glad to see you, I hope,' she remarked solemnly.

Adam's stern mouth relaxed into a smile. 'Overjoyed, but the sugar lumps she knows are in my pocket might have something to do with that.'

A wave of his hand invited her to sit down and help herself to food. She poured orange juice into both glasses, then sat sipping hers while he brewed coffee and toasted bread.

'You *look* less haunted this morning. Are

you feeling better?' he enquired calmly as if they'd been sharing their first meal of the day for years and there was nothing strange about her being there.

She recognized it as his personal way of dealing with their situation – simply ignore the bizarreness of it and it would become acceptable in time, he seemed to be insisting. But she knew that, however tempting it was to pretend that he might be right, she couldn't shelter behind a sham of normality they'd be unable to sustain.

'I tried to do what I should have done before,' she admitted slowly. 'I thought about the future.'

He set coffee pot and toast rack on the table, and then sat down himself. 'Constructively, I hope – not just going round in circles, as donkeys used to do when they were threshing corn in Greece.' He smiled suddenly, readmitting her into some kind of intimacy at last. 'Have you ever considered how unfairly donks have acquired a reputation for stupidity? In fact they're very sagacious animals.'

'According to my uncle, they calm restive horses if they share a field with them,' Leonie was able to contribute to the conversation. Then she managed to smile herself. 'Enough about donkeys! May I tell you what I worked out during the night?'

He nodded by way of answer, and she couldn't tell whether what she was about to say seemed any more important to him than the animals they'd been discussing.

'You agreed to my proposal,' she said as calmly as she could, 'and seemed yesterday to be prepared to go on with it. My ... my object remains the same ... to have a child, not only for the sake of my aunt and uncle but for my own sake as well – so I would like our marriage to continue. But I realize that ... that it might not work ... occasional p ... propinquity might not be enough to ... to...'

'...to propel us into forgetting that we didn't marry for love,' he agreed, unable not to help her out. 'We shall have to see whether we can manage without it.'

She eyed him uncertainly, having now learned to be most distrustful of him when he sounded most grave. But his sudden smile was full of understanding.

'I'm laughing at *us*, my dear, not at you,' he said gently. 'We shall only survive this odd experiment if we don't take ourselves too seriously.'

He was right, she realized – not only right, but wise and kind as well, and, knowing that, it was suddenly easy to go on.

'I can't help feeling guilty about *you*. Amy Wetherby confessed to me once how much she thought you needed a companion. I tried to explain that some people are solitary from choice. I think you're one of them, which makes me suggest that I should come here just at weekends – at least you'd have the times in between on your own. Would that be enough peace and quiet for you, do you think?'

The anxious question made his mouth twitch, but he was wanting now to seem as sensible as she was being, and he was touched by a concern for him that he realized was genuine. She was an extraordinary mixture – at once beautiful but unaware of the fact, maddening but enchanting as well, and not nearly as lacking in passion as she'd schooled herself to believe. He'd said earlier that he had no idea how this story would end. All he was certain of so far was that it wouldn't be dull.

At last he answered her question. 'So we'll settle for weekday life as usual apart, and weekend adventure together. I think my survival manual would approve of that.'

She saw one more hurdle looming that had to be faced. 'You mustn't wait on me when I'm here – the chores are to be shared, but I must also share in the extra expense. This *is* a business arrangement, remember.'

Adam smiled, but shook his head. 'What you really mean is do I work hard enough to make the shop pay! In fact it pays rather well, but it wouldn't greatly matter if it didn't. When my parents died I had a large house to sell in North Oxford – Shangri-la to academics! I'm not in James Wetherby's class, but I'm not poor either. So thank you for the kind thought but your being here won't strain my finances unduly.'

She was about to ask at least to be allowed to bring fruit and vegetables from the farm when they were interrupted by the arrival of a very large tabby cat who pushed open the kitchen door and sat down by the Aga.

'Home is the hunter from the hill,' Adam quoted. 'Meet Nimrod – obvious name, I'm afraid, but he seems to like it – now grown considerably since Matilda Dobson insisted that I needed a kitten for company.'

'I didn't know you were a cat-lover,' Leonie said, unnerved by Nimrod's unblinking, green stare.

'I don't love cats – they want respect instead. Nimrod is an independent spirit who merely expects me to provide his daily ration of milk. An occasional fish head doesn't come amiss, but he prefers to provide his own food as a rule.'

She tucked her ankles further under her chair in case the cat was still hungry, and asked a different question. 'May I ring the farm? I'd like to say thank you for yesterday's lunch party.'

Adam's sudden frown took her by surprise. 'Do whatever you like,' he said sharply. 'This is your home whenever you're here.'

At the risk of irritating him again, she had one more thing to say. 'I don't know how you normally spend your Sundays, but you must do what you would be doing if I weren't here – otherwise I shall become more of a nuisance than I can bear.'

'I walk to the newsagent's to buy whatever Sunday papers I feel like reading. After lunch I stroll to the vicarage to play chess with Andrew Rushton or argue with him about the translation of some Greek prose – he's a scholar as well as an exceptionally nice man. But he probably won't expect me today, even though I felt obliged to mention that we decided to marry first and get to know each other afterwards.'

'Was he ... shocked?' Leonie made herself ask.

Adam shook his head. 'Parish priests are impervious to shock; they have to promise that when they get ordained.'

'Well, please go and beat him at chess at least. I'm going to set about pruning every shrub your garden possesses – they're all much too overgrown.'

With Nimrod's milk ration attended to, Adam set off in search of newspapers, with no complaint about this way of ordering their first day together. God alone knew whether even their 'business arrangement' could be made to work, and to turn it into anything more rewarding than that would need all the stars in their courses to be shining down on them.

The weekday/weekend routine became a habit that everyone got used to. Leonie cycled or drove into Frantock after breakfast on Saturdays and returned to work at the farm after breakfast on Mondays. The shared days even became enjoyable – mainly, Leonie continued to insist, because both of them still had time and space to themselves. In fact more marriages, she said, would be improved by just such an arrangement.

But in one vital respect it posed a problem that grew more, not less, intractable as the days went by. Her bedroom was still hers alone; they shared the cottage but they didn't share a bed, and she could detect in Adam not the slightest hint of a desire to change this state of affairs. The relief of being left to sleep alone slowly gave way to resentment, and then to despair. Was he a man who didn't want a wife? Or a man who, at least, didn't want *her* as a wife? She had no idea which it was. All she was certain of was that she *couldn't* – not even for the child she wanted so much – stalk into his room one night and demand that he make love to her. If that was the only way it would happen, it wouldn't happen at all, and their ill-fated, insanely planned marriage of convenience would be at an end.

That was how matters still stood between them when Christmas was approaching and something unlooked-for happened. She was in the farm's office one morning, wrestling with the week's milk returns, when a telephone call from a hospital in London informed her that Mr Albert Smith was there, having suffered a serious heart attack the previous night. The foreign-sounding voice at the end of the line belonged to Smithy's employer. He understood, he said, that she would want to know the attack had been very serious.

'Will he survive it?' she asked unsteadily.

'The doctor here thinks not,' the slow answer came back. 'I'm sorry to have to tell you that.'

'I'll come – straightaway,' Leonie said, 'but I'm in Somerset. Please tell Smithy, if you can, that I'll be there as soon as I can manage it.'

Desperate as she was, it took four hours to reach the hospital, and she was met with the news that Smithy had died half an hour earlier. The man she'd spoken to on the telephone – a diplomat from the Swedish Embassy – had been kind enough to wait for her to arrive and introduced himself when she emerged weeping from having kissed Smithy goodbye.

'He was a good man,' Arne Larsen said gently. 'My wife and I will miss him.'

'He'd been my father's servant during the first World War and remained devoted to his memory,' Leonie managed to explain. 'He was my dear friend as well – my only friend at one stage of my life.' She wiped away her tears and tried to think what must be said next. 'I promised that he should be buried in the churchyard at home, where my father's grave is. I need to find an undertaker ... make the necessary arrangements.'

But she was interrupted by Mr Larsen. 'You need do nothing but give me the address,' he said with what she realized was wondrous kindness. 'My people will make the arrangements, you have only to tell me when the funeral can take place. If you will come back with me now to the house there are some things of Smith's that you should have.' He looked at her strained face and shook his head. 'The long journey home is too much for you, I think. I am sure my wife would want you to spend the night in London with us.'

Leonie thanked him unsteadily, but insisted that she was quite able to manage the journey home. Ten minutes later she walked with him into the house in Green Street, assailed by memories she had put aside for years.

Smithy's possessions amounted to not a great deal. The scrupulously cared-for clothes, Arne Larsen said, could be disposed of; the rest of the things – half a dozen books, a photograph album and a folder of papers – were packed up for Leonie to take away.

'It's not very much is it,' she asked, 'to represent a man's entire life, but he didn't set much store by things. It was what people were, he'd have said, that counted, not what they owned.'

'And he would have been right,' said Mr Larsen. 'If I'm not absolutely obliged to be somewhere else on the day of the funeral, I should like to attend – my wife also. Would that be all right?'

'Very all right,' she agreed unsteadily, and promised to telephone him when she'd been able to speak to Andrew Rushton the following day. Then she was put into a taxi for the brief journey back to Paddington. Her memory leaped back through the years to another taxi going in the opposite direction – utterly miserable, resentful of her then stepmother, and blindly unaware of what the next ten years would bring.

When she looked at Smithy's album the following morning she took another journey back in time – her dead mother was there, smiling and vividly alive; regimental groups, stiffly composed, showed her father as a young man in a captain's uniform; and she was even there herself, staring mulishly at the camera as her aunt told her she still did.

More surprising to find among Smithy's few documents was a copy of his will, in which he left to her all that he'd possessed in the way of capital – nearly £3000 slowly accumulated during a frugal lifetime of service and hard work. It was up to her, he'd written, to use it however she reckoned fit, and after some thought she donated it in his memory to the Star and Garter Home for soldiers incurably damaged in the service of their country.

The day of his funeral was a December morning of sparkling frost and brilliant sunshine rarely seen in Somerset's winter dampness. The Larsens *had* come down from London, and even local friends who hadn't known Smithy at all took their places before the service began.

Leonie had asked to leave the lesson to Adam, and he chose St Paul, writing to the Corinthians – 'For now we see in a glass darkly, but then we shall see face to face. Now

I know only in part; then I will know fully even as I have been fully known.' The lovely words could comfort any sadness, she thought, but there was more to acknowledge than that. A ray of sunshine fell on Adam's dark head as he stood at the lectern and she saw him clearly at last – for the kind, honourable and attractive man that he was. Any child he fathered would be fortunate indeed, and she, Leonie Vaux, was fortunate to be his wife. It was a mind-blowing revelation to have at a funeral, but she could hear Smithy saying, 'Seen the truth at last, 'ave you? Well, you took your time, but better late that never.'

After the service and committal in the churchyard, they took the Larsens back to the farm for a simple lunch, and then waved them off on their way back to London. It was time for the day to revert to normal and, having changed out of her funeral clothes, Leonie got ready to go back to the cottage with Adam.

'I know it's not the usual day,' she almost apologized, 'but I'd still like to come with you if you don't mind.'

'I don't mind at all,' he said with a hint of sharpness. 'I just wish you'd remember the cottage is your home as much as it is mine.'

With the early winter darkness came biting cold again, and Adam lit the fire in the sitting room as soon as they were indoors. She refused any more food, but sat nursing the glass of wine he poured for her, thinking what a strangely disturbing day it had been. That, she supposed, accounted for the tears that began to trickle down her cheeks. She brushed them away, hoping that Adam wouldn't notice; he was talking to Nimrod, ensconced on his knee and prepared for once to be a lap cat. But then his voice broke the silence in the room.

'If you're weeping for Smithy, out in the cold ground instead of here with us, there's no need. His spirit, the part of him that matters, is elsewhere.'

'I know,' she managed to say, '"my soul, there is a country far beyond the stars" ... I wasn't weeping for him, only for how wasteful life is. My daughter, Luc, my father and my Parisian friends ... they should all still be here, not just because I need them. This terribly disjointed world needs good people.'

In the firelight her face looked beautiful but sad, and Adam thought that she could just as justifiably have wept for the waste of herself. She was too young for despair, but too old to be offered love and comfort like a dose of medicine for an ailing child. He was aware of the terms of their arrangement, and although they were never more irksome than now, they still weren't for him to break; he was convinced of that.

'I can't pretend the world doesn't need your good people,' he said at last. 'God knows it does. But for as long as you remember them, live with them still in your heart and mind, I don't believe they *are* wasted. That is all the comfort I can offer you.'

The logs shifted in the grate, and Nimrod yawned and rubbed a sleepy eye with one paw. Then Leonie spoke again, so quietly that the words were only just audible.

'There'd be comfort in sharing your bed tonight, because I feel very lonely. Perhaps it's too much to ask – you've already done a great deal for me today.'

What she'd said, almost against her will, couldn't be unsaid, but the total silence in the room made clear the mistake she'd made – a social gaffe of unforgivable proportions. She tried to retrieve the situation by sounding wryly amused. 'I wasn't hoping for a night of unbridled passion – just a little of the shared warmth Nimrod seems to be enjoying! Forget I mentioned it.'

She stood up and made blindly for the door, but Adam's voice halted her.

'The cat was being kind, showing me that at least he welcomed my attentions.' Then his voice changed. 'My dear, I had to wait – it was for you to change the strange rules we live by. Passion, bridled or not, wouldn't be quite right tonight, I think, but you certainly don't have to feel lonely. Please share my bed, if it would help.'

Her eyes still questioned him. 'The survival manual would approve?'

'It would insist on it,' Adam said earnestly, '...Page 22, I think ... passion is dealt with a bit later on.'

She smiled then, but went upstairs without

answering. The room she went into presently was unfamiliar, and almost monastic in its neatness and simplicity. Adam's bed felt cold, and she shivered with a mixture of tiredness, grief and doubt that she should be there at all. But a small, insistent voice said that if she changed her mind now their fragile bond of trust would not only be broken but unmendable.

Then Adam walked into the room and it was too late not to stay where she was. But having his warm body beside her suddenly felt not strange at all. Gradually her shivering ceased and, held gently against him, she fell fast asleep. He lay awake himself for a long time, wondering whether he would ever be able to tell her that the story of the girl loved and lost had been dreamed up purely for Amy's benefit. Probably not, he decided, because she mustn't know that he, unlike her, hadn't done with romance and passion at all.

Fifteen

It was certainly morning, because grudging December daylight was creeping into the room, but it was coming from the wrong direction – her bedroom window faced west. The window itself was in the wrong place ... no, *she* was in the wrong place. But the mists of sleep were dissolving, and memory of the previous day and night now came flooding back. They had laid Smithy to rest in the churchyard, and she had rounded off an emotional day by asking to share Adam's bed – a night spent with her husband at last during which, she could only suppose since she remembered nothing else, she had simply fallen asleep. It seemed an anticlimax so shamingly complete that she didn't know whether to laugh or weep.

Beside her the bed was empty, but Adam was presumably still in the house. The temptation was very strong to stay where she was, at least for now, if not for ever; but even in her mind's present disordered state she recognized cowardice when she saw it beckoning. She must get up, take a shower, dress, and go downstairs. She must behave normally in every way, and Adam – a perceptive man, thank God – would understand that nothing had changed; they would simply resume the pattern that yesterday's events had interrupted.

Twenty minutes later she walked into the kitchen, warned by the smell of coffee brewing that he was there. He turned from the stove to smile at her, expecting a response, and got instead the cool good morning of a guest who happened to have spent the night in his spare room.

'No mighty hunter this morning?' she enquired, for something to break a silence that suddenly felt uncomfortable.

'He's in the back porch, sleeping off last night's indigestible dinner,' Adam said briefly. 'I trust *you* slept well?'

Colour rose in her pale face, but she answered in the same brittle voice. 'Very well, thank you.' She glanced at him for long enough to see that *he* looked tired. 'I shall be able to manage on my own tonight. Your bed will be all yours again, much to your relief, I expect!'

She didn't know what she was expecting, but not that he would throw down the spoon he was holding with a clatter that made her jump.

'Is that how it's always going to be with you – one step forward, two steps back?' he demanded in a voice that didn't lack anger for being very quiet; in fact it sounded worse, she thought, than if he'd shouted at her. 'I must tell you, Leonie, that it's not how it's going to be for me. Either we give this so-called marriage a chance to work as it should or we end it now. You seemed to need me last night, but now you're yourself again and I'm to be put aside until the next time a need arises. I can't accept that, I'm afraid. Either we go forward or we end our arrangement altogether.'

'You agreed,' she said, white-lipped now, '...you understood the sort of marriage it was going to be ... no pretence about being in love, because I loved Luc. If I didn't need a child so much ... for my aunt and uncle and the farm ... I'd stay lonely for the rest of my life. I made a vow *not* to love anyone else.'

Adam stared at her, aware that she believed what she said and his anger died because she deserved understanding, not anger. He came to stand in front of her, but didn't touch her.

'My dear, Luc is dead,' he said gently, 'but you are alive. You're also young and beautiful, and heartbreakingly loyal, but you're heartbreakingly wrong as well. If you're intent on emotional suicide I doubt if I can make you change your mind ... but I won't give up without one more try.'

There was no time to step back to safety out of reach; she was pulled hard against him, and his mouth found hers, as it had once before, she fearfully remembered. This time his lips demanded a response, and she knew that the hunger she felt in him was answered, indeed matched, by the longing in herself. She had been alone too long – her body ached to be loved.

When he lifted his head at last they were both trembling. 'I should take you back to bed right now,' he said unevenly, '...that is undoubtedly what I should do.' But suddenly she saw his expression change.

'You should ... but you aren't going to ... don't want to?' she murmured, shaken by the wave of disappointment that swept over her. The seesaw of emotions of the past few minutes was enough to cope with, but now all she could see in his face was unbelievable, sparkling merriment.

'Sweetheart, I'd rather stay here with you than do anything else on earth, but I'm committed to another lady – I promised to pay her a visit.' He was struggling not to laugh, and her sudden indignation made matters worse.

'It's Sunday morning – no time to be paying social calls,' she tried to point out crossly. 'If you won't take me to bed you ought at least to be going to church.' But she couldn't hold out against the tears of laughter now streaming down his face and, still not knowing why it was so funny, began to laugh herself.

At last he mopped his face, gently dried her tears, and dropped a kiss on the end of her nose.

'Now I'll try to explain,' he said unsteadily, still trying not to laugh. 'I promised to visit an elderly lady who has to dispose of her late husband's library, but she sounded frail, and nervous about a strange man turning up on her doorstep. I'd like you to come with me for purely selfish reasons, but *she* might be happier as well if I could introduce her to my wife.'

Serious again, Leonie nodded. She wasn't accustomed yet to thinking of herself in that way, but it was who she was – Adam Vaux's wife, and she vividly remembered the moment in church the day before when she'd realized that it was something to be proud of.

'Of course I'll come with you,' she said now. 'I can go to evensong this evening.'

'*We* shall go to evensong,' he corrected her, 'but first things first, don't you think? We haven't had breakfast yet.'

That was the moment Nimrod came strolling into the kitchen, miaowing for milk, and restoring normality, but the day felt different now. Every day would be different from now on, she realized. Adam had been right – they could only go forward, not back – better late than never, as Smithy would have said.

The house they drove to an hour later was on the outskirts of a village ten miles away. In summer, Leonie thought, it would be beautiful, but on a grey December morning the outlook over waterlogged fields and a lowering sky was more truthfully described as desolate. The small Georgian manor they'd come to had once been lovely but was now badly in need of repair, and its surrounding garden was an unkempt wilderness.

They stood in the porch waiting for their

knock on the door to be answered, and sadness seemed to be in the very air. Leonie put her hand in Adam's, for the comfort of knowing that he was there.

'How dreadful it will be,' she whispered, 'if there's nothing you want to buy.'

But his smile was reassuring. 'There *will* be something,' he insisted. 'Even if there's only rubbish I should buy it, but it won't be rubbish, I feel sure. This is the house of a man who read books.'

The door opened at last, and a tall, thin lady peered at them, apparently uncertain what she should do next.

'Mrs Carruthers?' Adam asked gently. 'I'm the book man you were expecting, and this is my wife, Leonie. May we come in?'

'It's Mr Vaux, isn't it,' she asked anxiously. 'Yes ... please, both of you come in.' She closed the door behind them and then limped along a wide passage to a room that was still beautiful even in its present state of shabbiness. Two walls were lined with bookshelves, and Adam's heart sank at the sight of what he could immediately recognize as rows of Victorian theologians' disputations on the lives of saints and martyrs, volumes of obscure local history, and leather-bound collections of poetry that probably hadn't been read for a hundred years.

But Mrs Carruthers had seen his moment of hesitation. 'A lot of what is here won't interest you,' she said sadly. 'My children seem to think nothing will, but I hope that isn't the case – my husband loved what he collected himself over the years.'

Adam moved across to the next wall and saw what he hoped to find – sets of Trollope and Henry James, E.M. Forster, Somerset Maugham, Evelyn Waugh, John Buchan, and even Sapper's Bulldog Drummond stories.

He turned to smile at his hostess. 'There's plenty here to interest me,' he said gently. 'Are you sure you want to sell them if they belonged to your husband?'

A less-disciplined woman would have wept, he thought, but she was schooled to conceal grief. 'I *have* to dispose of them,' she insisted. 'My children say that the house must be sold before it finally falls to pieces. They don't want it, do you see ... well, of course not, their lives are elsewhere. But all my married life was spent here, so it saddens me to be leaving it.'

Leonie was now in danger of weeping herself. 'What about you, Mrs Carruthers – where will you go?' she asked.

'Into some kind of home,' she said vaguely. 'I believe it's all arranged.' Then she almost smiled at the sadness in Leonie's face. 'It doesn't really matter now that my dear husband is dead; anywhere would be the same without him if I can't stay here ... and I do see that that isn't very practical.' Again she almost managed to smile at them. 'Old people are such a nuisance, living too long nowadays!' And she said it without a trace of self-pity in her voice.

Adam wandered along the shelves, making notes as he went, while Leonie explained the origin of her unusual Christian name to Mrs Carruthers and they then shared memories of pre-war Paris. He came back at last, briefly listed the books he would be happy to buy, and quoted a price that seemed to take the old lady by surprise.

'You should let another dealer see them, you know,' he suggested, 'not just accept my offer.' But she shook her head.

'Our dear friend Andrew Rushton advised me to get in touch with you,' she said. 'I don't need anyone else's opinion, Mr Vaux.'

He smiled at that, but didn't argue. 'Shall I take the books away now, or come back another time?'

'Oh, take them now,' she answered at once. 'It would be silly to bring you back again.'

Adam fetched boxes from the car and he and Leonie filled them with all that he had bought. Lunchtime came and went, unnoticed, but just as they were finishing Mrs Carruthers brought in a tray of tea.

'I should have thought,' she said anxiously, '...you must be hungry...' But having no idea what else to offer them, her voice trailed away, and Leonie hurriedly filled the silence.

'We breakfast very late,' she said firmly, 'and then don't bother about lunch. But a cup of tea would be very welcome, wouldn't it, Adam?' He almost never, she had had time to learn, drank tea, but now with her eye upon him he agreed that tea was exactly what he needed, and Mrs Carruthers was able to smile at them again.

With the tea drunk, and his cheque written for her, they drove away in the grey afternoon light. Adam stared at his silent passenger, and finally asked what she was thinking.

'How much I'd like to murder the poor woman's children,' Leonie said fiercely. 'I suppose she *can't* stay in that lovely, decrepit house, but surely *one* of them could make her welcome instead of bundling her into a home.' Her voice sounded so close to tears that Adam put out a hand to give hers a little pat. Then they drove home in silence.

It was getting to be too late for evensong as they approached Frantock and, as he firmly remarked, his thoughts ran in any case to a restorative glass of sherry, and to the not too distant prospect of food.

'A late breakfast indeed,' he quoted feelingly. 'One slice of toast eight hours ago does *not* keep a man's body and soul together.'

'I know, but what else was I to say?' Leonie enquired.

His smile suddenly embraced her. 'Nothing else – you said so exactly what was needed that I came close to falling in love with you. There's a little way still to go, but I'm getting there!'

She heard the laughing note in his voice, and found herself wishing that he'd meant what he just said. 'Meanwhile, you're hungry,' she suggested as matter of factly as she could. 'Will pâté, omelettes and cheese do?'

'Admirably – I was afraid you'd suggest something that will take hours to cook, and I'm ravenous.'

The sherry and the supper she'd proposed were duly enjoyed, but beneath the surface of easy conversation lay the hint of something that was different. For both of them the memory of how the morning had begun was in their minds, insisting that what had been left unfinished must be completed.

After supper, when they were sitting by the fire, it was Adam who led them towards it.

'The house feels different nowadays,' he suddenly remarked. 'Even Nimrod knows that. It's not just that there are flowers that weren't here before, and a definite improvement in the arrangement of the furniture – I had noticed, you see! I suppose it's what we have to call the woman's touch.'

Leonie stared into the glowing logs, wondering whether he resented the changes that she hadn't expected him to notice. 'Did you mind – have I meddled too much?' she asked tentatively.

'My dear, meddle away,' he said at once. 'I only meant that the house feels empty now when you're not here.' Then he got up, and fiddled with the record player. A moment later the closing music to Act 1 of *Madame Butterfly* filled the room.

'The finest opera Puccini ever wrote,' he said quietly when the last, high, rapturous notes had died away. 'Do you agree?'

'Yes, I do,' she agreed, 'though I expect that

most people would plump for *La Bohème*.'

But her mind was on the story as well as the music. At that point in the opera Butterfly and Pinkerton were approaching their marriage night together and the prospect of consummated bliss was in the air. It was just as inevitably what she and Adam were now going towards, and it could be postponed no longer.

Their coupling, a little later, was as easy and natural as breathing. He was the most tender of lovers and she was deeply content to be possessed. Lying awake early the following morning, she marvelled at the alteration in herself, but realized that their meeting with Mrs Carruthers had had something to do with it. The time for happiness was brief enough, and she'd wilfully wasted too much of it already. Emotional suicide, Adam had called it, and he'd been right as usual. She leaned over and kissed him awake.

'Promise me you'll try to make old bones,' she asked with sudden urgency in her voice.

'Sweetheart, I'll do my best,' he promised seriously. 'I'll do my very best.'

Sixteen

Edward Robert – named after both his grandfathers – was born the following autumn. He wasn't followed into the world by any siblings, much to his mother's private grief, but he was all the more precious for that. She and Adam had a son, and Elizabeth and Michael could share in the pleasure of watching him grow up.

They had agreed beforehand that the farmhouse should be his home. Much as they loved the cottage, it lacked space, and its courtyard garden could offer nowhere for a small boy to run free in. It was Adam, therefore, who now made the weekend trips from Frantock to the farm, but in between times he missed his wife and son. Even before Ned's first birthday they'd converted a wing of the old rambling house for their own use, but in practice the three generations shared the house so contentedly that Leonie reckoned it to be family life as it really ought to be.

The cottage in Frantock wasn't left empty. The Rushtons' younger daughter, Mary, now lived there, minded the bookshop when Adam was elsewhere and kept a caring eye on her parents at the vicarage. It wasn't a life to satisfy most young women, but Mary had already settled for being an observer, rather than a participant. Having completely missed her mother's hawklike beauty, she was endowed with Andrew's sweet nature instead, and she asked only to be surrounded by books. Her secret, long guessed by Jane Rushton and by Leonie as well, was to have loved Adam Vaux from the moment she set eyes on him. His marriage to another woman made no difference to her well of selfless devotion – she simply cherished his bookshop, and became the adoring godmother of his son.

Only once, feeling low in spirits, did Jane rail against fate to Elizabeth Wentworth. 'If I didn't like Adam so much I'd have to hate him for turning my poor girl into a confirmed spinster at the age of twenty-five!'

Elizabeth shook her head. 'Jane dear, your "poor girl" is quite content, I think. She loves keeping house for herself at the cottage, and she knows that Adam relies on her to mind the shop. If she weren't there *he* would have to be, but now he's engrossed in his writing instead.' Adam's novels set in ancient Greece – Periclean Athens to be exact – had begun as a pleasure for himself, but he soon had the reading public panting for more. 'Mary is beyond compare when it comes to the research he needs,' said Elizabeth.

Jane Rushton didn't insist that it was still life lived at second-hand. She would never have accepted it for herself, and couldn't help but feel that it was a shocking waste of a girl who should have been a loving wife and mother. But she was a fair-minded woman too, and knew that against Leonie Harcourt, her daughter had stood no chance at all. She switched the conversation to someone else who concerned her.

'Have you seen the Wetherbys lately? I thought James was looking rather frail.'

'Martha would agree with you,' Elizabeth said sadly. 'I think he drove himself too hard during the war. But Daniel is due back here soon, to set up his Wetland Research Centre at the Manor. Having him more or less resident there will make all the difference to James and Martha, and they expect Amy back too, as soon as she graduates.'

Jane stifled the comment that dazzling, blonde Amy would complicate her younger son's emotional life as surely as Adam had complicated Mary's – but one couldn't always be harping on one's childrens' problems. It was true, though, that having recovered from his youthful infatuation with Leonie Vaux, Jonathan now tried and failed to behave naturally with Martha's teasing granddaughter. His hands were sure and expressive enough when it came to shaping stone, but the poised, alluring creature that Amy had become left his tongue bereft of words when he most needed them.

Elizabeth stared at her vicarage friend, thinking how much they would miss her when the time came for Andrew to retire and, in accordance with the Church's inflexible rule, he and Jane had to move outside the parish they had served so devotedly.

'My dear, I know it isn't quite yet,' she said suddenly, 'but what will you and Andrew do when you leave Frantock? Don't go far away, please – we should be so lost without you.'

Jane shook her head. 'We shall find a small, convenient house somewhere nearby, I hope. Think of it: no leaking roof, no storage heaters that run out of heat when you need them most, and no getting up at some God-forsaken hour to say the office in a freezing church every morning. I shall feel as if I've gone ahead of time to heaven!'

Elizabeth smiled, and didn't say that that beginning to the day was probably what Andrew valued most throughout each twenty-four hours. Instead, she spoke of what filled the public mind – the imminent coronation of a new, young queen. It was just what a tired, jaded populace still impoverished by years of war needed to restore pride in itself and its history. There were few television sets in private homes as yet, but James Wetherby inevitably had one, and they'd all been invited to the Manor, to watch a ceremony most of them would never see again.

Country time was supposed to dawdle at its own slow pace, regulated by the merging of the seasons, one into another. It wasn't, Leonie often thought, how country life seemed to those who lived its endlessly busy days. The years rushed by and she wasn't nearly ready for Ned's schooldays at Wellington to begin, leading him as they eventually would to an agricultural college at Cirencester. Apart from his termly departures and returns, time was measured now by the recurring pattern of farm life and local anniversaries, overshadowed by the Cold War belligerence of a wartime ally turned potential enemy. But when she agonized about it to Adam he shook his head.

'My dear, the very thing you dread is what holds us in a sort of equilibrium – perilous, I grant you, but the USSR knows as certainly as we do that a nuclear war would mean the ultimate Armageddon. I'm reasonably sure Ned won't have to fight in another war. Is that comfort enough?'

Smiling because he wanted her to, she agreed that it was. But sadness overtook them soon afterwards when James Wetherby died after a brief illness, and Martha gave up the struggle to live without him a mere eighteen months later. But by then Daniel Wetherby's Wetland Research Centre had been established at the Manor, and he and his wife and young children had made their home there. In the course of time the Rushtons were succeeded at the vicarage by a much younger couple – pleasant enough in themselves but, as Elizabeth said regretfully, very Low-Church! She was more concerned by now, though, to watch the slow alteration in her husband. Michael, at sixty-nine, was well past the age when men in easier occupations expected to have retired. Love of what he did kept him working, but she and Leonie waited anxiously for the day when Ned could take over the reins at the farm.

Then, one spring morning, something extraordinary happened. Crossing the yard to go back into the house, Leonie saw a man she didn't recognize standing there, looking round. He took off his cap and smiled at her, and there was something faintly familiar about his toothy grin.

'*La maison*,' he said in a dreadful French accent, pointing at the house, 'and here's what, if I remember right, you told us we had to call "*la ferme*".'

Out of the mists of time she pinned down the memory of a small, thin-faced London urchin, and then his name suddenly came into her mind.

'It's Jimmy...' she stated delightedly, now sure of who he was. 'As I live, it's Jimmy Bates! Oh, my uncle will be so pleased. Let's go and find him – he's working in the barn.'

She led him to where Michael Wentworth struggled with the innards of a tractor that was refusing to start, and watched the two men recognize each other after a gap of twenty years. Jimmy, not tall but no longer scrawny, grinned happily at the large, kind man he'd remembered as the most reliable grown-up he'd ever had the luck to meet. The Guv, as they called him then, wouldn't call to mind now a promise made so long ago, but

Jimmy hadn't ever forgotten it himself, and he was here to prove it, just for old times' sake.

Michael wiped oily fingers on his dungarees and then held out his hand with a broad smile. 'It's good to see you Jimmy. You've filled out a bit since the days when you could wiggle under any bit of barbed wire known to man! You look as if you've done well – I'm glad about that.'

This, Leonie supposed, had been prompted by her uncle's glance at their visitor's smart clothes; Jimmy had obviously dressed with care for what he considered to be a social call.

'National Service,' he cheerfully explained. 'The Army turned me into a mechanic, then I got a job in a garage.' His professional eye wandered to the dismembered tractor engine. 'You've got a bit of a problem there, but I reckon I could fix it for you.' He hesitated for a moment, aware that his trousers were pristine and the tweed jacket was new, but they couldn't weigh against the chance to show the Guv that he had some skill to offer.

'Overalls,' said Michael, 'that's what you must have before you even look at Bessie here; she's been a good girl, but she's feeling her age a bit.'

Jimmy removed his jacket and climbed into the overalls that he was being offered, and Leonie knew that she could leave them now without it even being noticed that she'd gone.

She walked into the farmhouse kitchen, to describe the scene outside to her aunt and warn her that there would be an unexpected guest for lunch.

Twenty minutes later a contented rumble indicated that all was now well with Bessie's inside, and then Jimmy was brought in to be re-introduced to Elizabeth. He was ill at ease for a few minutes, but then she reminded him of the time she boxed his ears for laughing at the vicar behind his back, and stiffness was at an end.

Over lunch they heard about the other 'vacuees' who'd shared life at the farm twenty years ago. Billy and 'Shirl' had gone to Australia with their parents. Jimmy's younger sister had married and had two children. 'Father hopped it,' he admitted darkly, 'good riddance, so we muck in together me and Evie. She can't bring up the kids *and* work all on her own. It's a bit of a squash, but we manage.'

Leonie remembered the small, elfin-faced child who'd wept so bitterly when Jules' sick-leave at the farm had ended; she'd been a quiet, gentle child, unlike the rumbustious Shirl. Where had the years gone that she was now the mother of two children of her own?

'Garage work pays reasonably well, I suppose,' Michael Wentworth suggested after a pause, 'and you're obviously very good at it.'

Jimmy's shoulders lifted in a shrug. 'It's a job,' he said, 'but machinery's not like animals. It can't come alive, and snuffle into your hand or give you a nudge when it wants something.' He grinned rather sadly at them, gathered round the table. 'Still, it's bin a pleasure, coming back. I'll tell Evie, and we'll bring the kids down one day if that's all right with you. It's about time they understood where the food they eat comes from.'

'Bring them on holiday in the summer,' Elizabeth suggested, 'you could stay in the cottage old Tom Hobbs used to live in, it's empty at the moment.' As she said the words, her glance fell on Michael, and she saw in his face the very thought that had just occurred to her. He questioned her with one briefly lifted eyebrow, she nodded in reply, and then he smiled. Watching them Leonie thought how beautifully a good, happy marriage worked – words weren't even needed.

'The cottage is vacant,' Michael said quietly, 'but, as it happens, so is the cowman's job that goes with it. The man who took over old Tom's place wasn't happy. He thought he'd like a change from ploughing wheat fields in Norfolk, but he didn't really like livestock and you can't be a good dairy farmer without loving cows. I seem to remember that you did!'

There was a little silence round the table and then he spoke again. 'I can't offer you what I expect a good mechanic can earn in London, but you'd live rent-free at the cottage, you and Evie and the children of course, and perhaps they'd have a healthier life here. Go home and have a think about it – if the idea appeals at all, we can get down to details.'

Jimmy cleared his throat, but even so his voice sounded husky. 'I can tell you here and now the idea appeals all right, but I'd have to talk it over with Evie – she'd have to be happy about leaving London as well.'

'If she was too small to remember much about the farm, bring her down, Jimmy. She must be allowed to see what she might be coming to,' Elizabeth suggested.

He promised that he would, and then jumped to his feet when Michael invited him to share a stroll round the meadows.

'He won't be able to resist the calves,' Leonie said when the two men had gone out. 'I think my darling uncle knows that very well!'

Elizabeth smiled, but looked doubtful. 'It won't work unless they can all be happy here ... but what a mercy it would be to have some more help. For two pins I'd go down on my knees and beg Almighty God to whisper in Jimmy's ear how much we need him. He was a tough little customer all those years ago, but I never caught him out in a lie or an unkindness, did you?'

Leonie shook her head. 'No *and* he's looking after his sister and her children – that's what I call real kinship.'

They watched Jimmy climb into his little Austin Seven an hour later and, for fear of tempting Providence, refused to speculate what his decision would be. A week later he telephoned Michael to say that the details could be discussed because Evie had decided that she'd get used to cows in time, and in the country the children would forget the ill-tempered bully who'd blighted their lives before Jimmy took them in.

'An answer to Elizabeth's prayers, or yours?' Adam asked when told the news. 'Some pretty powerful lobbying *must* have been going on!'

Leonie didn't deny it, but gave a slightly different explanation. 'Elizabeth and Michael's wartime bread was cast upon the waters and it's now being "returned to them after many days" in the shape of Jimmy Bates, that's all.'

'He'll have to get on with Ned,' Adam went on thoughtfully. 'It won't always be Michael who is telling him what to do.'

Leonie looked unconcerned. 'Have you met anyone who can't get on with Ned?'

Adam's grin answered her first. 'Allowing a little something for maternal prejudice, I'll agree that Jimmy probably won't mind the new "Guv" when the time comes! What do you remember of Evie, though – will she settle down?'

'We must make sure that she does,' Leonie insisted firmly. 'From the little Jimmy's said, the poor girl has had a wretched married life. We can surely offer her something better than that.'

And so it turned out, even though Evie's courage wavered when she realized that urban life – to the extent that Frantock could be called urban at all – was three miles away. But her brother's face told her what the move meant to him, and she nodded when he asked her if she'd be all right.

'Course I will,' she said as calmly as she could. 'Mrs Vaux is going to teach me how to ride a bicycle. She mentioned something about a pony and trap, but I'm not sure I've got nerve enough for that. What happens if the pony doesn't want to go where I want to go?'

'You go where *you* want to go another day,' Jimmy said truthfully. 'There's no reasoning with any kind of horse; you'll get tired of it before he does.' Then he smiled at his sister's anxious face. 'I'll teach you to drive the Austin ... how about that?'

Evie thought it might be easier, all things considered. Life in the country offered some possibilities she hadn't dreamed of in London's Mile End Road, but it needed all her courage to look eager to move. She could make the cottage into a real home for them – no question about that. It was outside that her difficulties would begin – the animals, domesticated or wild, the darkness at night with not a single street lamp to light the way, and even their nearest neighbours out of sight. She feared she might die of loneliness when the boys were in school and Jimmy lost in the space around them. But he was looking anxious, and she managed to smile at him. God willing, she'd be able to cope all right.

Seventeen

As that summer approached they could relax; with Jimmy there, the problem of too little manpower was solved at last. There was no need now for Michael always to be working. Elizabeth could stop worrying about him, and she agreed with Leonie that it was an added happiness to have children running about the farm again.

Evie's small sons had been nervous, to begin with – the animals were so much larger than themselves; but their uncle's lack of fear was catching. Jack, senior in age at going on seven, was soon confronting them without blenching, and where he led little Harry hesitatingly followed.

One evening when they were alone together Adam asked his wife if the Bates family's uprooting from London had been a success. Leonie considered the question before answering.

'There was never any doubt about Jimmy,' she said finally. 'He's a good mechanic, which is very useful, but he understands how animals work as well, and given his backstreet upbringing, it's a minor miracle.'

'And Evie?' Adam persisted. 'What about her?'

'She misses what she's used to,' Leonie admitted. 'I doubt if we shall ever make a countrywoman of her. But since she ranks Jimmy only just below God and my uncle in the scheme of things, she'd put up with more than rural life to see him happy.'

'I've discovered something else about her that might help,' Adam said thoughtfully. 'She loves books the way Jimmy loves cows!' He grinned at the astonishment in his wife's face. 'I know that because I saw her outside the bookshop the other day, looking like a child at a sweet-shop window. She wouldn't have gone inside, but I insisted that she must meet Mary. It was like leading her into Aladdin's cave. At the moment she doesn't know where to start, but I could see Mary happily recognizing a kindred spirit. She'll take Evie in hand, and they will both enjoy themselves enormously.'

His own pleasure came, Leonie realized, from knowing that two women, different in almost every way except in being lonely, would find companionship in his bookshop.

'Now I'll tell you my good news,' she said next. 'According to Amy, Daniel and Rachel will be back at the Manor in time for Ned's birthday party. It seems ages that they've been away.' Then her dark brows drew together in a frown. 'Ned's being twenty-one will make me nearly fifty – I can scarcely believe it, but I'm afraid it's true.'

Adam smiled but shook his head. 'No need to worry, love – you're just approaching your prime.' And that was true too, he reflected; her crisp, dark hair and lovely bone structure could have graced a much younger woman.

She settled more comfortably within his encircling arm before going on. 'Michael wants to make an announcement at the party – about handing over the reins to Ned. It's time he did, I think; he's getting tired.'

'I know,' Adam agreed. 'Thank God Ned wants to be a farmer – he might have grown up with a different career in mind.'

She twisted round suddenly to examine her husband's face. 'Are you where you want to be? No, don't smile, please – it's a serious question. I can't forget how our marriage began. You certainly didn't have matrimony in mind when you came to Frantock to dispose of Eustace's bookshop. I simply marched into your life and took it over.'

Her face looked full of remorse, but he was accustomed to the emotional see-saw that could lift her high one moment and cast her down the next. He touched her cheek with gentle fingers. 'Dear heart, but for that train ride which Fate arranged for you to share, I should now be a lonely, ill-tempered bachelor instead of the supremely contented old gent you see before you! Does that answer your question?'

'You aren't old,' she insisted, reaching up to give him a grateful kiss. But memory replayed for her the moment when he'd stumbled, breathless and ill-looking, into her compartment as the train pulled out of Paddington all those years ago. It hadn't been in her plan, then or later, to fall in love with him, but the arrangement she'd suggested had turned into an enchanted marriage, whose only shadow was the fear that premature death might take him away from her.

Instead, a blow that was unlooked-for fell elsewhere. The preparations for Ned's party were well in hand then Michael Wentworth failed to return for the lunchtime break. Thinking that Bessie was playing up again, Jimmy went to the far meadow where he expected to find the Guv cutting hay. But Michael was slumped over the steering wheel, already beyond help.

Elizabeth, tragic-faced but calm, insisted afterwards that it was exactly the ending he would have chosen – working one moment, facing his Maker the next. But she'd been his wife for more than fifty years and from then on, it seemed to Leonie, although she remained with the rest of them at some surface level, inside she was attuned to conversations that only she could hear.

A special dispensation from the bishop allowed Andrew Rushton to return to Frantock church to conduct the private funeral Elizabeth knew her husband would have wanted. But the church was packed a fortnight later for the memorial service to a man who'd been esteemed and loved throughout the county.

The celebration of Ned's coming-of-age was abandoned, but Elizabeth insisted on a dinner party attended by their oldest friends. Its only unfamiliar guest was a young American staying with Daniel and Rachel Wetherby, sharing their youngest daughter's college vacation. Alice Newman was beautiful by any standards, but when Adam murmured 'the *princesse lointaine* herself', Leonie knew exactly what he meant; this girl was different – ethereally, delicately, lovely in a way that their sturdy Somerset maidens couldn't match. It was only as the evening wore on that Ned's reaction to her began to make his mother uneasy. He did his best to behave as he should to the rest of his guests, but he couldn't help looking bewitched by Alice Newman.

Later, in the privacy of their bedroom, Leonie aired her anxiety to Adam. 'She's lovely, I grant you, but you could search England and not find a girl who looked less suited to being a farmer's wife.'

'Mother-hen complex, my love,' he pointed out gently. 'Ned's only just twenty-one – I doubt if marriage is high on the list of things on his mind, Of course he found her beautiful; I'd be disappointed in him if he didn't. But there's no need for you to worry. She will go back to New York with Margot, and Ned will remember her for a while as being different from his friends here who know about livestock, share his love of hunting on Exmoor, and ask nothing better than to spend their life in Somerset. With one of them he'll eventually settle down.'

Leonie still looked doubtful. It was true that she'd handed on to Ned a strong streak of her own French practicality, but he was Adam's son as well, and he'd inherited his father's idealistic love of what was beautiful and out-of-reach.

'We'll have to wait and see,' she said finally, 'but Margot will oblige me if she leaves her exotic friend behind her when she comes back to Frantock.'

Her anxiety faded as time passed and Ned gave no sign of remembering Alice Newman. The joys and woes of farm life were more than enough to fill his days and send him, dog-tired, to sleep at night. Like Michael Wentworth before him, he loved the land and the animals in his care, and cherished the lovely landscape around him. Being very good to look at, as well as a pleasure to know, he didn't lack female friends; but Leonie could detect in him so little preference for one girl rather than another that she found herself complaining to her aunt that it was time he made up his mind.

'Is there any hurry?' Elizabeth asked reasonably. 'He's only twenty-five years old.'

'I know, but a wife would be good for him. He works too hard and he needs a companion.'

'He needs the right companion,' Elizabeth insisted. 'I think he's still waiting for her.'

The conversation faded from Leonie's mind until a morning when she went out to find

Margot Wetherby crossing the yard, home again for summer vacation. Beside her was a girl not seen since Ned's birthday party but immediately recognizable. Four years on she was, if possible, still more beautiful.

They exchanged greetings and then, as his mother had known would happen, Ned came out of the barn and walked towards them. She saw the expression on his face and realized at once who it was that he'd been waiting for. He remembered to kiss Margot as the dear friend she was, before holding out his hand to Alice Newman.

'We were expecting you back – why did it take so long?' he asked gravely.

She didn't seem surprised by the question, Leonie thought; her slow smile even welcomed it. 'I went travelling ... wanted to see the world; but it's a big place – that's why it took so long.' Then, politely, she turned back to Leonie to continue the conversation Ned had interrupted.

They parted company and Leonie went indoors to sit down at the kitchen table and stare blindly at nothing at all. She was still there lost in thought when Adam came looking for her.

'Sweetheart ... something wrong?' he wanted to know. 'You look as though you've seen a ghost!'

'Not a ghost, a living girl,' she said slowly. 'Do you remember telling me not to worry about Alice Newman? I almost believed you at the time. But she's back, Adam, and Ned has seen her. I know now that if she doesn't marry him he won't marry anyone else.'

Adam didn't contradict her; when she spoke in that tone of voice he knew that what she said was true. Instead, he cupped her pale face in his hands and smiled at her.

'Surely there's still no need to worry,' he insisted. 'Allowing for the fact that we're prejudiced, can you see any girl in her right mind turning Ned down? Alice was taking a risk, staying away so long.'

Leonie shook her head. 'She was taking no risk at all; she could have stayed away another four years and still been certain that he'd be waiting for her.'

Again Adam knew better than to argue; there were things clearly visible to women that a mere man couldn't be expected to fathom. But there was something he was obliged to say.

'If she understood that, I hope she also understands what else she'll be marrying besides Ned – us, the farm, Frantock, Somerset ... everything, in fact, that's dear to his loyal, loving heart.'

Leonie made an effort to smile at him. 'It's more than my crystal ball reveals, I'm afraid – we shall just have to wait and see. But poor Margot would have understood what will be asked of Ned's wife and perhaps she even loves him enough to teach her friend!'

They were married three months later – a wedding that Frantock never forgot for the beauty of the bride and the enchanted happiness of the man who held her hand as they left the church.

Jimmy's presence at the farm made a brief honeymoon possible, and they returned to find Elizabeth resettled with Leonie and Adam, so as to leave them the rest of the farmhouse. But the new arrangement wasn't needed for long as Elizabeth, now eighty and growing tired of life without Michael, died peacefully in her sleep before the year was out. She had been counsellor and friend for more than thirty years and not even the glad news that her daughter-in-law was now pregnant could outweigh Leonie's sense of loss. There were too few people left who mattered deeply to her – she could ill-spare any one of them.

As Alice's pregnancy advanced, not only was it clear that she was carrying twins, but also that she considered their conception a mistake. It was too soon, too much, when she was also discovering how endless were the demands of farm life on her husband. Watching her face, Leonie saw the gradual change from happiness to boredom and resentment, for the moment at least still tinged with sad regret. Alice hadn't quite given up trying to live the only life Ned could offer because she hadn't given up loving him; but it was like watching some exotic bird of paradise beating its wings against the bars of a cage. She was having to learn about the other passion of her husband's life besides herself: not even to keep her happy could he neglect the inheritance that had been handed to him. He would tend the land and the animals, day in, day out, from one year to the next, until his own strength gave out and the duty passed to his son.

The twins were born early the following summer – Simon and Jennifer – and, recovering health and beauty, Alice seemed content for a while. The improvement didn't last, and Ned insisted that she visit New York ... she needed a change, he said. But his private prayer was that, away from her entrancing babies and her home, she would miss them enough to come hurrying back.

In fact what brought her home was the news that her father-in-law had died after an operation to replace a damaged valve in his heart. The risk, weighed against Adam's increasing infirmity, had seemed worth taking, and for a day or two afterwards the operation seemed to have been a success. Then, without warning, his body rejected the replacement valve and his life was over.

Ned drove his mother home from the hospital, thinking that her tears would be easier to bear than the dry-eyed stoical composure in which she seemed to be wrapped. She was a woman of strong emotions, and he knew how intensely his father had been adored.

'Weep, love,' he pleaded gently when they were back at the farmhouse. 'Just to please me, give in and weep.'

Leonie shook her head. 'Tears won't help; not even you can help, my darling one, but I shall have to manage because I can't die to order, which is what I should like to do. It's not that I don't love you and your family; but they are your life. Without Adam my life seems to be over.'

It continued to seem so for several months after the funeral; then the bombshell came that Leonie had almost forgotten to expect: Alice confessed that she was returning to New York for good.

'Without you I shan't ever be quite whole or happy again,' she said calmly to Ned, 'but I have to go while I still love you. If I stay I might come to hating you for keeping me here, and I don't want that to happen.'

'Can't even the twins keep you?' Ned managed to ask, unable to plead for himself. 'Don't you see how wonderful they are?' She didn't answer, and his self-control gave way. 'Dear God, Alice, the children are four years old – they need you. Is it only what you want that matters?'

She stared at him with genuine sorrow in her face. 'What I want is not to destroy your life; it's what would happen if I stayed. By going now I can at least leave you the memory of a brief but happy marriage.' She came to stand in front of him, with pleading in her beautiful grey eyes. 'Don't try to keep me, Ned ... I can't be tied down; perhaps never, but not now and certainly not here.' Her hand reached out to touch him, then fell to her side instead. 'Your mother will take care of the children ... she needs a reason to go on living now that Adam is dead.'

Everything that she'd said was true, he realized and all he had to offer in return – that he would never stop loving her – could make no difference; she would go because she had to.

She left two days later, and it was only after she'd gone that he came near to his first quarrel with Leonie.

'You hate Alice,' he said suddenly, after they'd toyed with the food she'd put on the table. 'I can feel you hating her – I won't have that. You'll teach the children to hate her too.'

There was a moment's silence before she was able to answer him. 'I promise you that I shall never criticize Alice, to the twins or to anyone else. But my feelings are my own affair; they can't be turned off like a tap. I realize that yours can't either, and God knows I don't want you to be destroyed by bitterness. But I can't pretend what I don't feel, so it's useless to ask me to; I shall go on hating Alice in my heart. I might, in time be able to forgive Margot for ever bringing her here.'

A smile touched Ned's mouth for a moment, but there was sarcasm, not humour, in it. 'So much for the Sermon on the Mount, my dear Mama! – no compassion on offer, and very little forgiveness?'

'Not much,' she agreed quietly. 'I know it makes me a very inadequate Christian, but I haven't yet learned to forgive anyone who hurts the people I love, and I doubt if I ever shall.'

His anger with her died as quickly as it had risen. 'You need to forgive me, I think, my dear. You've good reason to hate the people you have hated; I only want you to accept that Alice went believing that she did the best she could for us.'

'Yes, I'll accept that,' Leonie finally agreed. 'I think it's true.'

A little silence fell before Ned spoke again. 'What about the twins? We must find some-one to help.'

Leonie shook her head. 'No need – I shall bring them up. Evie adores them too, and she'll help. They won't have a mother but they won't lack love.' She hesitated over what to say next. 'What will happen – a divorce?' She read the answer in his face even before he put it into words.

'A divorce only if Alice asks for it, but I don't think she will – because she still loves us all. I can't be certain she'll ever come back, but I shall wait, whether she does or not.'

Leonie stared at him, pierced by his likeness to Adam, not so much in looks as by the staunch, great-hearted man he was. 'Once long ago when I railed at the cruelty of Fate or God, who seemed to delight in wasting the good that we humans are capable of, your father smiled at me, and insisted that nothing was wasted unless we allowed it to be. I see now that it's what you believe too – by letting

Alice go, you still manage to keep love and faith intact.'

'Something like that,' he agreed gently, and then enfolded his mother in a loving hug.

Eighteen

The seasons – a more necessary measurement of time than years to working farmers – came and went. Abroad, they were marked by the horrors of the Vietnam war, the gradual disintegration of a once-monolithic Soviet empire, and the unending cycle of famine and genocide in one part of Africa or another. At home, there were years of social change and bitter industrial unrest. Turbulent years one way or another, but, looking back afterwards, Leonie more personally remembered them as a time of emotions 'recollected in tranquillity', as one of her father's poets had once said. With Luc and Adam dead, her own life had become unimportant. What mattered now was holding their fractured family together, helping Ned, and raising his children. She'd made good her promise to him – even without Alice, they hadn't grown up short of love. Now aged twenty-three, Simon was back at home, ready to put theoretical farming knowledge into practice. Like Elizabeth Wentworth a generation or two earlier, his twin sister had regretfully put aside the hope of a career in music.

'Good, but not quite good enough, that's

me,' Jenni had explained ruefully. 'I shall stay here and become a very good teacher of Frantock's future citizens instead!'

And so she had, to the secret contentment of her grandmother. Leonie would have preferred to think that Harcourt and Vaux blood alone had made Jenni the girl she was, but she admitted to herself that the woman who was her long-absent daughter-in-law had also contributed *something* to the child she'd found it possible to leave. Nearly twenty years on from that abandonment, the twins had long since given up asking questions about their mother. She just wasn't there, that was all, and, thanks to Grand'mère, they had managed very well without her.

But Jenni, adoring her father, grieved for the loneliness at his heart's core. Much as she loved teaching her class of infants, she was happy that the long summer holiday had now come round again – it meant more time at home working in the *potager*, and more time to spend helping her father. Just at the present moment, though, she was doing what she also loved, playing the organ in Frantock church. Best of all, she was there alone. Accompanying the hymns on Sundays was well enough – the swelling sound of choir and congregation filling the high, vaulted spaces was a weekly reminder of the glorious Anglican choral tradition, but nothing equalled the joy of having what pipes and pedals could produce all to herself. Lost in the intricacies of a Saint-Saêns prelude and fugue, she didn't hear the creak of the church door. It was only when the piece came to an end and a voice spoke from a pew beyond the chancel that she realized she wasn't alone.

The quiet 'good afternoon' didn't sound sinister, but she was brushed for a moment by a feather-touch of fear. The man coming towards her was a stranger, and he was between her and the door. Then he spoke again and her taut nerves relaxed.

'I didn't expect to hear French organ music being beautifully played in an English country church.' His voice was pleasant, and its faint accent told her where he hailed from.

'It wasn't a recital – I was only practising,' she explained. 'I'm sure you can hear it better played in your own country.'

His rueful smile was pleasant too, she decided. 'You have a musician's ear for accents, or perhaps my English is very bad!'

Jenni shook her head. 'It isn't bad at all, but I'm used to hearing English spoken with a French intonation.' She piled her music together and prepared to leave the church. 'Enjoy your visit to Frantock, monsieur ... *we* think it's beautiful, of course, but it doesn't attract many people from abroad.'

'I came with a purpose,' he confessed, 'but first I should introduce myself – Pierre Lacroix is my name.' He held out his hand and waited for her to respond.

'Jennifer Vaux,' she answered, and smiled at the sudden question in his face. 'My ancestry long ago was Huguenot, I'm given to understand. You said you had a purpose in coming here. May I ask what it is?'

Pierre thought the directness was probably typical of her – it seemed to match her candid grey eyes and clean-cut features. She wasn't conventionally pretty, but her eyes and her nut-brown hair were beautiful, and the intelligence and humour in her face made her attractive.

'I came looking for traces of a family called Harcourt,' he explained, giving the name its English sound as best he could. 'It's a difficult word for a Frenchman to pronounce and your pained expression says I didn't manage it very well, I'm afraid.'

He'd misinterpreted her expression but when she didn't answer for a moment he went on himself. 'The patron at The Bell couldn't help – he didn't know the name. I hoped to find some church records, but first, no doubt, I must locate *le curé* and ask for his help.'

Jenni nodded. 'The records will certainly be kept locked, but there's something in the churchyard that I *could* show you.'

She led the way outside into the warmth of early summer, crossed the grass towards the far corner of the churchyard, and stopped in front of Edward Harcourt's grave.

'My great-grandfather,' she said quietly, 'a very nice man by all accounts.'

The Frenchman by her side looked at the inscription on the stone, and then at the tiny, flower-decked grave next to it.

'She was just a baby,' he murmured, 'how very sad. A relation also, I'm sure.'

'My father's half-sister,' Jenni explained briefly. Then she walked to a nearby bench, waiting for him to follow and sit beside her. 'Why are you looking for the Harcourt family?'

He was staring at the lovely picture in front of him made by the old stone church amid its surrounding greensward and sheltering trees, and there was a moment in which she could take note of *him* – dark hair worn a little too long by English standards, suntanned face, observant, deep-set eyes below strongly-marked brows, and a mouth that seemed slightly at variance with a very square jaw. A self-assured and probably impatient man, she thought, although for the moment there seemed to be something unexpectedly hesitant about him. Then he turned towards her and she hastily stared at a busy blackbird instead.

'I came in search of Leonie Harcourt,' he finally said. 'Her grave is somewhere else?'

Jenny shook her head. 'She's my grandmother, and I'm glad to say she isn't dead.' His expression didn't change, but his hands betrayed some emotion that she couldn't understand and she couldn't help wondering how this stranger fitted into her grandmother's life. 'Why do you look for her?' she asked again.

He asked permission to smoke, then leaned back against the seat to begin his story. 'I'm a

Professor of Modern History at the Sorbonne. A sabbatical from teaching enables me to finish a book I've been writing – the story of the young men who answered General de Gaulle's call for Frenchmen to help fight the war against Nazi Germany.'

He broke off for a moment to smile wryly at the girl sitting beside him. 'It's a deeply entrenched English belief, I'm afraid, that we left you to fight alone. Our government did, but many of our people did not. My book might help us to understand each other a little better.'

He blew smoke into the air, waved it away and his digression with it. 'I set out to find survivors among those men before it was too late. One of them, called Jules Lefevre, told me a fascinating story of a house in London where volunteers like himself were made welcome. Its chatelaine was a Lady Harcourt and her daughter, to whom Lefevre himself happened to be distantly related, was called Leonie.'

'She was Christine Harcourt's stepdaughter,' Jennie corrected him firmly. 'Her mother was a French lady, Cécile Lefevre, married briefly to the Edward Harcourt who is buried here.'

The Frenchman simply acknowledged the correction with a nod and went on. 'Lefevre is an old man now, but his memory of that time in London is still vivid in his mind. I understood him to say that Leonie Harcourt might still be alive, and I wanted, if I could, to talk to her. But no one that I've asked so far has known of a lady by that name living here.'

'My grandmother's married name is Vaux. The Harcourt family home, Frantock Manor, was sold several generations ago, and the name of Harcourt is mostly forgotten now.' Jennie stopped talking, waiting for the question that would presumably come next.

'Madame Vaux must be old too, I realize,' Pierre Lacroix said, 'and perhaps frail. Is she too frail to meet with me, and talk about the past?'

Jenni rubbed her nose – a sign of uncertainty inherited from Adam Vaux. It made her look younger than he'd supposed she was; the magisterial playing of the organ prelude had misled him, he realized. She'd been helpful so far, but he sensed her doubt about him and half-expected her to turn his request down. It was more usual nowadays for young women to find their ageing relatives a nuisance, but he could see already that Jennifer Vaux would not fit into any of the stereotypes he knew.

'You are very fond of your grandmother, I think,' he said gently.

'She brought me and my twin brother up when my mother left to go back to America. Now it's my turn to take care of her, and she's very precious.' Jenni stood up as a sign that the conversation was over. 'I shall have to ask her whether she wants to see you or not. But don't be surprised, please, if she says no – those wartime years were sad, anxious ones for her. She may not want to talk about them.'

He nodded, remembering the tiny grave he'd seen – a child's grave and surely Leonie's daughter, but she'd been named Harcourt, not Vaux.

'Will you let me know?' he asked. 'I shall be staying at The Bell for a while.'

Jenni agreed that she would, then held out her hand to say goodbye. The grip of his fingers made hers tingle and she withdrew them too quickly, angry with herself for feeling disturbed. She hoped Leonie would refuse to talk to him, even though it seemed a churlish thing to wish for. The unhappy past was best left unvisited in her view. Pierre Lacroix should find his reminiscences elsewhere and leave her grandmother in peace.

But as she cycled home she could see no way of not mentioning his visit. A barefaced lie was out of the question and, in any case, she told herself, she was simply overreacting to a man used to making an impression. Leonie might agree to see him for half an hour and that would surely end his visit to Frantock.

It was at the breakfast table the following morning that she finally broached the subject. Her father and twin had already eaten and gone outside as usual, and she and Leonie had the kitchen to themselves. She poured coffee for them both, not sure where to start, and it was Leonie who spoke first.

'You nearly poured my coffee into the milk

jug instead of my cup! Something more important is on your mind?'

The question sounded amused, but Jenni knew that age hadn't dimmed her grandmother's powers of observation. Nearing eighty Leonie might be, silver-haired and physically frail, but she was still the formidable woman around whom their family revolved, and would be until she died.

'Grand'mère, I was thinking about your diary,' Jenni suddenly decided to explain. 'I reread the first part of it last night before I went to sleep.'

'For some reason I suppose,' Leonie suggested, 'otherwise why look at it again now?'

Jenni nodded, seeing in her mind's eye the man she had to talk about.

'I met someone in the church yesterday – a Frenchman called Pierre Lacroix. He's a historian, writing a book about de Gaulle's Free French's share in the war. We English don't do it justice, apparently.'

'Probably true,' Leonie agreed calmly. 'English and French have never understood one another,' but she smiled at the expression on her granddaughter's face. 'You still haven't explained why he's here.'

'To find *you*,' Jenni said with a rush. 'He'd met the cousin you mention in the diary – Jules Lefevre – and heard about the house in Green Street. Your memories of those days would be valuable, he thinks – that's why he hopes you'll talk to him about them. I said you'd have to agree – that I'd ring him at The

Bell if you didn't mind a visit.'

Leonie studied her granddaughter for a moment. 'Why didn't you like him? You don't normally make up your mind about people so quickly.'

Jenni considered the question. 'He's a professor at the Sorbonne – perhaps *that* makes him a little too self-confident for me. Pierre Lacroix isn't used, I fancy, to being refused ... especially by women.'

'Ah, so he's good-looking,' Leonie guessed accurately, 'and if he's at the Sorbonne, he's also clever and *cultivé* – I shall like him even if you don't! Of course I'll talk to him. Why did you think I might not want to ... because it was a time I didn't enjoy?' When Jenni nodded Leonie's thin hands brushed the past away. 'Professor Lacroix isn't interested in my private life, my dear, only in what I remember of the brave young men who came to London when the war seemed all but lost. In any case, I want news of Jules.'

'Then you shall have it, dearest gran, from our good-looking, clever and *cultivé* professor,' Jenni promised her with a smile. 'I'll ring and invite him to tea – this is rural England, after all, not sophisticated gay Paree!'

With the visit arranged for the following afternoon – a Sunday – Jenni reckoned that her part was over. She agreed to Simon's suggestion of a round of golf with two friends, and didn't defend herself when her grandmother accused her of behaving childishly – avoiding a man she'd taken an unreasonable dislike to.

'Papa will be here to help you welcome the professor, and Evie's going to look after the tea. You don't need me as well, Grand'mère,' she said firmly, then kissed Leonie's nose. 'You're the one he's come to see, *n'est-ce-pas*?'

'That goes without saying,' was the dignified reply, 'but good-looking, interesting men don't exactly grow on trees in deepest Somerset – you might have enjoyed Monsieur Lacroix's visit.'

'I might,' Jenni agreed with the slow smile she'd inherited from her mother, 'but sitting here won't help me get my handicap down. You can tell us this evening how you got on.'

So it was that Pierre Lacroix parked outside in the lane later that afternoon, paused to take in the mellow beauty of the house in front of him, and then walked towards the middle-aged man who'd come to stand in the open doorway.

'Welcome to Manor Farm,' Ned said with his pleasant smile. 'Jenni assured me that your English is much better than my French, which is a great relief to me. My mother, of course, will be only too happy to talk to you in her mother tongue, so I'll leave the two of you together after the tea ritual!'

Deducing rightly from this that Jennifer Vaux was absent, and thinking that he wasn't surprised, Pierre Lacroix shook hands with his host and followed him along a wide, stone-flagged passage to a drawing room that would have graced a Georgian manor, he thought, rather than the farmhouse it was supposed to be. He found a slender, still-upright, still-elegant lady, whose face, framed by beautiful silver hair, was alive and intelligent – no time-diminished octogenarian here.

He kissed the hand she offered him and murmured the usual '*Enchanté, madame*', thinking that in this case the courtesy was true. Then, with her son still in the room, he spoke in English. 'Thank you for permitting my visit. I'm delighted to have found you, and entranced by the beauty of your home.'

Her eyes sparkled with enjoyment. 'Very properly said, *Monsieur le professeur*! Now we can dispense with compliments and enjoy our conversation together, but first some tea, and news, please, of dear Jules Lefevre – our telephone calls had to cease when he became very deaf.'

'He is frail, of course, madame, but still enjoying life, I think. I was to remind you of him, he said, if I was able to find you in Somerset.'

'I remember him very well,' Leonie insisted. 'It's something you must now be grateful for that old people who hesitate over what happened last week recall vividly events of sixty years ago! Your book will presumably rely on such memories.'

Pierre nodded, but stood up as someone he took to be the housekeeper wheeled a trolley into the room. Introduced, her still-Cockney voice came as a surprise until his hostess explained the wartime visit as an evacuee that had led to a lifelong friendship.

With tea and cucumber sandwiches and succulent fruitcake disposed of, Ned excused himself on the grounds of work waiting outside. In French, now, Pierre Lacroix asked about the house in Green Street – the refuge, he said, that Jules Lefevre had called it.

'Yes, it was that, I think,' Leonie agreed. 'All sorts of foreigners washed up in London by the tides of war found their way there. I didn't like my stepmother for purely personal reasons, but she was a born hostess, and she made welcome men who were much in need of kindness – lonely, displaced and very unhappy, most of them were then, with their own countries under German occupation. Many were French, of course, answering General de Gaulle's call for volunteers. That's how Jules came to arrive, with a friend of his called Luc Gosselin.'

She looked across at her visitor. 'I don't know how much Jules has already told you. He became a fighter pilot, but Luc went back to France, to assist a Resistance group. I had known him before the war in Paris; he was going to be a famous artist, we all said.' Her voice grew husky for a moment, and he saw in her face the sorrow that Jennifer Vaux had warned him about.

'After the war I tried to find out what happened to him,' she went on unevenly. 'No one seemed to know ... or even to care very much. His wasted life was just one more tragedy.'

Pierre Lacroix hesitated for a moment,

choosing with care the right words to say next. 'I've been collecting information for a long time, you know. My book is in the nature of an official history, so I've been given access to records and archive material that wasn't available for a long time. When your cousin mentioned your friend's name, I searched for it at his request. Luc Gosselin was killed soon after the German occupation was extended to Vichy France. Resistance operations attracted cruel reprisals,' Pierre explained quietly. 'They were terrible times, *madame*. Thank God they won't be repeated.'

Leonie nodded, unable for a moment to say anything at all – she was seventeen again, rapturously in love with the exciting young man who complained that she moved too much while he sketched her portrait. It seemed a lifetime ago, a different life lived by a girl she scarcely recognized. But she could still see Luc's face in her mind's eye, and grieve over the waste of his life.

'Yes, they were terrible times,' she finally agreed. 'But I'm glad those young men are being remembered at last.' Then, a graceful gesture of her hands waved the past aside. 'What do you do next – return to Paris, *monsieur*?'

'No, I should like to stay here for a while,' he answered after a small pause. 'I am entitled to a little holiday, and I should like to spend it here. I've fallen in love with Frantock and the kind people at The Bell are prepared to put up with me for as long as I want. Jules

Lefevre warned me that I might find it hard to leave Somerset – I think he was probably right.'

'Très bien,' said Leonie, then reverted to English as Ned came back into the room. 'You know Jennifer already, but at dinner one evening you can meet my grandson as well – the two of them don't, I'm glad to say, play golf all the time.'

'We play golf in France too, *madame*,' Pierre reminded her with a smile.

'Good,' she said again. 'It will give you something to talk about with Simon. His other passion is cows, but you probably don't share that as well!' Her dark eyes twinkled again. 'In all other respects he's a delightful young man. My granddaughter teaches young children and plays the organ – but you know that about her already.'

Aware that it was time to leave, Pierre bowed over her thin hand, and thanked her for a fascinating visit.

When Ned returned from taking him outside he looked a question at his mother.

'I liked him,' she said after a moment's thought, 'intelligent, well-mannered, and very much alive. I wonder why my opinionated granddaughter didn't take to him.'

'Overlong hair?' Ned suggested, omitting to point out that she had an opinionated grandmother as well. 'She'd say it smacks of vanity in a man.'

'She'll have to get used to it, I'm afraid. Pierre Lacroix is going to stay for a while, and we can scarcely ignore him now we know he's here.' The amusement died out of Leonie's face as she remembered their conversation. 'He had news of someone I knew a long time ago. It makes a link between us, Ned.'

'Jenni will understand that,' he said gently, 'and overlook the long hair.'

Nineteen

The *'coup de foudre'* theory of falling in love was one that Jenni distrusted. She reckoned that it should be instead a gradual process of discovery and delight. Her grandmother's diary, handed over to her when she was eighteen, vividly described just such a slowly deepening dependence – on Adam Vaux in her case. Jenni's father's brief marriage was all the proof she needed of the opposite truth – that eyes meeting across a crowded room were no guarantee of lifelong happiness.

Whenever Jenni met someone she liked she waited for this gradual process to begin. It never had so far; liking usually remained, but the growing certainty of treasure finally found had never materialized. Nor would it, she felt sure, with a man like Pierre Lacroix, even though that electric tingle at his touch had been disconcerting.

She went to join the dinner party her grandmother had arranged, determined to be coolly friendly at the most, perhaps no more than merely polite, and discovered that she need scarcely have been there at all. The Frenchman got on easy terms with her father and Simon straightaway, and he was clearly enchanted with her wilful, autocratic, and delightful *grand'mère*. Will Shakespeare had the words for it, as always, Jenni realized – age couldn't wither nor custom stale, the remarkable woman who was her grandmother. Leonie slightly intimidated most of Jenni's friends, but Pierre Lacroix seemed to know exactly how to deal with her – teasing, firmness and judicious flattery made up a mixture she couldn't resist.

Jenni took little part in the conversation, wanting to leave the stage to Leonie, but it gave her ample opportunity to see that she'd been mistaken about their guest. There was nothing calculated in his behaviour – he *was* what he seemed, an intelligent, interesting and very attractive man. Proper pride wasn't vanity, and self-assurance wasn't arrogance; she would have to admit to Leonie that she'd judged their visitor unfairly.

Her now-slumbering intention to avoid him only stirred again when her services as a guide to Somerset were offered, on the grounds that she had nothing else to do now that the long school summer holidays had just started.

'You may not have realized yet,' she suggested to Pierre, 'that my grandmother is a very bossy woman, or you'll be too polite to point it out if you have.' Then she smiled at Leonie. 'Monsieur Lacroix may think he has "sights" enough in Paris to look at.'

'Monsieur Lacroix is determined to see whatever Somerset has to offer,' he said firmly, 'and a guide is indispensable, of course. May we begin with Wells Cathedral tomorrow?'

Feeling slightly breathless now, Jenni stared across the table at him. '*You* have work to do even if Grand'mère thinks I haven't. Truthfully, wouldn't you rather be left to get on with it?'

'The truthful answer is that I would prefer to go with you to Wells,' he said gravely. 'A sabbatical is meant to be enjoyable, you know, as well as productive.'

She accepted that with a nod, and spent the remainder of the evening trying to decide whether she looked forward to the following day's outing or dreaded it.

In the event it held nothing but pleasure from the moment he collected her at the farmhouse gate. They drove through a countryside looking its best, she decided contentedly – still vividly green after months of winter rain, ribboned by streams that were placid now, and sheltered by the ring of lovely surrounding hills – Quantocks, Mendips, Poldens, and Blackdowns.

When Lacroix commented that it seemed to be a very ancient landscape, she turned to smile at him approvingly.

'Of course – it's one of the oldest-inhabited parts of the kingdom. I think it's beautiful at any time of the year, but best of all is when the winter brings floods to the Levels, and they become a haunted, mysterious world of grey and silver.'

'You love it, obviously,' Pierre said, 'too much to ever want to go away?'

'Oh, I venture across county boundaries occasionally to Dorset or Devon,' Jenni answered solemnly. 'I've even travelled as far as France.'

His hand reached out to touch hers in a little gesture of apology. 'Forgive me – I didn't mean to sound patronizing.'

She nodded, but withdrew her hand and tucked it in the pocket of her skirt. Even so, her fingers remembered the feel of his, and she turned away to stare out of the window, defences firmly in place again. They drove the rest of the way in silence, and it was a relief to be able to escape from the intimacy of the car. A convenient parking space found for once, Jenni led him through the Penniless Porch to the green setting of the Cathedral, and there they both paused for a moment to stare at its golden glory.

'Grand'mère lived for a while in the shadow of Notre Dame when she was growing up,' Jenni commented. 'Even so she's ready to admit that this is perfect too.'

Pierre turned to look at her. 'Do we need to make comparisons? Why not just thank God that your countrymen and mine built these matchless places in His name.'

She knew then that whatever she showed him would be properly valued – whether it was the vaulted magnificence of the cathedral nave, the breathtaking curved sweep of the stone staircase leading up to the chapter-house, or the river-bordered Bishop's Palace.

Outside again at last, she suggested that it was too lovely to eat indoors – a nearby delicatessen would supply them with a simple lunch, and she knew just the place to take it to. With bread and cheese and fruit in the car, she directed him to Glastonbury.

'You can visit the abbey ruins another day,' she told Pierre. 'For now I want us to climb the Tor.'

She indicated the strange conical hill in front of them rising out of the flat land like a finger pointing to heaven. When they'd reached the ruined tower on the top and had got their breath back from the climb and the stupendous view, she explained why she'd brought him there.

'This was once a little island when the rest of Somerset was still covered with sea water, and it's haunted by legend and history as far back as records or imagination go. It was pagan first, of course, and people still come to spend the night of the summer solstice here. In medieval times the dying King Arthur of Camelot fame is believed to have been brought here for burial. Then, finally, a great Catholic abbey was built as a place of pilgrimage. There was even a legend that Christ himself came here. It's certainly true that the Glastonbury Thorn first planted by his uncle, Joseph of Arimathea, still blossoms twice a year, summer and winter.'

Bemused by this gallop across the millennia, Pierre held up his hands in mock protest.

'No more, please! I grant you it's a magical place, but it's too much to take in all at once.'

'You're entitled to feel light-headed the first time you come here,' she assured him calmly. 'It's time for our rather basic picnic, I think.'

Basic it was, but none the worse for that. Pierre's pocket-knife easily cut the crusty loaf and the wedge of Cheddar cheese, and a handful of grapes for each of them took the place of wine.

'Not one of your elegant French alfresco meals, I'm afraid,' Jenni said with a smile. 'Our picnics are simpler than that – no tables and chairs allowed – and they take place, if planned, despite the weather, usually wind and rain!'

He turned to look at her, sitting beside him on the grass. The sunlight would soon bring a dusting of freckles to her nose and warm her skin to pale gold, but even before that happened he thought he would never again see her as anything but beautiful.

'You have one dimple when you smile,' he said seriously, 'only one – why is that?'

Jenni shook her head. 'It's a scar, not a dimple – relic of my twin, Simon, bashing me accidentally with a sharp-edged toy when we were small. Do you have siblings? I see you as a much-indulged oldest son, telling your small fry what to do!'

'Only partly right,' he answered. 'No siblings; I was the only child – but certainly much-indulged – of parents who married late in life. My father is dead, my mother lives a very retired life in the south of France. I visit her when I can.'

She was chilled for a moment by something in his voice that suggested visits inspired by duty rather than affection, but he added something else. 'She is well taken care of, and she loves the Provençal *mas* that is her home – it's not unlike your father's farmhouse, though perhaps not quite so beautiful.'

It was a risk, because she would probably retreat again, but he needed the answer to a question of his own. 'Why don't you belong to someone here – are men blind in Somerset?'

'*They* are perfectly normal,' Jenni replied. 'I, according to Grand'mère, am not, being much too pernickety.' She smiled at the blankness in his face. 'Sorry – pernickety means choosy, hard to please!'

'I get the general idea.' Then he framed his next question. 'I wonder whether affection for your grandmother makes you determined to take care of her for as long as she's alive. You'd put her needs before your own, I think.'

'I expect I would,' Jenni agreed, 'even though she'd insist that I shouldn't, because she's the least sentimental woman I know – believes that it's all wrong to cling. But her life has been entirely devoted to us ... I can't see myself leaving her while she still needs me.'

'Which answers my question,' Pierre said quietly.

Jenni supposed she knew what that meant.

He *was* the impatient man she'd first thought him, and, being that, wouldn't wait for what he wanted – it was easier to move on to what *was* immediately available. She was grateful for the reminder; building castles in the air was a fool's occupation. There was nothing permanent about this new friendship, enjoyable though it was, and she must keep that firmly in mind.

'If you've had as much as you can manage of the Tor's atmosphere, we ought to make a move,' she finally suggested. 'Tonight is choir practice night, and the organist is required to be there.'

He nodded, then before she could guess his intention leaned over to gently kiss her mouth. She recovered her breath and even managed to sound calm and unconcerned. 'There was no need for that.'

'I think there was,' he said firmly. 'There's every need for you to know that I shall never forget this visit.' Then, without waiting for her to reply, he pulled her to her feet and they made their way down the hill to the car.

The sunlit days slipped by after that. Work forgotten, Pierre simply appeared at the farm each morning, and she could no longer believe that he wouldn't wait for her if she asked him to. They walked on Exmoor, battled their way along the Cob at Lyme Regis on a morning of blustery wind and racing clouds, and visited the stately homes and unspoilt villages strewn about the county. When Jenni insisted that she had duties to perform at home, he helped her in the *potager*, or walked the meadows with Simon, and regularly stayed talking to Leonie, comparing her memories of Paris with the city as it now was.

Part of his intense pleasure, Jenni thought, lay in sharing their family life. It seemed to be something he'd had no experience of before, and her conviction grew that even if his upbringing had been privileged, as he'd said, it had also been bleakly lonely. Watching him walk out with Simon and the dogs, or tease Evie in the kitchen when he taught her the French word for whatever she held in her hand, it was hard to remember a time when he hadn't been there. But behind the warmth and lovely ease of friendship lay the promise of a deeper relationship that coloured the days golden even when the fine weather turned to rain.

Then, one evening when they were expecting him as usual for dinner, he rang to say that he wouldn't be coming. There was a long telephone call he must make to France, and rather than keep them waiting, he would eat at The Bell. The following morning he arrived later than usual, looking tired and preoccupied, and Jenni laughingly chided him for a late night in the bar, playing darts. But almost at once she spoke again in a different tone of voice.

'Is it just that we've had our lovely holiday and it's time to go back to work, or did you get bad news last night from France? Is something wrong, Pierre?'

'Everything is wrong,' he said with a sudden violence that set her heart beating too fast. But her anxious face made him speak more gently. 'We need to talk, Jenni.'

Without argument she led him to the little summerhouse that filled the far corner of the *potager*. It had sheltered them from unexpected rain showers often enough, and felt reassuringly familiar even now when his manner, even his voice, seemed worryingly different. Sitting down, he reached for her hand, but then released it again, and gripped his own hands on the table in front of them instead.

'I'm going back to France,' he announced abruptly. 'It will seem unforgivably churlish and rude after the kindness I've been shown, but I can't stay any longer. The truth of the matter is that I shouldn't have come at all.'

'You came to find material for your book – what was wrong about that?' she managed to ask.

He turned to stare at her for a moment, then looked away again. 'It's all it should have been ... not what it has become.'

She was being told, she supposed numbly, that what it had become was a mistake, a summer holiday interlude forgotten as soon it was over. If she died in the attempt she must try to pretend that she herself had imagined nothing more than that. She schooled her voice not to shake, even to sound half-amused.

'You forgot to mention, I expect, that you have a wife and six small children at home.'

'No wife, no children,' he contradicted her fiercely. 'How could you think that?'

'I don't know what to think,' she said with the quietness of despair, 'except that you've grown tired of me and my family. We've been too ... too eager for your time and attention perhaps, and this is your way of saying so ... cruel now, but kinder in the long run.'

He should have expected her directness, he realized – she was the most honest woman he'd ever met. There was nothing to do now but match her honesty.

'I can't leave you like this ... I meant to go with everything that matters left unspoken,' he said unevenly, 'but you have to know – must know already – how very much I love you. I'd beg you to come with me to France, I'd wait however long it took for you to feel free to come, if things were not as they are.'

White-faced but more confident now, she was able to smile at him. 'You'll have to tell me how they are – I still don't understand.'

His hands reached across the table now to grip hers. 'Your grandmother spoke to me of the diary she kept – said she'd given it to you.' When she nodded he went on. 'So you know about her time in pre-war Paris. What you don't know is that before she married Philippe Lacroix after the war, my mother was Jeanne Gosselin – Emile and Luc were her brothers.'

He had to wait for her to find something to

say. ‘That’s how you knew Luc had died,’ she finally murmured, fastening on the least important part of the story, because the rest was too painful.

It was Pierre’s turn to nod. ‘But now I also know what Leonie believes: that Emile, and perhaps my mother too, were responsible for sending the Bernards and Max Reiner to die in a concentration camp.’

With what felt like an iron hand tightening round her heart, it was more and more difficult to speak, but at last, Jenni managed it. ‘Did you know that before you came ... about Genevieve and Pappi Bernard and Max?’

‘I knew of them, I knew that they had died ... no more than that, Jenni, until I spoke to my mother last night and asked her for the truth. There *had* been a quarrel with Genevieve Bernard, that was all she wanted to say. With so many people being taken away, who could be sure who’d been to blame.’

‘Grand’mère knows who to blame,’ Jenni had to insist. ‘Her information came from someone who was there at the time.’ She freed her hands and sat hugging herself because the day seemed to have turned grey and cold. It was how life itself felt; the golden summer had been lovely while it lasted, but it was over now.

‘What are we going to do about Grand’mère?’ she asked at last. ‘I’m a very bad liar. She’ll know at once if I try to pretend you’re leaving because we’ve had some stupid quarrel.'

'We'll tell her the truth,' Pierre said slowly. 'She deserves that and so does your father. I've been treated with such kindness here that nothing less than the truth will do.' He stopped talking and touched her cheek gently. 'I realize what it means, Jenni. Even if *you* can accept my family connections it's more than your grandmother will do. I could still sense her hatred of Emile Gosselin, and she knows that where he led my mother followed. I can't be sure of your feelings for me – much as I hope you're learning to love me – but I *know* you are devoted to Leonie. I can't ask you to choose between us.'

She shook her head as if trying to soften a blow that had hurt too much. 'At the moment I don't know how I'd choose. I can only take one step at a time, and the first one is to talk to Leonie. She loves me, and she's grown very fond of you – it might be enough to persuade her to forget the past and give us her blessing.'

'Does that mean that you *would* marry me?'

Jenni's slow, sweet smile reappeared. 'You're Pierre Lacroix to me, not Emile's nephew. If you could be patient and wait, yes ... yes, I'd marry you.'

His hands pulled her upright so that she could be held tightly against him, and it was all the response she wanted for the moment. Passion needed the right time for fulfillment, and the right time wasn't now. They had fences to jump first, starting with Pierre's revelation to her grandmother.

Having seen his car out in the lane, Leonie was waiting for his usual morning visit. After a glance at his face she asked, as Jenni had done, if he'd received bad news the night before. He kissed her hand, as he always did, and then said that he needed to talk to her – *she* had to be the judge of whether the news was bad or not. She waved him to a chair, saw Jenni sit where she could watch them both, and prepared to listen.

Twenty

He said what had to be said as briefly as possible, and made no attempt in the course of it to alter Leonie's opinion of Luc Gosselin's brother and sister.

'I intended to leave without telling you or Jenni of the connection,' he finished up, 'but in the end I found I couldn't do that. I love her, you see, and want more than anything for her to be my wife, but you both had to know the truth about me first.'

Looking at her grandmother's white, implacable face, Jenni realized how slight was the chance of reconciling her to Pierre's Gosselin connections – she would hate Emile, especially, until she died. But for the moment what he'd said about a love affair she'd seemed to approve of was ignored. There was a more important matter to pursue first.

'Your mother mentioned a "quarrel" with my dear Genevieve. Do you know what it was about?' she asked coldly.

Pierre studied his fingers, gripped together, as if he hadn't seen them before.

'Mademoiselle Bernard accused my uncle very publicly of collaborating with the Germans. He and my mother were hounded out of Paris after the war as a result.'

'And so they deserved to be,' Leonie calmly commented, but even this wasn't what she was intent on. 'The real reason for the quarrel was Roland Gosselin's gift to Luc before he left Paris. It was something his brother believed to be too valuable to lose track of. Luc must have told his father that he would leave it with me for safekeeping, but Emile clearly found out as well. He badgered Genevieve to tell him where it was, and when she refused he betrayed her and Pappi to the Germans out of spite.'

Staring at his set face, Jenni knew that he wasn't hearing it for the first time, but before he could even pretend otherwise Leonie's upraised hand insisted that she still had more to say.

'Perhaps you do intend to write your history of the wartime French, but I'm sure my memories are not what brought you here. The Gosselins are still looking for the suitcase Luc left with me. How happy you must all have been when Jules told you where to find me at last. Unlike Luc and me, I expect you even know what the suitcase contains.'

Heart thumping, Jenni waited for Pierre to deny what Leonie had said. Only Jules Lefevre's recollections could have led him, accidentally, to her grandmother; such coincidences happened often enough. But Pierre, not looking at Jenni, said something so different that it brought the taste of nausea to her mouth.

'I knew about the suitcase and, yes, I know what it contains.' His eyes skimmed Jenni's sheet-white face and looked away again. 'Understand if you can – I was brought up to believe that my grandfather had no right to give it to Luc – it belonged to our whole family. Justice seemed to have been done at last when, interviewing Jules Lefevre, I discovered that he knew where to find you.'

Jenni heard her grandmother give a little sigh of what sounded like relief – there could be no more lies now. Aware of it himself, Pierre went on in the same unemotional voice. It scarcely mattered; Jenni was lost to him. But he refused to leave her grandmother's contemptuous view of him unchallenged.

'My book *was* an honest reason for coming, but I admit to wanting to find the suitcase for my mother. Emile Gosselin died last year. It could have been sold, thrown away, or bombed to smithereens for all I knew.

'When I got here I could see at once that it hadn't been sold – this was a working farm, not the estate of a rich, idle family. After that the search for it soon ceased to matter – I was accepted so readily as a friend, and I was fast falling in love with your granddaughter. Last night I telephoned my mother about Jenni, and told her that I no longer cared what had happened about the suitcase – the search was over. She retaliated by telling me the truth – that it was my uncle who had betrayed the Bernards and Max Reiner to the Nazis.'

He lifted up his hands in a little gesture of despair. 'That's when I decided to go back to France, hoping that if I went saying nothing at all this saga of greed and hatred might finally come to an end.'

Tired but triumphant, Leonie had one last point to make. 'The bitter irony of it all, I hope your mother will realize, is that what Luc believed he'd been given was simply a collection of family papers.'

A faint, unamused smile touched Pierre's mouth for a moment. 'What his father had actually given him were a dozen signed Picasso drawings.' He heard Jenni gasp, but went on calmly with his story. 'When Picasso went to Paris before the first World War he was just another penniless artist. He rented a studio in the Rue de Ravignon where my grandfather had opened his first restaurant. Without the price of a meal, Pablo would often pay for his food by tossing off a sketch – they'd be worth something one day, he told Roland – quite rightly, as we now know.'

With even Leonie stunned into silence for a moment, Jenni was beyond imagining what would happen next. The drawings, even, seemed not to matter compared with what else her heart and mind had to accept. The past *wasn't* dead; it would continue to haunt them, at least until Leonie and Pierre's mother were dead; and still after that her chance of happiness with him was likely to be destroyed, because distrust was like acid, insidiously eating away everything it touched.

All she wanted now was for this dreadful interview to be over, but she had overlooked one last question. Typically, Leonie had not. 'The fate of the drawings remains to be settled,' she told Pierre calmly. 'They were given to Luc, obviously, as his patrimony. Your uncle and your mother had Roland's restaurants and presumably his wealth as their share. I promised to take care of the suitcase and that is what I shall continue to do. When I die it will be for Jenni to decide what happens to it – I shall no longer care.'

From her grandmother's point of view it was logical, Jenni thought numbly; from her own, it seemed cruelly unfair. But though heartsick and exhausted by too much emotion, she knew that both Leonie and Pierre waited for her to speak now.

'Nothing changes as long as Grand'mère is alive,' she said, addressing herself to Pierre. 'After that I'll decide what to do, and of course I shall let you know what is to happen to the drawings.'

It sounded firm and very final, he thought, and although his eyes searched her face for some hint of love surviving, all he could see was her desperate need for him to leave.

'I shall give my mother your message,' he said with equal formality. Then his voice changed. 'If I thought either of you would listen, I'd beg you to understand how much I've hated being here under false pretences. As it is, I can only thank you for the kindness you've shown me. I shall remember it always.'

Then he walked out of the room and a moment later they heard his car start up and drive away. The silence left behind seemed to be suffocating them. Jenni threw open a window, partly for something to do and partly so that some of the emotion in the room might escape. When she turned round again Leonie was on her feet, looking exhausted and, for once, defeated.

'Will you try not to hate me for insisting on the truth?' she asked quietly. 'I can't, not even for you, my dear, forgive the Gosselins for what they did, but that need not matter to you. My life is almost over; yours is still to live. If you can be happy with Pierre, you must forget the past and go with him.'

Jenni shook her head. 'Dear Gran, you might *just* put up with me marrying Pierre, but I can see no hope at all of his mother accepting me as a daughter-in-law. He's all she has left; he can't be made to choose between us.' Tears trickled slowly down her face, but she smeared them away and came to rest her hands on Leonie's thin shoulders.

'It was a little summer madness, lovely while it lasted, but over now. We'll go back to the real world – it's what suits us best, I think.' She even managed a faint smile. 'The sun's come out – let's take a stroll round the garden.' But at the door she halted again.

'I'll tell Papa and Simon that Pierre was suddenly recalled to France. Then we won't ever mention his name again. *D'accord?*'

Leonie nodded agreement, afraid that her

voice would refuse to function if she tried to speak. Then they walked out into the September sunshine, to begin the struggle to put their peaceful life together again.

Walking to church to play for the service the following Sunday was hard, but the congregation were already filing into their usual pews – it being tacitly agreed that custom gave some sort of ownership. Jenni knew that only wishful thinking of the most delirious kind could suppose that she might see Pierre's dark head there. He was back in Paris by now, and gradually her present ache of loneliness *must* dull to some bearable and fading sense of loss.

It was time for school to start again, and the Christmas term was always a busy one culminating in the time-honoured ritual of the Nativity play and end-of-term carol concert. She was even grateful for the customary parental in-fighting that determined whose daughter got to star as Mary, and whose treble-voiced son became King Wenceslas's page at the concert. It was almost Christmas – time to try to forget the state of the world and remember what the incarnation of the son of God really meant.

For once the weather was coldly seasonal – there was even talk of snow. And, for once, Leonie was finding the winter a trial. She was still in bed one morning, recovering from what she called a cold and the doctor insisted was bronchitis, when Evie came back into the kitchen to report that a woman she didn't recognize was hovering at the gate into the lane.

'She doesn't seem to be able to make up her mind,' Evie said, 'to come in or leave, but it's funny either way.'

'An old lady?' Jenni asked hesitantly.

'Not young, but not old,' was Evie's considered verdict. 'I 'spect she'll have gone by now in any case.'

But relieved of the fear that Jeanne Lacroix had come in person to demand her brother's suitcase, Jenni let herself out of the front door into the freezing morning air. The woman had heard the door open and turned to walk away, but a glance at her still-flaxen hair told Jenni who she was. A four-year-old child's memory of that lovely hair remained in her mind. She didn't doubt that it was her mother who stood there, half-wanting to run away again, half-wanting to be called back.

'Don't go, please,' Jenni said quickly. 'Surely you can spare the time to come inside for a moment, it's too cold to talk out here.'

Turning towards her now, she could see a thin face browned by long exposure to some tropical climate. Its once stunning beauty – known from old photographs – was only visible now in bone structure that would be lovely until she died; its colouring and texture had been lost.

Alice Vaux hesitated for a moment, then ducked her head in what Jenni took to be a little gesture of acceptance. Inside the house she was led to the drawing room, where Jenni poked the smouldering logs on the hearth into a more cheerful blaze. Then she turned to look at the visitor.

'My father and Simon are on their way to a livestock market, my grandmother is in her bedroom, not very well. There's only me for you to talk to at the moment.'

'You know who I am, it seems,' Alice said, still with a very faint American accent. 'My worst fear was that I wouldn't even be recognized. What should I know that I don't know about what's been happening here?'

Jenni shook her head. 'Nothing,' she said shortly, unable to mention the brief appearance in their lives of Pierre Lacroix. 'Michael and Elizabeth Wentworth had both died before you went away, and so had my grandfather. Grand'mère brought me and Simon up, with help from Papa of course, and the four of us live together in complete contentment with each other.'

It wasn't entirely true, of course, even apart from her own sadness. Leonie still missed Adam Vaux, and Jenni had caught glimpses enough over the years of her father's valiantly concealed loneliness. But she wouldn't say so to this stranger who was probably there merely to disturb them again before disappearing to some exotic destination. Her mother acknowledged what she *hadn't* said with a wry smile.

'I think you're telling me politely that I shouldn't have come! I didn't intend to. I meant to fly back to New York from Africa without stopping. Then suddenly, I couldn't *not* stop; I needed to know what you've just told me – that you've all managed very well without me. It's what I wanted to happen, though I expect you'll find that hard to believe.'

The wistfulness in her mother's voice made Jenni tell her the truth.

'Simon and I grew up knowing what Papa believed – that you'd gone while you were still happy with us, so that nothing was spoiled. We accepted that because it was what *he* wanted.'

Alice shook her head. 'But what you and your brother really thought was that I was a selfish, spoilt fool who didn't deserve what she had!'

Her daughter's silence answered her, but before it grew too awkward there was a sudden noise outside that took Jenni to the window.

'That's strange – the market must have been cancelled. They're back again already.' She looked from the Land Rover outside to the woman who sat by the fire. 'I'd like to tell my father that you're here, then Simon and I can disappear.'

Once again, but catching up an anorak this time, she ran out into the cold morning and briefly explained what had happened – their mother had decided to look in on them on her way to America. She was in the drawing room, and Grand'mère was still upstairs.

Unable to look at the expression on her father's face, she spoke now to Simon. 'I'll help you to unload the animals while Papa goes indoors.' She doubted if her father even heard what she said; he went towards the house like a man sleepwalking.

'Is it the worst thing that could have happened?' Simon asked quietly, watching him go. 'Is she an out-and-out bitch who doesn't care what damage she does, or is she just too stupid to know?'

'Neither, I think,' Jenni had to answer. 'I'm not sure she realizes it yet, but she's discovered at last that she needs us. It may be too late, of course, but that's for Father to decide.' She stared for a moment at her twin. 'If you can remember how beautiful she was you'll be rather shocked. But there's still something magnetic about her. I wanted to hate her and found I couldn't.'

'No surprise there,' Simon pointed out with a smile. 'You're the worst hater I know!' That made him remember someone else. 'You'd better leave the beasts to me – you must go and warn Grand'mère. God knows what *her* reaction will be to a daughter-in-law she hasn't seen for twenty years.' With his hand raised to lift the back of the trailer, he stopped again. 'I take it this *is* a flying visit – our mother hasn't come to stay?'

Jenni shook her head. 'Brief visit only, I think.'

It was the question that Ned Vaux was asking in the drawing room, having stared for a long moment at his changed, but to him unalterable, wife.

'Alice, have you come home, or not? I need to know the truth, please.'

'I only came to see how you were,' she answered slowly. '*My* need was to know that I hadn't done great harm after all.'

'Where have you come from?' It didn't seem a very important question, but there was so much he didn't know that he could only start at the end and work back from there.

'I've been in Africa – the Sudan most recently,' Alice said, 'working for Médecins sans Frontières. I've seen hardship and tragedy enough to last me a lifetime. To begin with, it seems wonderful to be helping, but soon you realize that all you're doing is making life a little more hopeful for a few people – the causes of all the misery are still there.'

It explained her ravaged face, Ned thought. The girl who'd wanted to experience the world had seen as much of it as she could bear.

'What now?' he asked gently. 'Christmas at home with your parents in New York?'

'I suppose so.' Her little shrug expressed no enthusiasm for the idea. 'My sister will be there, with her self-satisfied husband and their noisy, over-indulged children! It's odd, going from people who have much too little to those who have far too much.'

Ned stared at her, resisting the temptation

to stretch out his hand to touch her thin cheek.

'Why not stay here?' he suggested unevenly. 'The contrast wouldn't be quite so great!'

She looked round the room, comparing its ordered loveliness with what she'd left behind. It was contrast enough, but at least conspicuous consumption wasn't part of this family's way of life. The house was beautiful simply because generations of people living there had loved it and taken care of it.

Alice blinked away the tears that threatened to overflow, and tried to smile instead. 'Thank you, dear Ned, but the children won't want me here. Jenni only just managed not to say that I should have stayed away, and heaven knows I've no right to blame her.'

He thought he understood what she was really saying and shook his head. 'My dear, I'm not trying to tie you down – I know that doesn't work. Just rest here over Christmas – you can leave my mother and the twins to me.'

It was as if a lamp had been lit behind her drawn face, bringing back its beauty. 'Then I should like to very much,' she said simply. 'I'll go back to London to collect my luggage – if the taxi's still waiting outside – and take the train down on Christmas Eve.' Then she hesitated for a moment. 'Should I see your mother before I go? Jenni said she wasn't well.'

'She'll have recovered by the time you're back – wait till then,' Ned suggested.

Alice agreed, not sorry to put off the ordeal of meeting Leonie Vaux again. 'Then I'll leave right now ... I'd rather, Ned.'

He didn't try to change her mind, but simply took her outside to find the waiting taxi. 'You won't *not* come?' he said anxiously.

The smile he'd never forgotten lit her face again. 'It's a promise – Christmas Eve.' Then she kissed his cheek and got into the car.

He watched it disappear out of sight, then was joined by Simon who'd walked under the archway from the yard. Father and son linked arms and walked into the house, not saying anything. They met Jenni shepherding her grandmother down the stairs.

'Alice has gone already?' Leonie asked sharply. 'Could she not have waited long enough to speak to me?'

'She knew you hadn't been well. I said you'd be feeling better by the time she comes back' – his grin reappeared – 'and more amenable!' Then his face and his voice changed. 'It's only a Christmas visit, but while it lasts we shall have her back again. She needs kindness, and if you love me you must love her too. I expect it of you.'

Then he went outside again, leaving them to the awareness that when he spoke in that tone of voice expectation had somehow to be met.

Twenty-One

True to her promise, Alice returned late in the afternoon of Christmas Eve, having refused to be met at Taunton; she'd catch a train when she could, she'd said, and take a taxi to the farm. Thinking it would be easier for mother and son to meet alone, Ned asked Simon to watch for the taxi to arrive. So it was he who hurried to the gate as Alice began to unload parcels from the back seat of the car.

'Hello, Mum,' he said simply. 'Father's instructions are that I'm to deal with all this, including the fare. You've got to go inside – it's perishing out here.'

There was no strangeness about meeting him – he was exactly like his father, she thought, with tears suddenly catching the back of her throat. 'I promise not to say how you've grown,' she managed as he bent down to kiss her cheek. He smiled at her, and it was Ned's smile, too.

She walked up the path to the open door – another hurdle there, because her mother-in-law stood waiting. Still upright, still elegant, only the silvered hair and fine mesh of lines around her eyes and mouth showed the passage of twenty years.

'Welcome back,' Leonie said formally. 'Ned is visiting a sick cowman and Jenni is practising in church, but they'll be home soon.' She glanced out of the window to the frosted beauty of the garden. 'I gather you've come from Africa – I hope you've brought warm clothes.'

'I shopped for them in London,' Alice admitted, 'but I nearly froze to death when I first arrived.' She hesitated, unsure what to say next. 'It was Ned's idea that I should come ... I hope you and the twins don't mind too much.'

Even Leonie wasn't proof against the plea contained in those last words.

'Why should we mind? As far as he's concerned this is still your home.' Then, rather to her relief, Simon walked in behind them, laden with parcels and luggage, and made for the stairs.

'I must leave Simon to show you to your room,' she said almost apologetically. 'I'm forbidden to climb the stairs at the moment.' Her still-dark eyebrows sketched a frown. 'It's one of the tiresome things about growing old – people *will* keep telling you what you mustn't do.' Then irritation faded as she looked more closely at Alice.

'*You're* tired, too. Would you rather go and rest in your room, or drink tea first in the drawing room?' Now her face sparkled with sudden amusement. 'You haven't, I hope, forgotten the English passion for offering guests tea the moment they arrive!'

Alice smiled and chose the tea, realizing that as far as her hostess was concerned, she *was* a guest, not a long-absent daughter-in-law; at least that made it easier to know how to behave.

Over the tea trolley she was reintroduced to Evie, and told that they were in the habit of attending the Christmas Eve midnight service since cows still had to be fed and milked on Christmas morning. 'Jenni, of course, must go both times, being the organist,' Leonie further explained.

Alice hesitated for a moment, but remembered from the past the directness of the woman she was facing. 'Simon made me welcome at once. Jenni is biding her time before deciding whether to accept me or not, but I hope she will in the end.'

Leonie met frankness with frankness. 'She's more complicated than Simon, and she adores her father. I expect she's afraid it will hurt him all over again when your visit is over. In the circumstances it isn't unreasonable to think that, is it?'

'Not unreasonable at all,' Alice agreed. 'I probably shouldn't have come – it was selfish of me. But it seemed so beautiful and peaceful when I called here that I wanted to be part of it again.'

Leonie accepted this with a nod. 'Jenni will work her way through whatever resentment she's feeling – she's hopeless at bearing grudges. Now go upstairs and rest before dinner or you'll disgrace us by falling asleep during the sermon. Your room is the second on the right at the top of the stairs, and there's a bathroom leading off it. Dinner's at eight, as usual.'

Suspecting that Leonie was also ready for a rest, Alice stood up, kissed her mother-in-law's cheek as she passed her chair, and made for the door. The worst hurdle was over; perhaps, now, she could begin to feel accepted again.

Supper that evening was an uncomfortable meal – probably, Jenni supposed, because they were all trying to pretend that nothing unusual had happened. With the possible exception of Simon, who was content to live in the present moment, they were remembering the past and wondering about the future.

Looking at her father's entranced face as he listened to Alice talking about Africa, Jenni found it hard to believe that he could bear to be bereft all over again when her visit was over. But if she decided to stay, would Grand-'mère ... *could* she ... retire gracefully and relinquish her place as mistress of the house to a daughter-in-law she hadn't thought kindly of for twenty years?

Plagued by these worries, Jenni was thankful when it was time to leave for church and the lovely, familiar ritual of the midnight mass. But while the candlelit church began to fill, and the choirmaster reminded his sopranos that he wanted a firm top A on the last descant, not a wavering G sharp, there was time to think about Pierre. She supposed that Christmas would be spent with his mother – had *they* somehow come to terms with the past and left bitterness and grief behind them?

The vicar's gentle hand on her shoulder as he went past said that it was time to begin, and her fingers obediently found the opening notes of *O Come, All ye Faithful*. It was the eve of Christmas, and the child was about to be born in a stable all over again.

With the service over there were friends to greet, some who remembered Alice failing to hide their surprise at seeing her again so unexpectedly. The contingent from the Manor, forewarned by Leonie, managed better. But watching Margot, Amy's daughter, come face to face with her one-time friend, Jenni wondered how hard it was for her to smile a welcome. According to Grand'mère, it was Margot who had first brought Alice to Frantock, and then had to see her bewitch the man on whom her own heart was set. With the Wetherbys due to spend Christmas evening at the farmhouse, it would make the chances of an enjoyable dinner party more slender still.

Jenni returned from playing at the morning service to find that her father and Simon had taken Alice to inspect their newly planted stretch of woodland.

'There's not a lot to see – it's mid-winter,' Jenni pointed out.

'Enough,' said her grandmother, 'if you look at it with the eye of love as your father does. He'll be explaining to Alice how beautiful it's going to be in the spring.'

Cold hands hugging the mug of coffee she'd been given, Jenni voiced the anxiety in her mind. 'Gran, what are we going to do about Alice? I can only call her that, I'm afraid, not Mother. Do we try to make life here seem so irresistible that she'll *want* to stay? Simon won't mind – he's won over already. But I don't know about you, and nor do I know about myself. Suppose she hasn't changed as much as she seems to have done? What if this is just a convenient rest house while she decides what she wants to do next? I suppose the truth is that I don't trust her.'

Leonie's set face answered before she spoke. 'I know no more than you do, my dear. Legally she's still your father's wife and, legally, this is still her home. The beauty she's lost makes no difference to him. In fact it probably makes him want all the more to take care of her. My *guess* is that a visit will be enough to remind her that she hated farm life, especially in winter. If I'm wrong, we shall have to put up with her. Your father will be a happy man at last – which heaven knows he deserves – and we shall comfort each other, you and I!' She inspected her granddaughter's face and risked a question that might be resented. 'Or are you thinking that this would be the moment to bury the past once and for all and mend things with

Pierre?'

She strove, as she said it, to sound calm and unconcerned. If that was how it was to be, she would manage well enough on her own. She wasn't decrepit yet, nor dependent on a girl she loved more than anyone else in the world except her son. But Jenni wasn't misled; the faint idea of escaping life with a mother she might come to dislike withered and died. For as long as Leonie needed her, escape wasn't possible.

'I haven't heard from Pierre,' she said as evenly as she could. 'By now there's probably nothing left to mend.' Now she managed a smile as well. 'If life gets too unbearable here I could always marry John Rashleigh and instal *you* in the vicarage as well!'

Leonie took this in the spirit it was meant but shook her head. 'He's a good man, my dear, but I should hate to see you married to the Church of England. In any case you're not nearly biddable enough.'

Like Jenni, she smiled as she said it, but the suggestion was disturbing nevertheless. John Rashleigh, a lonely, scholarly widower verging on middle-age, liked his organist very much – that was obvious. Leonie didn't find this unreasonable – any man who wasn't blind or stupid *should*. But Leonie remembered her dear friend Jane Rushton, and *her* long struggle to bear the demands and frustrations of vicarage life. The danger was real because Jenni grieved over John Rashleigh's loneliness and his inability to communicate with at least half his parishioners – he was coming to share their Christmas dinner that evening simply because she was sorry for him. If she believed that Jeanne Lacroix or the memory of the past would always block happiness with Pierre, she might see rescuing John as an alternative to wasting her life.

Leonie hoped that she managed to sound amused. 'Vicarages are always draughty – on the grounds, I suppose, that their incumbents' flesh is better for being mortified. I think I might prefer to stay here! But right now we have this evening's dinner to think about – Daniel and his son James, Amy and her daughter Margot – four Wetherbys plus John Rashleigh and ourselves; we must pray the goose is big enough for ten people.'

'Smoked salmon canapés will blunt their appetites,' Jenni suggested, 'and Stilton and Christmas pudding will finish them off. Darling Gran, of course there'll be enough. This is going to be a moderate, modern repast, not a Victorian blowout! I shall start by laying the table in the dining room and decorating it with suitable sprigs of greenery. Anyone who expects lunch as well will have to eat in the kitchen.'

Leonie smiled at her, accepting that it was time to put worry aside. The future would reveal itself in due course, and no amount of agonizing on their part would make it more or less acceptable.

In the event, the goose, carried to the table by Jenni on a lordly dish, *was* adequate, and the evening was a happy one. It ended with music in the drawing room, because Daniel's son, called James after his grandfather, and his cousin, Margot, had come with instruments. A violin and a cello added to Jenni's piano provided them with lovely chamber music. Perhaps to his own surprise, John Rashleigh's tenor voice rendered *Danny Boy* very beautifully, and Simon's mouth organ contributed a haunting version of *Moon River*. Then the assembled company was invited by Jenni to round off the concert with one of the best-loved carols, *Stille Nacht, Heilige Nacht*.

No singer herself, Leonie did little more than mouth the words, and watch Alice as she did so. She wished she could be certain what her daughter-in-law was thinking, but it was hard to believe that any woman in her right mind could fail to understand the value of the life she could have here. Maybe, this time, her choice *would* be to stay with Ned.

Twenty-Two

Ned often talked to his cows; he told them things he found it hard to share even with his family, because they looked at him with large, peaceful eyes that never asked questions he couldn't answer. The news that Alice was back at the farm had been met with only a gentle swish of their tails – nothing that required him to say what it meant for the future.

He'd done his best only to make her feel welcome and loved; to have given away his long, lonely need of her would have been unfair. His family had had their own effort to make too, he recognized that. But he also knew, with the sadness that accepts what can't be changed, that persuading Alice to return for good would alter *their* lives as well as his, in ways they would probably resent.

Patient man that he was, he realized that the uncertainty couldn't go on. Christmas was over, it was time to face the future. Alice could be asked to do that now, because with rest, good food, and clean air to breathe, she was already a different woman.

With the intention that they shouldn't be interrupted when they talked, he asked her to go with him to visit a friend who had animals to sell. On the way home he stopped the car and turned to look at her. He longed to take her in his arms, but the words he was finding it hard to frame had to come first. Alice thought she guessed the reason for his hesitation and spoke first.

'You think it's time I went away, but you're too kind to say so,' she suggested quietly.

'It's time you told me what you're going to do,' he said instead. 'I hope it *isn't* to go back to Africa – you were ill when you arrived. Let someone else struggle with its miseries for a while, please.'

A wry smile twisted her mouth. 'I was told to leave Africa by a remarkable French doctor who said that my intention in being there wasn't to help desperate people at all but to punish myself. He didn't even know then that I'd abandoned you and the children – he just doubted my crusading spirit! I was indignant at the time, of course, but in my heart I knew he was right.'

She looked out of the car window at the landscape around them – no dust, no scorching heat, no teeming crowds of clamorous, hungry people. This was Somerset, beautiful even in mid-winter, peaceful, rain-blessed and fertile. Then she went on with what she had to say.

'Knowing that the doctor was right was what made me come here instead of going straight back to New York. If I could be sure that you'd all got on perfectly well without me, I hoped I needn't feel guilty any more.'

Ned thought of all the years spent without her ... survived certainly, but very far from perfectly. Even now, though, he refused to blame her. He longed for her to say that what she wanted was to stay with them, but first he must be sure she understood what that would mean.

He took hold of her hands and held them in his own warm grip. 'I promised myself that I wouldn't try to persuade you – what would be the point? I'm still the man I was, with only the same life to offer you that wasn't enough twenty years ago. It may not be enough now, but if you are tired of travelling, then come home, my dear.'

She was distracted for a moment by his likeness to Adam Vaux, as noticeable as Simon's was to him – male characteristics seemed in this family to run very strongly from father to son. It served to remind her of what must be admitted next.

'I'm not sure that what I want is important now,' she suggested sadly, 'at least I've learned that much! It's true that I've seen all of the world that I shall ever want to see, and I'm sure that you, and probably Simon too, would make room for me. But Leonie wouldn't, Ned, and my daughter doesn't want me here either. They don't trust me, I think, not to make you unhappy again.'

Sensing that by some miracle he might be about to win, Ned smiled blindingly at her. 'My dear one, they've only to see now how far from unhappy I am to cease worrying. *Will* you live with me again and be my love, till death itself parts us this time?'

Her answering smile almost restored youth's lost beauty. 'So much for Monsieur le Médecin's theory of self-inflicted punishment! I'm being given a lovely, undeserved reward instead. Dear Ned, I promise you that I didn't come expecting to be taken back, but I do want to stay ... I know that now.'

He pulled her into his arms, and buried his face in her hair. 'Even when I didn't know where you were I could still feel the cord that tied my heart to yours,' he said unsteadily. 'As long as it didn't break I could say to myself *she'll come back one day.*'

His mouth brushed hers in a brief, sweet kiss and then he released her and started the car. 'Let's go home,' he said with sudden, huge contentment.

At the farmhouse when they got back, Jenni was preparing dinner in the kitchen. She explained when they came in that Evie was still enjoying a visit with 'young' Harry, now a married man himself with two small children. Immersed in the tricky recipe she was following – yet another way of disguising the remains of a Christmas side of ham – she scarcely looked up as her father and Alice walked past her into the hall. It was Leonie, sitting by the fire in the drawing room with an unread book on her lap, who guessed what had happened as soon as they came into the room. Happiness lit Ned's face and her daughter-in-law also smiled, albeit defensively, knowing that whatever Ned liked to believe, Leonie had been waiting for the moment when her 'guest' would decide to leave. As usual, Ned bent down to kiss his mother, and waited for her to enquire about the animals he'd set out to buy.

'A wasted journey as far as the livestock was concerned,' he said cheerfully, 'they weren't worth the price Nick Holden was asking for them. But the rest of the trip was a glorious, shining success! Mama, I hardly know how to tell you that Alice has come back for good. I can scarcely believe I had the courage to ask, but she is content to stay and our family is complete again. I shall go about from now on, I'm afraid, with a permanent grin on my face ... I may even serenade the cows this evening!'

'I've no doubt they'll enjoy that,' Leonie managed to say calmly, but it took a huge effort of will to smile at her son and the woman at his side. 'Then I shall say "welcome back" all over again,' she commented to Alice. If she had to bite her tongue in half rather than admit what was in her mind, she would *not* remind Alice Vaux of the marriage vows she'd undertaken all those years ago. If they were to share the farmhouse amicably she herself must forget the past and accept that Ned's wife was now its proper mistress.

'Do the twins know?' she thought it reasonable to ask.

'Of course not. We told you first,' Ned pointed out, sounding surprised that the question was needed. 'Anyway, Simon is out looking at the boundary fences with Jimmy, and Jenni is muttering to herself over a saucepan in the kitchen. We'll tell them at dinner.'

Leonie nodded, aware that something else needed to be said before she could decently escape and take a welter of anxieties to the privacy of her own room. 'Be happy together, please,' she begged them gravely. 'Life's too short for even one more day to be wasted.' A glimmer of amusement then lifted the strain from her face. 'Let's hope that what Jenni is toiling over in the kitchen will make a celebratory enough feast. Perhaps a glass of champagne to go with it, Ned?'

'Suitably chilled of course,' he agreed solemnly. Then, with a loving smile, he moved to open the door for her as she stood up to leave the room.

Things changed slowly but inevitably after that, as Leonie had known they would. Now man and wife again, lovers again, Ned and Alice's changed relationship not only altered the emotional climate in the house, but affected other relationships as well. Watching from the sidelines to which she knew she must be relegated, Leonie sadly observed that it was Jenni who was suffering most. The previous closeness of father and daughter, precious to both of them, was being lost in his anxiety not to repeat a previous mistake; whatever time he could spare from the farm now *had* to be devoted to his wife. Almost worse, the twinship that had linked her and Simon seemed to be breaking down as well. It was Alice, now, who must be taught how to play golf, Alice who had to be given riding lessons so that she could join in the traditional Somerset custom of going out with the hunt. It was even Alice he sided with in their usual discussions at the dinner-table – the only time now when they were all uneasily together.

'It's not deliberate or personal,' Leonie felt obliged to say one morning when she was alone with her granddaughter. 'In a way I wish it were, then I could dislike her with a clear conscience. She just absorbs the attention of men as naturally as she breathes. It doesn't leave her much time to notice other women.'

Jenni shook her head. 'Not quite right, Gran. With me at least it *is* personal. I can feel that she doesn't want me here. Alice can spare some of Father's love for you, because she knows that she must, but generosity stops there.'

'It's a thousand pities my darling Adam isn't here to teach her the different kinds of love that the Greeks very sensibly had five different words for,' Leonie said sadly. 'That stupid woman sees you as some kind of threat – as if Ned or Simon loving you means there's less for her.' She hesitated for a moment and then risked the question she needed to ask. 'What are you going to do about it? Marry

John Rashleigh? My dear, not that, please. I could bear to see you as a vicar's wife if he were a young, vigorous, warm-blooded man, but our saintly priest is none of these things. His place is in a monastic cell, interpreting the mysteries of the Book of Revelation for foolish Christians like me who can't understand a word of it.'

It made her granddaughter's strained face smile, but Jenni had no intention of commenting on that opinion of John Rashleigh or any other escape route she might be considering. Instead, she gave a different answer as cheerfully as she could. 'I'm not about to do anything but stay here. Gran dear, I *can't* wish that Alice hadn't come back because she makes my father happy. She's taken Simon over for the moment, but he'll find a girl to love one day, and that's as it should be, too. Twins aren't meant to be yoked together emotionally for life. You mustn't worry about me – I'm not going to dwindle into crabby old spinsterhood – at least, not for a year or two!'

It was as much as she would say, Leonie realized. The past year had taught her how to hide her feelings, and any tears still shed for Pierre Lacroix were shed in private. She cycled to Frantock School every day to teach her class, and to church every Sunday to play the organ. She took her place in the kitchen when it was Evie's day off and, as soon as spring allowed, she went outside to work in the *potager*. She seemed content, but her face had grown thinner and more reticent, and Leonie wondered how much longer she could bear to be there.

It was a careless remark of Simon's at the dinner table one evening that threatened to destroy the fragile equilibrium in which they lived. Conversation had ground to a halt, and he'd cast around for something they *could* talk about.

'So Pierre Lacroix's book *has* seen the light of day,' he said cheerfully. 'Our French friend must have got down to some serious work on it after he left here.' He met his grandmother's pained glance and realized too late that he'd chosen the wrong thing to mention. 'Evie asked me to fix the window catch in your bedroom, Grand'mère – I couldn't help noticing the book on your desk, that's all.'

'You didn't tell me,' Jenni said in a stifled voice.

'It only came this morning,' Leonie explained as calmly as she could. 'Pierre has been kind enough to dedicate the book to me. I was going to show it to you later on.'

Feeling that Alice was being left out of the conversation, Ned started to explain. 'The book is about the Free Frenchmen who volunteered to come to this country during the war. Mama's family home in London at the time became a meeting place for them, and the author came to talk to her about the men she knew. He liked Frantock enough to stay here for a while.'

Bored with the subject, Alice gave a little

shrug. 'Isn't it time people stopped raking over the ashes of what's better forgotten? Do we have to keep being reminded that dreadful things happened?'

'History is *not* better forgotten,' Leonie pointed out. 'If the human race weren't as insanely stupid as it is we might even learn from it.'

Alice's smile, dismissive of such an elderly, pathetic view, propelled Jenni fiercely into the argument. 'Pierre's object in writing the book was to ensure that at least history is correct – not biased and not leaving out chunks of the truth. If that's what you call raking over the ashes I hope to heaven that more people do it, that's all.' Then she turned her flushed face towards Leonie. 'It's a lovely mild evening, and I want to show you something in the *potager*. Let's take a stroll outside.'

When they'd left the room Simon broke the silence at the table. 'I shouldn't have mentioned the bloody book at all – I'm sorry,' he said to Ned. 'But we didn't seem to be finding anything else to talk about.'

Which only, his father reflected sadly, made bad worse. But Alice smiled at Simon. 'Such a fuss about nothing, don't you think? I suspect that the Frenchman was attractive and very willing to be admired while he was here! Poor Jenni ... she seems not to have got over him yet. It's time she found someone here who might be more available.'

Ned frowned, not so much at what had been said as at the spirit in which Alice had spoken. 'They became very good friends, Jenni and Pierre,' he said quietly, 'but something happened to send him back to France. We were all sorry ... we liked him very much.'

'Poor Jenni,' Alice said again. She looked at her husband with apparently sincere sadness in her face now. 'She should go away, I think ... Staying here she's simply reminded of how happy she was when he was around.' Then she turned to Simon. 'I'm *glad* you mentioned the book. I couldn't understand Jenni at all ... could never feel I was getting close to her. It's a relief to know that it's this man she's unhappy about; I was afraid it was me.'

Ned hesitated for a moment. 'My darling, you still don't fully understand,' he said gently. 'Jenni stays here for her grandmother's sake. However hard it is for her she'll not leave while she thinks Leonie needs her. Our daughter has a very constant heart.'

He didn't intend it as a reproof, and it didn't occur to him that it might have sounded like one until he saw the expression on his wife's face. 'Here's something else you'll have to explain to me,' Alice suggested sweetly. 'Must it be Jenni that your mother needs? Can't *we* take sufficient care of her?'

Ned faintly shook his head at Simon, who, trying to be helpful, was likely to suggest that his sister most certainly thought of Leonie as the mother who had brought them up.

Ned's hand reached out to cover Alice's lying on the table. 'Let's forget about the past, shall we? It's the last we'll hear of Pierre

Lacroix, and one of these days Jenni will realize that she no longer thinks of him. Then the two of you will become the friends you ought to be.'

Alice produced for him the smile that still made his heartbeats quicken, and agreed that it was only a matter of patience and time.

Twenty-Three

The inside cover of Pierre's *The Forgotten Men* showed a photograph of him. Jenni sat looking at it for a long time. She'd seen him in her mind a thousand times without remembering the man pictured in front of her now. Had that frosting of silver in his dark hair been there before, and the deeply carved lines from nostrils to mouth? Was it anger or frustration or grief that made him look older than he was?

This sombre Pierre Lacroix was not the man who'd happily climbed Glastonbury Tor with her one day, or laughed until he cried when, asked to jump over a very small hedge, the elderly mare he was bestride had simply turned and shaken her grizzled head.

She read the book, and then immediately read it again. Eloquently written in French, she hoped its translation into English was being done with equal care. There was generous mention of Christine Harcourt's wartime hospitality, and a moving tribute to Luc Gosselin and the men like him that Jenni supposed had reduced her grandmother to tears.

'Pierre was right,' she said when she handed

the book back to Leonie. 'The story needed telling. Maybe we and the French will understand each other better as a result.'

'He sent the book to me because of the dedication,' Leonie tried to explain.

'Of course ... it was the right thing to have done,' said Jenni gravely.

'An even better thing will be to make his mother read it. Then she might begin to understand how Emile Gosselin and others like him betrayed what Luc gave his life for.'

Jenni nodded, still unable to talk about Jeanne Lacroix. 'I suppose you'll write and thank Pierre for the book – presumably a letter to the Sorbonne will still find him. I don't know where he lives.' She hesitated before going on. 'It's odd, but I realize I've never asked you whether my father and Simon know about the suitcase.'

Leonie considered the question for a moment. The answer was simple enough, but the reason for it seemed harder to explain. 'They haven't seen the diary – it wouldn't have been of interest to a man – and as for the suitcase I suppose there seemed no point in mentioning something that didn't belong to me. There still doesn't, especially now we know about the drawings. For me they're covered in the blood of people I loved. I'd burn them rather than have anyone in my family or in Pierre's see them as a commodity to sell.'

'Someone reasonably might,' Jenni pointed out, 'who hadn't read the diary. Will you consider showing it to Father now?'

Leonie's firm shake of the head was answer enough. 'No, my dear, I won't. A man shouldn't be asked to keep a secret from his wife, and I would need his promise not to tell Alice. We know what she thinks of past history – something better relegated to the scrapheap.'

She frowned over what Jenni had said. 'You're right – the diary and the suitcase must stay together. Neither of them is mentioned in my will, of course, but the diary you already have, and *you* must have the suitcase, too. Then there'll be no question about it when I die because no one else here knows of its existence.' Her frown faded into a relaxed smile. 'I'm glad that's settled – it's been a worry to me.'

Jenni didn't answer, but from her expression Leonie made a guess at what she was thinking. 'I know, dear girl – now I'm asking *you* to keep a secret instead. You must say if you think it's too unfair a burden.'

Jenni brushed the burden away with a wave of her hands. 'I was thinking something else altogether – how sad it is that we don't know my mother well enough to be sure that we can trust her not to see the drawings as something to sell.' Then she managed to smile at her grandmother. 'I'll hide the suitcase in *my* cupboard, Gran, and then we'll forget about it for at least another ten years!'

Leonie agreed to this and chose not to say that in the fraught atmosphere in which they now lived, ten years was too long to expect her to survive.

The truth of it was brought home to her soon afterwards when Alice insisted on driving her into Frantock to keep an appointment with the dentist. Before starting the car on their way home from the surgery Alice turned to look at her passenger's set face.

'Poor *Maman*! Was it a very unpleasant half-hour?' she asked with a sympathetic smile.

The French word, copied from Ned, to whom it had been taught as a child, sounded bogus coming from an American woman of forty-five, but, on her best behaviour, Leonie forbade herself to say so.

'Half a minute is unpleasant enough for me,' she admitted instead. 'I've always hated going to the dentist – the result of a recurring childhood nightmare that involved having teeth pulled out without an anaesthetic!'

It was true, but she knew the real cause of her distress was the sight of the house across the street. What had been Adam's beloved book shop was being gutted by its new owners. Mary Rushton, now old like herself, had come to the farm to apologize for what she, as much as Leonie, considered to be heartbreaking vandalism.

'Those lovely old shelves being ripped out,' she'd said, on the verge of tears. 'They never admitted that they were going to do that, Leonie. In fact they let me believe that they intended to keep the book shop. When they finally said they were going to turn it into a new dining room I'm afraid I accused them of a deliberate deception. They didn't seem to mind – just smiled pityingly at me. I was a stupid old creature who didn't understand how business is done these days. It's true, of course, but one doesn't like to have one's nose rubbed in the fact, so to speak!'

Leonie had to smile at the phrase on her old friend's lips, but agreed that people of their generation *were* now regarded as a dying, if not quite dead, weight on the young, holding back a brave new world they didn't like or understand.

Recalled to the present moment, Leonie put the memory of that conversation aside and gestured at the cottage in which her married life had begun. 'I expect you'll think I'm raking up dead ashes again, but it hurts to see a place you've loved pass into the hands of people who want to do something different to it. Mary Rushton is upset that she didn't guess what was going to happen.'

'I remember her,' Alice said. 'She seemed old even then, but she couldn't have been. What has happened to her?'

'She's gone to live with her younger brother and his wife.'

'As an elderly spinster I expect she considers herself lucky – provided she gets on with her sister-in-law, of course,' Alice commented.

Spinsters, Leonie realized, were one step lower than elderly widows in Alice's scale of nuisances. They must be grateful for any mercy, however small, that came their way. But she still schooled her tongue and merely answered the question she'd been asked.

'Mary Rushton would get on with anyone except the devil. Unlike me, she has a gentle soul.' But the woman suddenly in her mind now was her granddaughter, not Mary, and, please God, not destined to be another lonely spinster. Alice's next remark confirmed that she had made the same connection.

'Don't you think, *Maman*, that we should do something about Jenni? If there's no man here capable of helping her to forget that tiresome Frenchman, we shall have to persuade her to spread her wings. There's a great deal more to the world than Frantock, or even Somerset.'

The road they were driving along was empty, and Alice could safely turn and glance at her passenger before she went on.

'Ned and Simon explained about Pierre Lacroix, but now let's face the truth. Jenni is venting her resentment with him against me, because I'm here and he isn't. Ned insists that she stays because of you, but what she's really doing is reminding me all the time that *you* brought her up, not me! I understand, of course, but it's cruel all the same. That was then, this is now.'

Leonie considered this speech – deliberately timed, she felt sure – knowing that what had just been said could easily be true. Maybe Jenni was doing exactly what her mother accused her of. And there was the added possibility that her parents' obviously reignited love affair was rubbing salt in the wound of her own lost happiness. Desire fulfilled was apparent each time they looked or smiled at each other. She was still trying to dredge up something to say out of the confusion in her mind when Alice spoke again.

'I can't help Jenni, much as I want to – she would ignore anything I said. But she listens to you. Please say that what she needs is to go away, make a fresh start somewhere not in Frantock. It's absurd for her to be anxious about you when Ned and I are here to take care of you.'

It sounded so right and reasonable that Leonie found herself trapped for once in a feeling of uncertainty and helplessness. What if she, and even more so Jenni, were wrong about Alice Vaux? What if instinct, relied on for so long, couldn't be trusted any more? She hadn't found an answer when Alice spoke yet again.

'*Chère maman* – I call you that because Ned does! – my husband and my son both love me, and even you, I think, begin at least to like me. It's only Jenni who refuses to give in and makes life so uncomfortable for the rest of us. Can you not explain to her that if she isn't happy here *she* must be the one to leave?'

Her voice sounded sincere, and her eyes were pleading. Leonie might almost have been convinced, but she was suddenly reminded of something Ned had let drop, probably without meaning to. The French doctor who'd sent her away from the Sudan hadn't been convinced, because a woman had protested to him too much, just as she was doing now.

At last Leonie knew what to say. 'It's true that I'm concerned about my granddaughter, but you mustn't overrate my powers of persuasion. Jenni will stay or leave according to some decision that she makes for herself. If her stubborn heart believes that I need her to be here, nothing that I or Ned or you can say – short of telling her to go – will change what she decides to do. Our only hope of a peaceful life in future lies in my convincing her that I can manage perfectly well without her.'

'But you've just admitted that whatever you say will make no difference,' Alice objected with a note of genuine frustration in her voice.

It was Leonie's turn to smile. 'I shan't *say* anything. I shall have to find something to do instead, and I believe I can. Be patient, though, it will take a little time.'

Aware that the conversation was better left there, Alice returned her mother-in-law's smile, and then concentrated on turning the car under the archway of the farm, into the yard. All would yet be well, she told herself. A little patience was what was needed.

Rewarded for a dismal winter by a spell of fine spring weather, Jenni spent most of her time in the *potager* – it was the busiest couple of months of the year, with the ground empty of winter crops to be re-dug and planted. Engrossed in plans to reshape some of the beds, she was slower than she might have been to notice a change in her grandmother. Leonie listened to her description of the new layout, nodded and sometimes made an alternative suggestion, but all the time Jenni was aware that only half her mind was on what they were discussing – the old eager sharing of ideas was no longer there.

'Gran dear, you look tired, and I don't think you're enjoying this stroll very much,' she said one afternoon when they were out in the garden together. 'You'd tell me, wouldn't you, if you weren't feeling well?'

'I feel exactly as I should,' Leonie said sharply, 'but if you keep squinting at me to make sure I haven't collapsed I shan't come out walking with you in future.'

Then she smiled at the girl beside her, apologizing for her ill-temper. 'My dear, I swallow the battery of pills that idiot doctor prescribes, I do very little in the way of anything useful, and at this rate I shall live to be a hundred – which I don't very much want to do. Does that satisfy you?'

Jenni bent to kiss her cheek. 'Sorry ... I should know better than to fuss over my redoubtable Grand'mère! It's just that I can't spare you ... so you have to be here for a long time yet.'

Leonie promised solemnly to do her best and the subject wasn't raised again between them. Instead, Jenni took her faint sense of unease to her father and asked *him* to tackle Leonie. Finding her still working in the garden one evening when he returned from his check that all was as it should be outside, he came to where she was cleaning tools before putting them away.

'You work too hard ... spend too much time out here alone. Does it have to be like that?' he asked sadly.

'It's what I like doing,' she insisted. 'A garden is a lovesome thing, God works, and so do I! Thirty small children can make a fair amount of noise given the chance. After a day in a hot classroom it's lovely to be out here in the coolness and the quiet.'

Ned nodded, accepting that what she said was true and knowing that what else they might say was better left unsaid.

'I tackled Leonie, by the way,' he commented instead, 'and got the verbal equivalent of a box on the ears that I expected! She was *not* going to be checked up at the surgery, and no, she wouldn't swallow yet more pills to enrich the pharmaceutical industry still further. All she needed was to be left in peace and not be badgered to death by her son and granddaughter.'

'It sounds just like her,' Jenni had to agree with a rueful smile. 'I *know* she's getting more frail and tired, but there's nothing wrong with her mind or her ability to choose what she will or won't do. She still misses Grandfather Vaux very much – in fact, I suspect that all the people she loved long ago seem almost more important to her now than we do. Perhaps the same thing will happen to us when we grow old.' It was said with a note of sadness that made Ned reach out and clasp his daughter's grubby hand.

'I'm sorry, Jenni love,' he said quietly, 'sorry for whatever it was that went wrong between you and Pierre ... sorry for what stops things going right between you and your mother. I don't know what to do to change that.'

She turned to smile at him in the gathering dusk, thinking how easy it was for them to talk out there, and how difficult inside a house that now seemed to belong to Alice.

'There's nothing to do; we can manage well enough as we are.' Then she pointed up at the darkening sky. 'Look, there's a new moon just rising. Turn your silver over, and I'll bow to her three times. That ought to bring us good luck!' Then, when these precautionary measures had been taken, they went indoors together.

Jenni only remembered that pious hope a few weeks later when she knocked at her grandmother's door one morning and got no answering '*Viens, petite*'. A sharper knock and still no reply made her go in. Leonie was apparently sleeping peacefully, but Jenni's desperate fingers at her wrist could find no pulse, and her grandmother's hand felt very cold. It seemed impossible that so vital a human being should no longer be there, but Leonie's still face confirmed the truth that she was dead.

Afterwards, all that had to be done was done. The doctor certified that his elderly patient had died of heart failure – not unexpectedly, he pointed out kindly to Ned and Jenni. She could have slipped away any time, and surely this was how she would have wished for it to happen, in her sleep. The funeral, intended to be private but in fact quietly attended by most of Frantock, took place a week later. Jenni chose the music that was played and sung, and made the service a celebration of Leonie's life, not a mournful wake for her death. Ned and Simon read the lessons and, helped by Jimmy and his son, carried her afterwards to join Adam and her father and daughter in the churchyard.

It took days for Jenni to steel herself to go back into her grandmother's room, but there was work to be done there – clothes to be sent to Oxfam and a lifetime's collection of books and trinkets to be dealt with. When this was done she opened, almost by chance, the drawer of the bedside table and made a discovery that turned her heart sick and cold – the bottles neatly placed there were still full of the pills they'd believed her to be taking. Beneath them lay an envelope addressed simply to Jenni in Leonie's immediately recognizable hand – Adam Vaux had taught her to use the Greek way of writing the letter 'e'.

Before facing what was inside, Jenni wrapped the bottles in a bag and took them to her own room. Then she opened the letter dated several weeks earlier.

Dearest Child,
Another secret for you to keep, I'm afraid – but it will be safe because I know you won't allow anyone else to clear out my bedroom. I don't know when that will be, but I must write this while I still can so that you understand. People are thought to end their lives in despair or mental confusion – I forbid you to include me in that number. Our dear doctor strives to keep me alive with pills and potions, but I choose to make my adieu while I can still do it with dignity. There is nothing left here for me to do, and I am tired of being without Adam.

So, Jenni love, weep no sad tears for me. Think of your own life instead. If you still love Pierre, as I believe you do, don't let that wicked old woman stand in the way of happiness. The bitterness between us must die with her and me. I can't guess what you'll do with the suitcase, but whatever you do will be right.

Now, lose the stupid pills, please, that I can't get rid of, and destroy this letter.

Á bientôt, petite,
Grand'mère

Jenni let the letter fall in her lap and sat for a long time staring out of the window. For the moment her only coherent thought was that Leonie had done things her way, and been true to herself to the end. No humiliating infirmity, no descent into mindless senility for Leonie Vaux.

But there was something else to be considered as well, and Jenni finally made herself confront the idea that *she* had been, indirectly at least, involved in her grandmother's death. She'd insisted often enough that she was content with her life as it was, but Leonie had probably guessed both the truth of her unhappiness at home and the reason for her refusal to leave. It was tempting to blame someone else – Alice, of course – who had wanted to get rid of her, someone who had pointed out to Leonie the sense of obligation that kept her granddaughter at home. But there was no comfort there. Alice had been rather proud of her formidable mother-in-law; *she* would have done nothing to persuade her in the direction of suicide.

Don't weep, Leonie had written, but it was one instruction that suddenly couldn't be obeyed. One moment unnaturally calm, the next she was adrift on a sea of tears, alone on it, with no one to share her sadness.

At last, exhausted and shivering, she wiped her wet face and remembered what she had to do – destroy the letter and take the pill bottles to the dustbin. As Leonie had planned it, so must her death always remain – a dignified and entirely natural ending to her life. With the bag of bottles safely buried, she turned to go back into the house and met her father crossing the yard. He stared at her for a moment, with his hands on her shoulders so that she had to look at him.

'I know how much you miss her, Jenni love, but is there something else wrong as well?'

The gentle enquiry almost made her weep again, but she shook her head. 'Nothing's wrong ... everything is as it should be now,' she said calmly. Could she hear Leonie murmuring *'très bien, petite'*? Yes, she rather thought she could.

Twenty-Four

The school summer term came to an end and, with it, Jenni's feeling of uncertainty. She would stay with the children of Frantock, who'd learned to trust their teacher, but she'd find somewhere else to live – a small cottage nearby, with some land attached; she couldn't be without a garden. She would visit the farm, of course, and stay in close touch with her father and Simon. But they would understand that it was time for her to establish herself as an independent woman. She must accept the freedom that Leonie, in dying, had given her.

The summer holiday stretched in front of her. Six weeks might seem a long time but it wasn't too much for all she'd set herself to do. She must dispose of the suitcase, which seemed to hang like a burden round her neck, but there was something else to do before she parted with the drawings. Jeanne Lacroix had to be found and told what was going to happen to them; she must be made to understand *why* it was happening.

All she knew of Pierre's mother was that her home was in Provence, but that *département* stretched across almost the entire southern part of France. Jenni realized now how reticent Pierre had been in talking about himself and his family. All she even knew of *him* was his connection with the Sorbonne. She could try to reach him there and ask for the address in Provence, but her heart and mind were set against it. There'd been no message for her when his book had arrived, and she knew that Leonie's letter of thanks had not been answered. He probably hadn't sent the book at all – it had been merely a courtesy on the part of the publishers.

Something he'd once said, though, hovered at the back of her mind, tantalizing, but refusing to solidify into a fact she could get hold of. Tired of trying to pin down that elusive memory, she picked up his book, willing the image of him inside to give her the clue she needed. At once she was aware of the smell peculiar to a book that was new, compounded of ink, the paper it was printed on, and the glossy material of the jacket. Then, as that thought came into her mind, she grasped the connection she'd been trying to make – in one conversation or another Pierre had mentioned his familiarity with the centre of France's perfume industry, Grasse. It was, at least, a destination to head for in searching for his mother.

She set about making arrangements for the journey, and then broke the news to her father that she was going to visit France.

'The long holiday you need so badly, I hope,' Ned said at once. 'But it's better shared with a companion. I'd spare Simon, my dear, if you'd like him to go with you.'

She smiled gratefully but shook her head. 'It's not exactly a holiday – there was something left undone between *Grand'mère* and the Gosselin family that I must finish now.'

Ned stared at her for a moment, thinking how dear she was and yet for the moment so out of reach. 'Why do I get the feeling that Pierre Lacroix has something to do with this?' he ventured.

'Probably because he's related to the Gosselin family through his mother,' Jenni answered gently. 'But what I have to do doesn't involve him – it concerns Jeanne Lacroix, if only I can find her.' She hesitated a moment, knowing that there was something more to say. 'When I get back from France I'm going to look for a little house that I can buy. Don't be hurt, please – it's high time I found a home of my own.'

She expected her father to look sad, and he did, but equally she knew he was too honest a man to pretend not to know why she was leaving.

'You won't go far,' he said simply, 'you'll always be in touch?'

'Of course.' Her smile reassured him, and then she kissed him goodbye because she would set off early the following morning while he was still busy with the milking.

By noon the following day she was in Paris. The métro took her from the Gare du Nord to the terminus for the trains to the south, where she locked the suitcase safely away in a *consigne*, and then waited for the train that would take her to Grasse.

A town of the Midi, it turned out to be far hotter than Somerset, or even Paris. It was dramatically sited, beautifully flower-decked and did indeed smell of perfume. She would have liked to be just a normal visitor, free to roam about and enjoy it, but the reason she was there drove her to the main Bureau de Poste and the telephone directories she would find there. With her heart beating too fast, she ran her finger down the lists of names, and gave a little sigh of relief when she found what she was looking for – Madame Jeanne Lacroix lived in the Rue des Lilas and her street map indicated that it was on the outskirts of the town, less than a mile from where she was.

But it was growing late; she must find something to eat and a bed to sleep in. Tomorrow would be time enough to look for Jeanne Lacroix.

The next morning she hesitated over whether or not to telephone and ask to be allowed to call. Better not, she finally decided. If she was already on the doorstep her quarry would find it hard to refuse to let her in.

Remembering that Pierre had said his mother lived in a provençal *mas*, much like the farmhouse at home, the tree-lined street came as a surprise, but she could see how the surrounding fields had gradually been built on. The wide door of the house stood open and, even as she hesitated, an elderly woman came out and saw the stranger standing at her gate.

'I don't know you,' she said truculently, 'why do you stare at my house?'

'I came to see *you*, Madame Lacroix,' Jenni answered, also in French. 'Perhaps you remember my name – Jennifer Vaux. I think your son has spoken to you about me.'

Dark eyes glared at her out of a brown, lined face. 'Then you're the granddaughter of Leonie Harcourt, and I have nothing to say to you.'

They'd have been a good match for each other, Jenni reflected sadly – each as stubbornly unforgiving as the other. But she'd come too far to be refused now.

'Please, *madame*, I need to talk to you,' she insisted firmly. 'My grandmother died three weeks ago. I'm here to settle what was left unfinished between you.'

The woman in front of her gave a little shrug. 'Then you'd better come in, but I shan't make you welcome.'

She turned and walked back inside the house, and Jenni followed her into a wide hall that seemed too cool and dark after the hot brilliance outside. The kitchen that it led to was less gloomy, but all, it seemed, that an unwelcome visitor was entitled to be shown to.

Settled at the table, Jeanne Lacroix opened

the discussion at once. 'I assume you've come about the drawings – have you brought them with you? They belong to me now that both my brothers are dead.'

She was a strong, thickset woman despite her age, and Jenni realized that it was her intention to sound intimidating. Instead of healing a still-running sore, their conversation now seemed more likely to make it worse than better.

But she refused to be flustered by the hostility, and managed to speak quietly. 'The drawings were given to your brother, Luc. He in turn gave them to my grandmother to keep because, had he survived the war, they would have married. She had his child soon after he returned to France, but the baby died two days after it was born.'

Leonie and her daughter were swept aside by a wave of Jeanne Lacroix's hand. 'My father had no right to give the drawings to Luc – they were family property. They still are.'

Jenni took a deep breath and battled on. 'I didn't come here to argue with you, only to let you know what is going to happen to the drawings – which are not yours any more than they are mine. They're in Paris at the moment and that is where they will stay – at the Musée Picasso. The bequest will be made in the name of Luc Gosselin.'

Jeanne Lacroix's heavy hand moved again, and this time Jenni half expected to feel its weight against her face. But it was banged down instead with a force that made the table shake.

'I don't believe you,' she stormed. 'You think I'm a fool to be taken in by such a story? You'll keep them yourself and make a fortune out of selling them. You English, you say one thing and do another. No wonder we can never trust you. I suppose your grandmother reckoned that a child would mean Luc had to go back to her after the war, then she'd be sure of a share in the value of the drawings.'

For the first time in her life Jenni felt an almost overwhelming urge to strike another human being. She forced her hands to relax from the tight balls they were screwing themselves into, and then faced the malevolent old woman across the table.

'Leonie Harcourt, as she was then, was eighteen when her child was born. She waited for Luc until long after the war was over, and then – finally certain that he was dead – married my grandfather. The suitcase Luc had left with her remained locked, as it still is. She didn't even know what it contained until your son told us about the drawings. Now, have you any more insults to hurl at my grandmother's memory before I leave?'

There was a long moment of silence in the room, broken only by the insistent tick of a pendulum clock hanging on the wall. At last Jeanne Lacroix spoke again, the anger in her voice now replaced by a kind of bitter despair.

'Even my clever son is a fool at times. He

should never have mentioned the drawings, but I expect your grandmother disarmed him – she was attractive to men, I remember.'

Her eyes examined Jenni now – not beautiful, but something about her had snared Pierre. She was more delicately built than most Provençal girls, and her voice was soft, but in her own quiet way she'd been irritatingly in charge of the conversation. It was certain that she knew about the Bernards – Leonie would have told her. But nothing gave her the right to judge what had happened all those years ago.

The pain of it was still in Jeanne Lacroix's voice when she suddenly burst out, 'You know things about my brother Emile and me that you don't like. But you *can't* know what it was like to be young and afraid when the Germans marched into Paris. No one who didn't live through those years can understand how hard it was just to survive. You blame us for what we did, but you have no right to.'

'I'm not judging you,' Jenni insisted gently. 'But whether you believe me or not the drawings your father left to Luc are being given to the Musée Picasso – it's where they belong now.'

Ravaged by resentment now, rather than disbelief, the other woman cast around for something that might wound her opponent.

'I expect you came hoping to see my son. Well, you won't, because he's not here in France at all.'

'I had no intention of even looking for him,' Jenni replied. 'Too much past hurt and bitterness got in the way of our friendship – I suppose you could say it was another casualty of the war, small to anyone but us.'

The sadness in her voice trapped Jeanne Lacroix into revealing a grief of her own. 'My son left without coming to see me because I made him very angry. Perhaps he won't ever come again – my only son. I have your grandmother to thank for that.'

Her conviction that only she still suffered would never change, Jenni realized, but instead of being intimidating, she was now just an old woman who looked desolate and lonely.

'Pierre *will* come back,' Jenni said with as much firmness as she could, deciding not to add that holding on to anger for years was something women seemed better at than men. 'Thank you for talking to me – now I must get back to the station.'

She felt the weight of loneliness in the house and thought how sad it was. Jeanne Lacroix had the look of someone who chose to spend a lot of time out-of-doors, growing things. They could have had *that* in common, as well as love for her son.

But she got up to leave and then, in a gesture that astonished her when she thought about it afterwards, suddenly leaned over to kiss the old woman's cheek, before letting herself out of the house.

* * *

She was back in Paris by late afternoon, looking for somewhere to stay the night. The small, back-street hotel that she found was homely and comfortable enough to persuade her to spend a few more days there. Once the suitcase had been handed over she could become just another summer visitor – take a river trip on a *bâteau-mouche*, go to Versailles, window-shop in the Rue de la Paix, and eat in Left-Bank bistros like the one in which Roland Gosselin had befriended a struggling artist all those years ago.

The following morning she found the museum easily enough, housed in an old hotel. A severe-looking receptionist looked unimpressed when a young *Anglaise* clutching a shabby suitcase asked to see the director.

'Without an appointment that's not possible – he is a very busy man,' she announced with pride. 'I could perhaps see if his assistant is free.'

Jenni smiled pleasantly but sounded firm. 'I can't stay in Paris long enough to make appointments, and my story is too complicated to tell more than once. Please be kind enough to ask whether he could see me.'

The English, the receptionist's shrug said clearly, were all the same – still thinking that they ruled the world. But she spoke rapidly into the intercom on her desk, and a moment or two later a middle-aged, bearded man walked into the hall.

'Good morning! You have a story to tell me,

I understand, and – unusually for an English person – you will tell it to me in French! Come this way, please.'

She was led into a pleasant room, half office, half scholar's study, and invited to sit down.

His manner, though polite, didn't hide a faint hint that French civility was being worn thin by a visitor who could have nothing of interest to say. Jenni began by surprising him; she leaned across the desk and handed him her suitcase.

'It's always been locked and I don't have a key, so I can't promise that I know what's inside,' she explained quickly. 'But I've been told that there are a dozen sketches signed by Pablo Picasso. If there aren't, there's no point in bothering you with my story. Could you get the suitcase open and find out?'

For a young woman she was commendably direct and sensible, he thought, even if almost certainly mistaken about what the suitcase contained. He took a small tool from his desk drawer, fiddled with the lock, and finally got it to yield. 'I was a juvenile criminal,' he explained solemnly, 'long since reformed!'

Liking him better for this unexpected glimmer of humour, Jenni watched, heart in mouth, while he lifted out the sheets of paper. One glance at them made him gather them together carefully and spread them out on the table behind his desk.

They were a mixed bag of rough drawings in pencil, crayon, charcoal – anything that had come to the artist's hand. The sketches had obviously been tossed off at lightening speed by a young man who was just discovering what he could do. But each line brought to vivid life the people who had been his companions in the bistro – a waif-like girl caught smiling at whoever her companion had been, a lonely sad-faced student, a rotund priest, and young, laughing children who, Jenni supposed, might have been Roland Gosselin's own sons and daughter.

At last she looked away from them and stared at the silent man beside her. 'Are they genuine? Do I need to tell my story now?'

'I think you do,' he said faintly. 'We'd need to make some tests, of course, but they look entirely authentic to me. Begin your story, please.'

Jenni returned to her chair, took a breath, and plunged in. 'It starts, as you'll have guessed, before the First World War, when Picasso moved to Paris from Spain.' She told the story as briefly as she could, omitting any mention of the Bernards and Leonie's hatred of the Gosselins. At the end of it the director asked the obvious question.

'I understood you to say that Luc Gosselin believed the suitcase to contain only family papers. What made you bring it here?'

Faint colour tinged Jenni's face but she answered calmly. 'Luc's nephew – a history professor called Pierre Lacroix – happened to visit my grandmother for a reason that had nothing to do with the drawings. He knew about them and told us.'

It left out so much that would have made it credible that she wasn't surprised to be asked another, tactfully-phrased question.

'Mam'selle Vaux, you're suggesting making a gift to the museum that is not only breathtakingly exciting but also very generous. You must forgive me for needing proof that it is yours to give! Are there members of the Gosselin family still alive who would dispute your ownership of the drawings?'

'They aren't mine, any more than my grandmother believed they were hers,' she answered firmly. 'They belonged to Luc Gosselin.' She drew out of her bag Leonie's old, leather-bound diary. 'This is my grandmother's account of what happened from the time she met Luc in Paris in 1938. It's too precious and personal to leave with you, but I've marked for you to read the paragraph where she describes Luc handing over the suitcase for her to keep in London while he returns to France as an agent of the Resistance.'

The director read it, and handed the diary back. 'But what of the Gosselin family still alive?'

'Professor Lacroix has no interest in the drawings,' she managed to say. 'His mother, Luc's sister, knows the drawings are going to stay here. I went to see her in Grasse before coming to the museum.'

He stared at her across the desk, aware that there was a good deal more that his reticent

English visitor was minded not to tell him.

'Do I, unfairly, suspect Madame Lacroix of *not* wanting the drawings given away? It would be understandable – they're very valuable!' he suggested with a faint smile.

'She wasn't enchanted with the idea,' Jenni was forced to admit with magnificent understatement. 'The truth is that she and my grandmother disliked each other for a reason that only indirectly touches on the drawings. But the animosity has been kept alive too long. With no one benefiting from Luc's inheritance, perhaps it can now be allowed to die.' She looked across the desk at the man watching her. 'Professor Lacroix, who teaches at the Sorbonne, could confirm all this for you, but he's abroad until the end of the summer, I believe.'

The Director nodded, then made an expansive gesture with his hands. 'We shall make our tests of course, but it seems likely that we have been given a splendid bequest. It will be recorded, as you ask, as the posthumous gift of Roland and Luc Gosselin.' A charming smile suddenly lit his face. 'Mademoiselle Vaux, may we also keep the suitcase? I can't help feeling that after all this time it should stay with the drawings!'

She resisted the temptation to kiss him for the sheer relief of getting rid of it at last, and solemnly assured him that he was welcome to it.

With a disclaimer form signed and her address given, she was conducted personally to the entrance, under the reflective gaze of the receptionist. Then, free to leave, she could walk out into the brilliant morning and choose which of the pleasures on her list she would enjoy first. She felt content now, certain that Leonie would have been happy with what had become of Luc's inheritance.

Twenty-Five

Pierre returned to Paris to find himself bludgeoned by its speed and noise. He'd taken the stress of city life for granted until a short time ago, but over the past few weeks he'd become accustomed to a different world. Speed was reduced to how fast his feet would carry him along the Camino de Santiago, and in place of noise he'd had quietness and solitude and time in which to think. He had some idea now of what it had been like to make the medieval pilgrimage along the route that still stretched from France to Santiago de Compostela in the far north-west corner of Spain.

He'd left Paris consumed by too much emotion – sadness, anger, and regret – knowing that he must cure himself before it was time to return to the routine of university life. The ache of losing Jenni would remain, but he must at least come to terms with his mother before hatred destroyed him as it had destroyed her. During his long and sometimes uncomfortable march across Spain there'd been time enough to understand that she and Emile and others like them had done what they did in order to survive. He had no right to believe that, in their desperate circumstances, he would have behaved differently.

There remained the battle over the drawings and somehow he must convince his mother that they had no claim on them. He would go down and see her before the new term began, and start by making his peace with her.

Then with only one more stage to go before reaching Santiago, he fell heavily on a rough piece of track, gashed his head and ripped his right leg open. A nearby farmer who'd seen him fall drove him to the nearest hospital and, patched and released two days later, he'd stubbornly finished the walk. In the wondrous cathedral at Compostela he received the scallop shell that proclaimed him a pilgrim at the shrine of St James.

But the accident had cost him time he couldn't spare and, back in Paris, there was no hope of fitting in a visit to Grasse before term began. Knowing his mother's hatred of telephone conversations, he wrote to her at length instead. He would spend Christmas with her without fail; then they would heal the hurt they had done to each other and not quarrel again. There was no mention in his letter of the drawings; he knew they must be dealt with when they were face to face. She didn't answer, but he hadn't expected that she would. He needn't worry – her housekeeper's instructions were to telephone him if anything was wrong.

Now he would settle down to work again, doing what he enjoyed most. His students belonged to a younger generation; they spoke a different language among themselves, loved music he couldn't listen to. But he knew that he reached them when he taught. His book had caused much comment, but he was surprised and touched to find them impressed by the young men he'd written about. Courage was still 'cool', apparently.

It wasn't until Christmas was approaching that his usual routine was interrupted by a telephone message asking him to contact the director of the Musée Picasso. A meeting was arranged, and the following evening after the museum had closed he went to keep the appointment.

The director made him welcome, first by pouring wine, and then asking interested questions about the Camino while they drank it.

'But you didn't invite me here to talk about my pilgrimage,' Pierre suggested as soon as he decently could.

'No, I wanted to show you these,' the director said, pointing to the sketches spread out on his table. 'I'm assuming that you can guess how they got here.'

Pierre got up to glance at them and then returned to his chair. 'My assumption is that they belonged to my grandfather, Roland Gosselin. The rest you'll have to explain – I thought they were still hidden in a farmhouse in an English village.'

'They were until a young Englishwoman brought them here during the summer. To jog your memory, Professor, she had beautiful grey eyes and a smile one doesn't forget!'

'You've just described a girl called Jennifer Vaux,' Pierre said unevenly, 'but I still don't understand. Nothing was to happen to the drawings while her grandmother was still alive.'

'Madame Vaux had died some weeks earlier. I'm sorry if that comes as a shock to you.' He poured more wine, then went on quietly. 'We were offered the drawings as a posthumous bequest in the names of Roland and Luc Gosselin. Mademoiselle Vaux told me the bare outline of the story attached to them, and seemed to think that the surviving members of the Gosselin family wouldn't contest such a generous gift. She gave me your name, however, and I needed your confirmation of what she had said.'

'I should have guessed,' Pierre said slowly. 'How like Jenni to have known exactly what to do!' Then he looked at the man watching him. 'Of course I confirm it, on behalf of myself and my mother, even though she doesn't yet know what I've agreed to.'

'I think she does,' the director corrected him. 'Mademoiselle Vaux had been to see her in Grasse before she came here.'

Pierre closed his eyes, imagining that interview. Jenni's distaste for the Gosselin family must now be complete. On a good day his mother could be charming; on a bad day she was capable of being as unpleasant as anyone he'd ever met, and Jenni's arrival would have made it a very bad day. 'Did she say that my mother objected?' he managed to ask.

'Madame Lacroix wasn't given the chance, I suspect. She was merely told what was going to happen!' The director took a sip of wine and then smiled at his visitor. 'I realized that there was very much more to the story than I was being told, but Mademoiselle Vaux assured me that it need be of no concern to us – it was time to bury the past, she said, and I was very content to do that.'

'And so, God knows, am I,' Pierre agreed quietly. 'It all happened sixty years ago, and perhaps this brings the story to an end at last.'

He stood up to take a last look at the sketches, and, standing beside him, the director pointed at the ones of the laughing children. 'I thought they might be Roland Gosselin's own sons and daughter, but my research suggests they weren't born when these children were drawn.'

Pierre certainly saw no resemblance to his mother, and didn't say that if she'd had the habit of laughing as a child, it was something she'd lost long since. Instead he shook hands with the director and was shown out into the damp December evening. But his mind was still on Jenni's visit to Grasse and her likely reception there. Somehow he would have to forgive his mother that she hadn't mentioned it or told him that Leonie was dead.

Jenni's new home was to be a Victorian terraced cottage on the outskirts of Frantock.

'It will "benefit" from improvement, as your estate agent friend, David Chant, rightly says,' she admitted to her father at the farmhouse, 'but it's cheap, it's the right size, the garden is spacious because it's at the end of the row, and it looks out across the lovely Somerset Levels.'

'Let me guess – the improvement is needed because it's a wreck,' Simon suggested.

'Nothing that a few coats of paint won't fix, and kind David says that I can start work before the formalities are completed. He knows I want to move in before term starts.' She smiled hopefully at her brother. '*We* can start work, if you're willing to lend a hand!'

He would have insisted on helping anyway, as he was well aware of the female antagonism – not to be understood by a mere male – that had spoiled their mother's return for Jenni. She needed to escape from the farmhouse.

'Nothing I like better than a little interior decorating,' he agreed, 'and not to be selfish about it, several of our friends will be allowed to share the treat as well! Just lay in a big enough stock of paint and brushes.'

She blew him a kiss and then, at her father's invitation, climbed with him up to the farmhouse attics. Here, furniture from Adam Vaux's Frantock cottage had long been stored, on the good country principle that a need for everything came round again sooner or later. With her choice of furnishings for Willow Cottage made, she brushed her hands free of the dust of ages and smiled at her father.

'It's a great adventure – a home of my own. Simon *will* think it's a wreck at the moment – the old lady who lived there obviously hadn't been able to look after it very well – but it's just waiting to be loved.'

'Who better to take it in hand then?' her father agreed. But he stared at her, regretting with all his heart the need for her to leave. 'You didn't say how the "unfinished business" went in France. I'm assuming you didn't see Pierre while you were there.'

'He was abroad,' Jenni admitted briefly. 'I saw his mother instead, down in the South. She and Grand'mère had a quarrel going back to the war years that I hoped I could finally end. I don't think I succeeded with Madame Lacroix any more than I could have persuaded Grand'mère to change *her* mind, either. Even now the bitterness won't end until Jeanne Lacroix dies.'

'And that's what wrecked your happiness with Pierre?' Ned asked incredulously. 'Dear God, couldn't the pair of you have left these warring old ladies to fight each other?'

Jenni shook her head. 'It was more complicated than you realize. I'd like you – just you, please – to read Grand'mère's diary that she gave me. Then you'll understand. She said it would be of no interest to a man, but I think the real reason for not showing it to you was that she didn't want you to know she loved someone before she met

Grandfather. Read it, please, and then I'll tell you the rest of what I did in Paris.'

Ned nodded, and then risked one more question. 'Leonie was afraid you'd marry into the church out of pity for a lonely man. I assume that *isn't* in your mind, or you wouldn't be buying Willow Cottage – there's more than enough room for two at the vicarage!'

'John Rashleigh did suggest it.' Jenni smiled ruefully at a word that merely sounded like an invitation to go out to tea. 'But Grand'mère was right as usual; it wouldn't have worked out.' She smiled suddenly at her father. 'Don't worry about me. I shall probably measure every other man I meet against Pierre, but Grand'mère thought that about a Frenchman called Luc Gosselin, and ended up most happily married to someone else.'

Ned wiped a smudge of dust off her cheek with gentle fingers, but all he said was, 'Just let me know when you're ready to take delivery of the furniture.'

He gave her back Leonie's diary some days later and asked to be told the rest of the story. Jenni described her visit to Jeanne Lacroix, and the handing-over of the suitcase at the museum.

'Have you heard anything since?' he asked at the end of it.

'A courteous note came from the director, confirming the authenticity of the drawings and saying how grateful they were for them.' She struggled to sound casual about what she said next. 'There was also a brief letter from Pierre. The museum people had been in touch with him and he'd assured them that the gift wouldn't be contested. He was sorry to hear about Grand'mère, of course, and thanked me for going to see his mother – but *that* was just a meaningless politesse; he quite clearly blamed me for upsetting her.'

'Don't *you* now hate Jeanne Lacroix as much as Leonie did?' her father asked. 'You have got reason to, God knows.'

'No, I don't,' Jenni answered slowly. 'I've had time to realize that there are two ways of looking at everything. Emile Lacroix probably believed that the Germans couldn't be beaten and so had to be lived with and it's perfectly true that resistance to them led to cruel reprisals on innocent people. Nothing's ever completely straightforward, is it?' She hesitated for a moment. 'Now that you know what I gave away to the museum, can you think of anything else I should have done with the drawings?' She waited anxiously for what he would say, but felt reassured when she saw him smile.

'My dear, if you mean should we have sold them and made a killing for ourselves, the answer is a very definite no. If you mean should they have been given to Luc's sister, my answer is *still* no; she has no claim on them.'

'That's all right then,' Jenni said gratefully. Then she brought up a happier subject. 'Shall we forget it now? Christmas is nearly here ...

something to celebrate instead.'

Even missing Leonie as they did, it *was* a happy time. With Jenni established in her own home, Alice could make her welcome as a visitor, and if it was an odd sort of relationship between mother and daughter, at least it worked on those terms and kept the atmosphere in the house peaceful.

Jenni was back in her own cottage, but not yet back at school after the holiday, when her telephone rang one morning. It took a moment to identify the hoarse voice shouting in French at the other end of the line.

'It is Jeanne Lacroix here in Paris ... can you hear me? I hate this telephone.' Assured that she could be heard, she hurried on. 'My son is ill – that's why I'm calling. He's *very* ill, you understand.'

'I *don't* understand,' Jenni shouted herself into the telephone. 'Tell me, please – why is he ill?'

'He had an accident in Spain; the leg healed, but the poison is still inside, and it's stronger than the drugs they're giving him.' Her voice quavered on the edge of tears. 'I ask *you* to come because it might help him ... he's not fighting, the doctors say.'

Jenni asked as calmly as she could for the address of the hospital, and said that she would get there as soon as it was possible. A silence at the other end suggested that Pierre's mother had simply hung up, and Jenni replaced a telephone she'd been gripping so hard that the blood had been driven from her hand. Then she lifted it again and rang the farm – she needed a lift urgently to Bristol Airport, she told Evie, who answered the call.

'Harry's here – he'll come straight over,' she said at once. 'What else do you need – money?'

'Some more pounds that I can change would help,' Jenni agreed. 'Thanks, Evie dear – tell my father for me, please.'

By the time she'd packed an overnight bag, changed into travel clothes and locked up the cottage, Harry was at the door. In less than an hour they were at the airport and she was in Paris by mid-afternoon. Obsessed by anxiety to get there, her mind had only focussed on the needs of the journey, but in the taxi to the hospital she understood the extremity of Jeanne Lacroix's despair in asking her to come. Only the fear that Pierre was going to die could have overridden an implacable woman's dislike of Leonie's granddaughter.

She was waiting in the hall when Jenni walked in – a now-countrified figure in the inevitable black of a southern widow – and her drawn face warned Jenni to expect that Pierre might already have died. But she grabbed Jenni's hand and muttered, 'Tell Pierre he must fight – the doctors say he's not trying to help them. It's Room 25 you want, on the second floor.'

Impatient of the lift, Jenni ran up the stairs, asked a nurse if she might see Pierre Lacroix, and was led to his door. The fading Januaryafternoon light showed her the intravenous tube dripping something into his arm, and his gaunt face shadowed by several days' growth of beard. His eyes were closed and he didn't hear her walk towards him. She hadn't seen him for more than a year, and it seemed longer than a lifetime.

His hot hand rested on the counterpane and she grasped it in her cold one, while she forced her voice to speak the only words she could manage.

'C'est moi, Pierre.'

The faint hum of a machine by his bed was the only other sound in the room, then his fingers suddenly clutched hers. At least there was still strength left in his hand. Eyes open now, he slowly pulled her hand towards his mouth.

'I'm not dreaming,' he murmured, 'you *are* here. I don't believe it, but somehow it seems to be true.'

'I've come to tell you to start fighting – you haven't been trying hard enough.'

The faint smile that touched his mouth made him familiar again. 'You sounded just like Leonie then! If you promise not to leave I'd like to sleep now. Will you be here when I wake up?'

'I'm going downstairs to persuade your mother to get some rest, because she looks even more tired than you do, then I shall come back.'

She found Jeanne still sitting where she'd left her, deaf and blind to the comings and goings around her.

'Pierre wanted to sleep,' she explained gently, 'and you must rest as well. Can I find you a room at a hotel?'

'I have one – it's just across the road, Les Marronniers it's called. I told them to expect you tonight as well.'

Jenni thanked her for the unexpected kindness, and insisted that she go and lie down, and then eat some dinner. 'I'll see you later on, madame. Only one of us needs to be here.' She waited for her to agree to leave, and then went back to Pierre's room. He was asleep now, and she sat down to wait.

Twenty-Six

Two days later anxiety was at an end; the doctor confirmed that Pierre's high fever was abating, the haematoma had been dealt with, and the lethal skin infection was finally coming under control. He wasn't going to die, and there was no more risk of having to amputate his right leg.

In the time spent with him Jenni had heard about the pilgrimage to Santiago and the fall that had caused the injury. But he hadn't explained why his long trudge along the Camino had been necessary, and nothing had been said about the inheritance she had given away.

Jenni had talked in turn about her grandmother's death and – more easily – about her new home at Willow Cottage; but she, equally, hadn't explained why *that* had been necessary.

They were at ease with one another as they always had been, but the moment of joyous recognition when she'd first walked into his room hadn't been repeated. They were merely friends meeting after a long time; there was some catching up to do, but no going forward. What had separated them was still there – would always be there, she realized. She could go home now.

She broached the idea of leaving with Jeanne Lacroix first, and wasn't surprised to see the Frenchwoman smile with unexpected warmth. With anxiety over, it was time to forget that Leonie Vaux's granddaughter was there at her urgent request. Pierre was mending, and it was safe to remember that the *Anglaise* had wilfully given away a fortune that rightly belonged to them.

'No doubt you are anxious to go home,' she agreed graciously. 'I shall stay, of course, until my son is well enough to travel. He will get strong again in the warmth of Provence.' She hesitated for a moment, and the dreadful thought occurred to Jenni that she was about to be offered back the cost of her visit, but habitual meanness got the better of Jeanne Lacroix and she merely smiled a goodbye instead.

Given her permission to leave, Jenni booked a flight home then steeled herself for one last visit to the hospital. She'd practised how the conversation would go; if she died in the attempt, she would smile and keep on smiling, and never for one moment hint that this must be her final meeting with Pierre because she couldn't survive walking away from him again.

It was far easier than she expected because he'd already been primed about her going. 'My mother says you're anxious to get back to Somerset.' He smiled pleasantly at her. 'I remember you telling me once that the Levels were at their most beautiful in the winter!' He sounded unconcerned at the prospect of hundreds of miles soon separating them again; she lived in south-west England, he lived in Paris – that was how things were. Then his smile faded as if he'd remembered, she thought, that he had something he must thank her for. 'I can't say how grateful I am to you for coming, Jenni – it was an act of friendship far beyond the call of duty! My mother is just as grateful to you, too.'

She could bear the empty phrases no longer, and said what would burst the bubble of unreality they seemed to be floating in. 'Perhaps she'll think my "act of friendship" wipes out the sin of having given away Luc's inheritance! Probably not, though – she has not brought herself to mention the subject, and nor have you.'

She saw his expression change, but he was given no chance to reply. Walking back towards the door, she halted there to smile at him. 'Get well soon, Pierre, and, if you feel inclined to repeat your pilgrimage, do it on horseback next time – it might be safer than shanks's pony!' Then she gave him a farewell wave and left the room. Salvation lay back in Somerset.

Simon, warned of her time of arrival, was at Bristol to meet her. 'All well?' he asked hopefully, even though she looked preoccupied and tired.

Jenni produced the needed smile. 'Pretty

well – Pierre has a little way to go yet, but he's on the mend. Paris was cold and wet, but he'll be heading south soon to recuperate.' Her tone of voice said that the subject of Pierre Lacroix had now been fully dealt with, and they could talk about something else. Simon took the hint and began to explain that lambing had already started at home – as always, there was no off-season in running a large farm.

Delivered to her front door half an hour later, she gave her brother a grateful hug – not for the ride home, he thought, but for accepting that she had nothing more to say about her visit to Paris.

'You look weary,' he said gently. 'Have a rest – we won't expect you to come rushing over to the farm.'

Her wholehearted smile reappeared at last. 'What it is to have an understanding twin brother! I shall follow your kind advice and potter about gently here until the new term starts.'

She let herself into the cottage with a feeling of overwhelming relief. Even its smallness was a comfort; it had become her private place. She could weep her heart out there, and come to terms with the hurt that had been done to her in that last conversation with Pierre. Then, free of the whole damnable French connection at last, she would await the healing and hope that would come with the arrival of spring.

* * *

Easter was early enough for the church flower ladies to be able to plunder Frantock's gardens for pure white cherry blossom and the gold of spring flowers; the bareness and the sombre purple of Lent were gone. In the afternoon of Easter Saturday, when the decorating had been done, Jenni walked into a blaze of colour and scent. The music the following morning must match the splendour around her that shouted Christ was risen, He was risen indeed.

Her practice was scarcely necessary – she knew the notes by heart, but time spent alone in the peace and quietness of the empty church had become precious to her. She closed the organ at last, gathered up her music and headed for the porch door. Then time stood suddenly still; not still, it was running backwards, out of control, because she was imagining that she saw someone who'd been there a long time ago. With a hand gripping a pew to steady herself, she ducked her head for a moment, then lifted it again, but what she saw was still there, and then Pierre Lacroix found his voice and spoke to her.

'I went to the cottage first, but I hoped you'd be here – I wanted to hear you play again.'

In command of herself now, she could answer him. 'I'd rather you came to admire the church – it's looking beautiful, don't you think?' Her voice was courteous – just as he realized, she would have greeted any stranger who happened to have wandered in. Worse still, she was quite ready, now, to walk away with the pleasant smile that she'd have offered any stranger she wouldn't be likely to see again.

'I'm aware that you don't want me here,' he said quietly, 'and I understand why that is. But will you let me talk to you, and promise to listen to what I say?'

She took so long to answer that he expected her to refuse, but at last she seemed to remember something that brought a faint smile to her face. 'My grandmother used to say that the English can't come face to face with visitors without offering them cups of tea! Perhaps you'd like tea in my cottage? I rather like showing it off, as a matter of fact.'

She was still the friendly citizen making a foreigner feel welcome, because that was what good citizens were required to do. With equal politeness he agreed that tea in the cottage sounded delightful.

They walked through the churchyard together, and she noticed that he didn't limp, but she couldn't say so – because that would acknowledge that she remembered other meetings that she refused to talk about. There were people to greet as they walked along, which made conversation between them unnecessary. Then they were at her cottage gate, and she could lead him into a charmingly furnished sitting room. Behind it, she explained, lay only a combined kitchen and dining room.

'"Two up, two down" we call these cottages,' she said cheerfully, 'but I love being here. Make yourself comfortable – tea will arrive in a minute or two.'

'It isn't really needed, Jenni,' he admitted. 'What *is* necessary is that I should be allowed to talk to you – it's why I'm here.'

She was ready to agree, only because she couldn't sustain her bright social manner much longer, and he wouldn't leave until the speech he'd obviously prepared had been delivered. But she had something to say first herself.

'Before you begin I need to make things clear. I don't regret giving the drawings to the museum. I can't judge your *mother* for what happened during the war, but Emile Gosselin's betrayal of the Bernard family will always seem inexcusable. I went to Paris to help you if I could, *not* to gain your mother's good opinion or to regain yours. All that being so, is there any point in going on with this conversation?'

It was her usual response to a challenge, he remembered – she'd meet it head on. But now it was his turn. 'There is certainly a point for me,' he said hoarsely. 'I've needed this conversation since I let you walk out of the hospital in Paris hurt and angry, you *were*, weren't you?'

'Yes,' she agreed, content to leave it there, but he nodded as if the admission was something achieved at least.

'When you came into my room it seemed

the most natural thing in the world – you were there because I needed you. Then my mother told me the truth: she'd asked, if not commanded, you to come, and I realized that only forgiving Christian kindness had prevented you from refusing.'

A silence fell that Jenni broke by going to a side table to pour wine. 'A glass of sherry instead of tea,' she suggested, offering it to him, and then sat down again with her own glass cupped in her hands. After a moment's thought she decided what to say.

'At the hospital we seemed to be talking through a glass wall – we were both visible but there was no contact. I thought it was because you shared your mother's undying conviction that I'd given away something valuable that belonged to you. She hated me for that, probably for more than all the past history.'

A gleam of amusement unexpectedly lit Pierre's face. 'Will you try to believe me if I say that she admires you? She's still angry, of course, but in her heart she knows that the drawings are where they belong. She's also angry because she couldn't browbeat you – something she's usually rather good at. She'd got used to the idea that it was safe to despise the English!'

Unable to find anything to say, Jenni got up again and walked to the window. Her neighbour was painting his gate bright green. Whenever she looked at it in future she would remember this conversation.

Then Pierre's voice spoke just behind her – he'd been drawn to the window too. 'When I first came to Frantock I had an ulterior motive that I concealed from you and your grandmother. That being so, there's no reason I can think of why you should ever trust me again or feel obliged to keep a promise you made before you knew the truth about my family. I wish with all my heart we could cancel out the past and start again.'

She turned to face him then. 'We can't, though, can we?' she suggested gravely. 'I knew that when you went back to Paris and I had to put my life together again without you. I've managed it, but probably changed in the painful process. You'll have changed, too, I'm sure, so going back isn't an option.'

Goaded by the certainty in her voice, he suddenly pulled her into his arms. '*This* hasn't changed,' he murmured before he kissed her. She couldn't resist the sudden overwhelming urge to answer his need with her own but, released at last, she wiped a trembling hand across her mouth, a gesture that he realized was meant to deny that moment of weakness.

Pierre tried to keep his voice steady. 'You *can't* pretend that we don't still need each other.'

'Need?' she queried fiercely. 'I know all about "need". I live here because my mother is back at the farmhouse after a long time away, and she's tormented even now by my father's affection for me. I've watched him ever since, nursing their marriage as you'd have to shelter a candle flame from going out. That's a marriage based on physical need, and I know that I don't want it – I'd rather do without passion altogether.'

A rueful smile touched Pierre's mouth for a moment. 'You make it sound as if you're determined to give up an extra spoonful of sugar in your tea, but I'm not convinced that you're ready for placid, passionless spinsterhood!' Then he grew serious again. 'My dear, I understand what holds you here – your family, the children you love to teach, the home you've made, and this corner of England that your heart is tied to. All I can offer instead is myself. I *haven't* changed, and I shall love you until I die, but I'm afraid you're going to say that isn't enough.'

'Someone *else* hasn't changed,' Jenni made herself point out. 'Your mother loves you, all the more intensely because you're all she has left. I must be the last person on earth she'd want to share you with. She couldn't wait for me to leave the hospital.'

Pierre shook his head. 'I went to see her before I came here, to explain that, if I could, I would persuade you to marry me. Instead of imploring me not to go, she suddenly began to talk about your visit to Grasse. She hadn't mentioned it before. She said that you'd kissed her goodbye, and she tried to sound indignant about it, not realizing that her eyes were full of tears. I doubt if anyone but me had kissed her since my father died.'

He lifted Jenni's hands to his mouth and held them there for a moment. 'She'd probably tell me to browbeat you into forgiving us, but I know you don't respond to that sort of treatment. I can only ask and pray that you will.'

Her eyes searched his face before she answered him. '*You* suggested starting again. Well, I think it's what we have to do, but it won't be possible if you've now got to hurry back to France.'

'I have three weeks before term starts,' he said. 'If that isn't long enough I'll come back in the summer, and then at Christmas and however long it takes after that, until for pity's sake you tell me either to go or say that you'll come with me to Paris.'

Her slow sweet smile finally reappeared. 'It will serve me right if you get tired of all that travelling.' She reached up to leave a gentle kiss on his mouth. 'Now, shall we put *us* aside for a little while? Tomorrow is Easter, and it's quite enough rejoicing to be going on with, don't you think?'

'Quite enough,' he agreed gently, 'seeing that this time, thank God, we shall at least be rejoicing together.'